E. P. MACLACHLAN

Colours in the Mist

First published by Kindle Direct Publishing 2021

This novel is entirely a work of fiction. The names, characters and incidents portrayed in it are the work of the author's imagination. Any resemblance to actual persons, living or dead, events or localities is entirely coincidental.

First edition

ISBN: 978-1-7399955-1-5

Editing by Thomas Button
Editing by Lisa Edwards
Cover art by Natasha MacKenzie

This book was professionally typeset on Reedsy.
Find out more at reedsy.com

For Mum and Gran,
Thank you for showing me the love of reading.

Acknowledgement

There are so many of you I wish to thank but I know what it will be impossible to do so, so know that if you have spoken, encouraged or even asked how my writing is going within these past years know that you have made an impact. Given me a little push, and kept me going. I couldn't have achieved what I have without you.

But there are those that I wish to put into the spotlight that I know Colours in the Mist wouldn't exist without.

Arnella - meeting you through an online group and building up a critique partnership and friendship with you have been some of the best experiences throughout my writing journey. You saw my draft in its infancy and helped me develop it into something stronger, you were always around when I questioned something and wanted someone to run it by. I can't thank you enough for the help, support and encouragement you have given me, but most importantly friendship.

Emma - you have literally been my number one cheerleader since I first told you I was writing, reading my manuscript numerous times, at all different stages of its development. And completely coming up with its title. This story wouldn't be where it is now without you.

Hannah - Thank you for being an amazingly supportive friend, you have put up with my constant rambling about writing and helped me through some tricky issues I've come across!

Gee - Thank you for your unending support and for being a sensitivity reader and for helping me identify anything that could be triggering. Thank you for making me feel welcome within the online writing community and becoming such a wonderful friend.

Emily - Thank you for making me feel so welcome and becoming such a supportive friend. I am so pleased we have met through the Writing Community.

My family and boyfriend, Kristian - this truly couldn't have been done without you. You have all supported my dream of writing asking how I am getting on and listening to me on so many occasions talk about my characters and their journey. I hope I have made you proud.

Online writing community - There are so many of you I wish to thank, Esme, Rosalyn, Selena, Tracey, Erin and many, many more. You have all been so incredibly supportive of my writing and answering so many of my questions. I don't think I could have built the confidence I have without you.

Reader - And you, my dear reader, I thank you. I thank you for taking a chance on my book, a book that has been with me for many years. I thank you for helping an aspiring author achieve their dream. I hope you enjoy the journey.

Can you see the colours?

Content Warnings

- Attempted rape
- Attempted sexual assault
- Beating (mild)
- Child neglect
- Emotional abuse
- Graphic injuries, blood and violence
- Loss of a loved one (mentioned)
- Physical and verbal abuse
- Physical assault

Prologue

17th November 1918

Dear Diary,

It happened again today. Why? Mother just makes me so nervous, and I can't seem to get anything right. Even if I do, it is never perfect ... never enough. I had to plead with Miss K. not to drop me from this winter's ballet performance after I twisted my ankle during practice. Miss K. tried to say that I would not be ready to perform and I had to insist that I would be. Mother will be so disappointed in me if I don't. It's an endless struggle to satisfy her, and I know my efforts are futile.

God, I wish Father was still here.

It feels as I grow older, my resemblance to Mother becomes less obvious than before. Sometimes I like to think that her distant, almost cold, nature is merely a result of me reminding her of Father. But in truth, I know it is not so. I was not lucky enough to have inherited his warm chocolate hair, and sun-speckled mahogany

1

eyes either; my only similarity to him is my fondness for nature. I bear no physical resemblance to Father or to the mother that bore me. It baffles me to think about how two polar opposites could have found such happiness in each other. Yet, the saying rings true that opposites attract, I suppose.

Father always seemed to know what I was thinking, which, I suppose should have been unsettling; but I always found it comforting, as words have not always been my strongest ally. Mother, on the other hand – her ice-blonde locks are always a shade of platinum; as if all the warmth was stolen from them. I suppose they are fitting, matching her glacial blue eyes and cold demeanour.

The only time I have seen her soften is in the presence of Hugh. Even for his icy soul, he is the spitting image of our father, though it seems my dearest brother may possess more of Mother's characteristics than you may first think. His spiteful, cruel behaviour may take on a different form than her heavily veiled disinterest, but he has taken after her in many ways, ensuring I feel like an outcast from my own family, going as far as to imply I was adopted.

Truthfully, there are times that I dream that his slight is true and that I am adopted. To believe that out there is a family who possesses the same hair as me: a colour resembling the last dregs of a candle wick burning ... begging for just a few seconds longer to remain ignited. My eyes – large and so far removed from either of theirs – are emerald, which in the sun can change colour as if held within are all the green hues of nature. Funny, really, my hair resembles the colour of destruction, whilst my eyes hold a variety of the colour of life.

Alas, these are my circumstances and I must endeavour to make the most of them. To continue trying my hardest to satisfy this family, from whom I feel so far removed.

It is times like this that make me miss Father. I know I complain about him a lot – how he was always away on business and even when he was home he did not seem to have time for me – but Frank, Mother's new husband, is terrifying. Hugh's cruelty, which has always terrified me, withers in the face of his.

I still remember the time I spoke of flowers, and he shut me away. I sometimes wonder if it was the context of my conversation or the mere fact that I had spoken at all that had encouraged his response. So, to help refrain from spouting pointless talk, I turn to eating, keeping myself silent, which has also been the result of many arguments between Mother and me. She insists that I need to be mindful, or else I will struggle to be suitable for the show next month at all... It begrudges me to know that she is right.

Looking in the mirror has become harder as of late, knowing that the reflection looking back has caused my family so much discontent for not being like them, for looking so different. People make jokes that Mother and Father stole me from someone else. This too has given me pause, wondering whether it is true.

I must go, someone is coming...

Lorian.

Lorian

The suffocating darkness.

The never-ending pain.

The numbing loneliness.

It all came rushing back as if a stampede of horses were running through my skull.

Then light.

Cracks of light, ever so slowly, creeping, tiptoeing into my vision – timid, and almost apologetic, as if they knew what sort of pain washed through me and tentatively crept closer, knowing their impact would be just as brutal.

What could be happening?

I dived deep into my fragmented memory. This pain made it so hard to focus. Deeper, I pushed past the hurt that laced through my head, begging for a scrap of something that might help me decipher this moment.

A cottage, slightly ramshackle, sitting between other wooden houses.

Maria's cottage.

Then pain…

Excruciating pain.

Was this another fever dream? Or was this the ointment finally burning away the sickness? Was I going to wake up looking into Elijah's face?

Just as Elijah's face came into focus, the hooked claws of a headache took hold, willing me to keep my eyes shut. Closing off the memories that tried to flood me, I banished everything from my mind.

I couldn't think about that yet.

I couldn't think about him yet. At that moment, all I could know for sure was that I was alive.

The first thing I had to do was to find somewhere to wash. Although my eyes still remained shut from the thrumming still pulsing in my head, my imagination could discern what I must have looked like: dishevelled to say the least. Death, I've no doubt, would cower at the sight of me.

Trying to regain my composure, I was forcing myself to take a deep calming breath when I was infused with a deep earthy smell. It seemed to fill my whole being, not leaving an inch untainted.

In an effort to try and make sense of the situation I found myself in, I pulled at a thread of memory. I was transported back to The Slums. The sickness had just broken out, and within the local crypt, even the candles could not mask the damp stench of the dead.

Fear doused me in one sudden flood, pulling me back to the present, and I began to feel more conscious of the space that surrounded me. My mind was fighting to comfort me that I was very much still alive. None of this made sense… Why was I in the crypt? If I was there, surely I was not buried?

Seeking clarity to my situation, I sought out my other senses, my sight still hindered from the weight of the pain held behind my eyes. Listening intently, I strained to hear the sound of anything around me. Nothing. Confirmation that I was alone, adding fuel to my rapidly increasing fear.

I concentrated harder, willing my hearing to return.

One.

Two.

Three.

Four.

Five.

I kept counting until slowly, tauntingly, a small sound tickled my ears. But … everything around me appeared muffled as if I was listening through a door; as if nature itself was guarding against me.

I'm being silly, I told myself, willing my terror to subside. Realisation flooded through me. I flexed my fingers. I was lying on compacted dirt. This couldn't be the stone floors of the crypt.

Bolting into an upright position, my body protesting with every movement, I felt a dull ache spread slowly through my very being, like oil spreading through water, as feeling began to return. The earthy atmosphere had infected my taste buds, leaving my mouth dry, as if full of soil.

Forcing my eyes open I was immediately blinded. Patiently, and against every sense of self-preservation I had, I waited for my eyes to adjust to my surroundings. The black fog of my headache still clung to my mind like fog clings to a heavy sky.

Blinking my eyes to try and clear the remainder of my vision I took in my surroundings. I was sitting in the middle of the floor of what once must have been a barn, but it was now abandoned. The building was dilapidated, and the roof, once a barrier sealing out the night, was caving in, allowing the silvery light of a moon that I could just see, to shimmer through the gaps.

Glancing around the rest of the room, I picked out other recognisable objects, confirming my suspicions: feeding troughs, hay forks and old tractor tyres that I had only seen in books. There was also something else – it wasn't anything I could see but I could not shake the feeling that there was something wrong, something I was missing that should be as plain as the nose on my face.

After a few minutes of deliberation over my odd feeling, and coming to no conclusions fast, I hauled myself off the floor and stretched up to my full height, onto my tiptoes. Everywhere ached like I had been asleep for a hundred years. Moving across the room I tried to rotate some of my joints to ease the stiffness cocooning them; even walking felt strange. I'd managed to make my way over to a set of old hay bales. Their deep musty smell was oppressive, clinging to everything, making the air heavy.

Feeling a little claustrophobic, I hurried towards the exit and out of that cursed place to find my way back home. As I stumbled out of the barn, I was engulfed in a white blinding light, which caused my head to spin. The sudden assault scrambled my already frayed senses; my knees buckled from under me and sent me hurtling onto the soft damp grass below.

Gasping for breath and trying to calm myself, I took small pleasure in realising the earthy taste in my mouth had subsided, and my eyes began to adapt to the increased amount of light. As they began to focus, albeit too slowly for my liking, my pulse thick in my ears, I silently prayed that I hadn't strayed too far from home. Yet as my surroundings grew clearer, I could feel my panic rise further, along with my already-throbbing pulse.

The place looked ravaged, devoured by some sort of disease. A sickly hue clung to every living thing in sight, causing it to appear a grey shadow of its former self. The trees were like dark silhouettes against the bright white of the sky, as if painted there just moments before. A light drizzle had just begun, adding to the eerie atmosphere, and drained me of what little warmth my body dared cling to, pooling into the cold lifeless ground below me.

Where was I?

A muffled sound drifted in the distance; my ears struggled to capture it as they roared with the sound of my pulse. There it was again, but louder this time, as though it was coming closer. I concentrated hard as I focused on the sound again.

"Hey, excuse me. Are you okay?"

I heard the voice, but it was still slightly muffled. A shadow fell over me where I was still kneeling, looking at the damp grass as I concentrated on deciphering the sounds. The shadow blocked out the pale light of the sun – it was the sun giving off this strange light not the moon as I had thought. Someone cleared their throat.

A pair of strong legs and heavy boots came into view, each covered in what looked like a dusting of snow. I did not dare raise my head too quickly for fear of being thrust back into my previous affliction, but as a gentle breeze drifted past, stirring up the snow-like substance and chilling my damp skin, I realised it was not snow. Focusing more acutely on the boots, I realised it was sawdust. A woodsy smell lingered.

Before I dared to risk using my voice, which was sure to be raspy from the feel of my throat, the stranger cleared his throat again. Though this action could have been a sign of agitation, I could tell from the slight shuffle of his boots, it was more an awkwardness from my lack of response.

A few moments passed as I willed my voice to cooperate with me as it had failed to do so on so many occasions, forcing myself to answer for fear of appearing rude. "Oh, um, I'm sorry. What was it you said?" My voice was coarse, quiet, as my mouth was still trying to find moisture but to no avail. Raising my eyes slowly I took in the stranger that the shadow belonged to. Strong, and broad, I had to tilt my chin up to look into his face.

To my shock, I received a smile. His eyes glinted in amusement at my predicament. His skin, although pale, had a slight inkling of a warm honey tone. If I was not hunched embarrassingly on the ground, I would put him standing at least a foot taller than my five foot three inches.

He had deep grey eyes, which turned up at the corners as he smiled. They were framed by black lashes that had been dampened by the rain, which grew finer as each moment passed, now only hanging in the air like mist. His hair hung limp with moisture, falling flat over his ears; he kept trying to tuck his hair behind them. His most striking feature, however, was a birthmark branded on his right cheek. Initially I mistook it for soot, and it wasn't until he brushed his hand across his face to remove the lingering rain droplets that clung there, that I realised what it was.

Chastising myself for staring, I averted my eyes. Behind the young man was a large wagon with a single horse harnessed to it. Why was everything so bleak? Everything was so bland, colourless… Was something wrong with my eyes? Before I could contemplate this further, I was drawn back to look at the man as he spoke. Even the honey colour had gone from his face.

"I said, are you okay? I was coming up the track and saw you fall. You annoy someone?"

Sounding bewildered, and slightly irritated, his words – although seemingly innocent –were betrayed by his curt tone.

In an effort to compose myself I flung my aching body upright, my legs quaking from the suddenness of my movement. Willing strength into my legs I pulled myself to my full height and responded with a glare. "What are you talking about? Why would it mean I have annoyed anyone? Simply falling over isn't anyone's fault, or business, for that matter…"

My response only seemed to amuse him further, as he tried to conceal his laughter with a cough, stealing the last of my patience.

"What? What is so funny? Do you know it is rude to laugh when someone isn't themselves?"

He stood, momentarily looking at me, as perplexed at my response as I was with myself. But soon enough he regained his aloof attitude.

"What are you talking about? You know that it is a childhood prank to spell someone to fall down? You're bound to have had it done to you when you were younger. Everyone has…"

He was outwardly laughing at me now. This young man was clearly insufferable and completely mad. I was in the middle of nowhere with someone intent on believing people 'spelled' one another to fall, for nothing more than their own amusement.

Heaving a huge sigh, I pushed past him. I wasn't going to

just stand there and spend another moment of my day with a man hell-bent on making me feel like a fool – well, more of a fool than I already felt.

Eager to put some distance between myself and the tall stranger, I stomped further into the dismal-looking field. The cold drizzle that had settled on my light clothes began to seep through, encouraging goosebumps to spread along my skin. I had no idea where I was, but there was bound to be a town not too far from there. If the situation was a result of one of my fever-induced deliria, I knew I couldn't have got far.

Before I could make up my mind as to what to do next, I heard the man's voice, as if it was carried on the chilling wind. His footsteps sounded behind me before I could make a decision, his tread heavy so I could feel the slight vibration through the ground as he closed the distance I had made.

"You're not going to get very far that way barefoot," he said.

Stunned, I looked down, realising he was right. I was barefoot. Why hadn't I noticed before? I would surely notice something like that. My feet also looked slightly grey. Blinking rapidly, I willed my eyes to clear. As if I had only just regained feeling in them, I began to wiggle my toes in the soft, dewy grass.

With a sigh, I turned to face the stranger and grizzled, "Even barefoot, why do you think I would not be able to make it back to the town? I bet it isn't that far."

"Well, for one thing, the town isn't that way, and for another, it is just woodland, which I believe would tear your feet apart," he said, still with his smirk on his face

"Fine. Show me which way the town is and I will go that way," I said, raising my eyebrows at him, just as my mother would do when she was getting towards the end of her patience.

"Well, it is about ten miles to the south. I don't know how you got this far out in the first place with no shoes on. Must have been one hell of a walk."

Astonished, I just stared at him. How could I have got so far out without even knowing it? Surely someone would have realised I was missing and come to get me. Moments went by before I realised he was still talking, and any distance that had once separated us had dissolved. God, did he not know about personal space?

I took a large and slightly exaggerated step back to try and convey my special desire; pasted on my best aloof impression and responded, "Hmm, what did you say?"

Still grinning, he said, "Do you want me to take you back to the town? I'm going that way now."

"Oh…" I blinked, clearing my thoughts and averting my gaze. "Yes please."

I clamped down on my annoyance at the stranger, realising he was just offering to help me. Chancing a glance at him, I saw he was still looking at me. This time, all the humour drained from his face and was replaced by utter concern, which was worrying.

"Are you sure you're okay?"

"Umm, yes, no, I mean…" In an effort to distract him from my own uncertainty, I countered: "What colour is your horse? And why are you riding a wagon and not a car?" I pointed to the horse that was standing on the muddy track a good thirty feet away from where I was standing in the field. The large wagon looked like it had seen better days. "Or is that not your horse?"

The stranger turned and looked at me quizzically. "Yes, she

is mine and well, she is a pale grey. What other colour would she be, besides another grey on the spectrum? And what is a car?"

"Well, she could be any colour, couldn't she? Why would she be only grey? And a car is a type of automobile. It has four wheels and takes you from place to place without having to use a horse. How have you never heard of one?" I responded feeling equally confused.

"'Cause that is all there is – grey," he responded, baffled, "and I've never heard of such a thing as a car."

My heartbeat quickened again – it had only just begun to quieten. "So, there are only grey horses? And no cars?"

Looking at me now as if I was insane, the man cautiously explained, "Grey horses, houses, flowers, people … everything is a tone of grey – as it always has been." Concern continued to embed itself into his face as he continued: "How could you have not noticed before? Surely you're not blind? Colour has been gone for hundreds of years. And nope, no cars."

As quickly as his concern had come, it was gone. A smile began to plague his face again. Even after everything he had just said, I couldn't help wondering if his lips were slightly pink?

Ignoring his questions but latching onto the little revelation he had casually announced about colour, I asked, "But how could it be gone?"

"Well, colour was stripped from Sòlas three hundred years ago, allegedly by a curse."

His tone took on an undertone of boredom as if he was reciting common knowledge. But nothing he had just told me was common. In fact, everything since my awakening was borderline bizarre, and the more information I received the

13

harder it was for me to make sense of my circumstances.

My mind and mouth sped onto another question: "What about electricity?" There was no lights on the wagon as there would have been before.

"What the hell is e-le-c-tric-ity?" he asked as my mind whirled to absorb the information.

Nonetheless, I sought out more information. "Sòlas? What are you talking about? We are heading back to Temford, aren't we?"

The fear I had managed to trample down was beginning to bubble its way back to the surface of my mind. The blank look received from this stranger only fuelled my panic. I looked down at my hands, my skirt, my feet, but this time I really looked. I blinked a few more times as the realisation dawned. This wasn't just my eyes waiting to adjust, this was what they actually saw.

Turning on my heel I began to walk. The barn – I had to get back to the barn, where this nightmare had begun, in the hope that I could find further answers in the place I had awoken. What had happened to me? If this was one of my fevered dreams, it was a damn good one.

"Hey, wait," called the stranger.

I know it is a ludicrous thought, but I immediately became suspicious. What if this man's intentions for me were not amenable and I was just allowing him to lead me astray?

I hitched up my skirt and quickened my pace, all but running. Mother would chastise me if she knew I was running, and not just running, but showing my ankles too. But my mind soon raced back to what he had said: no colour. A curse.

Soon enough he caught up to me. "Hey. Let me take you into town and I will tell you what happened on the way. Perhaps you can see if you recognise anything?"

Against my better judgement, I caved, slowing as I got to the barn and conceding to go with the stranger to a town I didn't know. Had I not been overwhelmed, and riddled with desperation for answers, I might have been more cautious (like Maria my old maid insisted I should be). But at this moment, I only had him. "Fine, if I go with you, you will tell me what happened to Temford … or Sòlas, whatever you want to call it. Deal?"

He quickly glanced to the sky and the bright white sun marking its position, cursing himself under his breath. "Yeah, sure, whatever you want. But we should go now, I have things I need to do and you need to tell me what this e-lec-tric-ity is."

We began making our way back to where he had left his horse and wagon. I nearly had to skip to keep up with his long strides. As we got closer, I couldn't help but take a proper look at the horse. It was beautiful. Even though all the colour had been taken from the creature it still stood with a quiet sense of tranquillity. Its only concern at that moment was trying to edge itself closer to a juicier-looking patch of grass with the wagon still attached.

It was all but a small jaunt to the wagon, but I couldn't help but steal a few glances at the man beside me in the peaceful quiet that surrounded us. It also soon became apparent that he couldn't help sharing his curiosity for me either.

Aware of his gaze, I felt the overwhelming need to justify myself. I could only imagine what he was seeing when he looked at me. In an effort to sound dignified I said, "Contrary to appearances, my common-sense is very much intact. The only questionable judgement I may have is getting on that wagon with you. And electricity powers the lights in your home."

A small smile curved his lips but he did not respond, simply checking the harness was correctly strapped, making a few adjustments. Giving the horse a firm pat, as if forgiving it for trying to wiggle its way to the grass, he turned, walking to the other side of the wagon. "Alright then, climb on up and we can agree to disagree on your state of sense, and we use candles or fires for light," he said playfully.

In one graceful move, he was situated on the seat of the wagon and held out his hand to me. "You'd better hurry, I am already late as it is."

How could they not have electricity? All of Temford did, other than the poorest of people.

Storing the thought for later, I looked at his outstretched hand. Hesitantly, I took it in mine. His palm was warm but firm. The connection of our hands, though brief, brought a slight blush to my cheeks and a flutter to my stomach. Childish embarrassment, I told myself. Hoping he hadn't noticed my reaction, I took a deep breath and hauled myself up, being sure not to close the gap of what little distance there was between us.

"My name's Maverick by the way," he said, glancing over at me.

"Lorian," I whispered back, shyness cocooning me as it so often did in social situations.

But what was strange was that it hadn't reduced me to silence until now.

Maverick

Both of us deep in thought, we made our way in silence to Sòlas' town. The girl, Lorian, was a bit strange. She had looked so young but when I asked her age she surprised me by saying she was eighteen – only three years younger than myself. What puzzled me the most was that she had been all feisty and argumentative to start with, but now she seemed quiet and subdued – shy even. How could she not know about the balance-trick spell? How could she not know anything about magic at all? She literally had no clue, staring at me as if I was a mad man. Then there were these things called 'cars' and 'electricity'; what were they and why did she think I would know about them?

I told her the tale of how colour had faded from the world over three hundred years ago when the witch, Stravaig of Bròn, entered Sòlas, on the night of the Samhain festival. With everyone in the centre of the town, on the festival green, that foul excuse of a witch was able to sneak in and put the curse over the whole of Sòlas.

"So I'm not colour-blind?"

Lorian's small voice interrupted the swirling replay in my mind. Refocusing on the here and now, I looked down and saw my knuckles going white. By the God and Goddess, she infuriated me with her lack of understanding. How could anyone get to eighteen and not know anything about magic when Sòlas was built upon it?

Sighing, I answered her childish question: "No, it is the curse. Everything has lost its colour and ever since, it seems as though no one is able to be truly happy. It is all a mask, an act of sorts."

She opened her mouth to ask another question, but, anticipating what she was about to say, I carried on, cutting her off: "…and yes, we can still laugh and have fun but no one is ever happy, not really." I finished with another huge sigh, trying to release some of the tension I could feel building, the longer the journey lasted.

"I'm sorry, I don't mean to keep asking the same thing, it's just…" She paused, wringing her hands in her lap impatiently.

"Go on, what were you going to say. It's just…?" I prompted, rolling my shoulders, easing the stiffness that had settled over them.

"I don't know how I would have got here. If what you say is true, then I'm not where I should be. My world was bright and colourful but most of all there is no magic where I am from…" Her voice dropped to barely a whisper and I had to strain my ears to hear her… "no matter how much I wished there was."

Shock and an odd sense of loss clawed through me at Lorian's statement. How could she be from another world? And a world without magic? Her world sounded so different, so full of … colour. But nothing compared to casting your first spell or knocking a bully over with the balance-trick spell. Even if no one could feel true joy, what could compare to magic? If it was true and she had never known it, no wonder she was so confused when I asked who had played the childish prank on her. It was everywhere in Sòlas, everyone could perform some sort of magic; even the smallest of babies had been known to express their abilities at an early age. Yes, there were different types and strengths, but everyone in town knew their neighbour possessed magic. I had never known anyone to not possess some kind of power.

"Are there no other towns around Sòlas?" Lorian asked as she stared out to the rows and rows of passing fields.

"No. Nothing. The curse seemed to lay waste to the land for miles. We get trade from towns, but it can take months to get to us. There is nothing close. The only one remotely close to us is Brón and you wouldn't want to travel over there."

She seemed so naive. I didn't know how she would make her way around town safely. But I guess that wasn't really any of my business, I had my own things to do.

"Months," she whispered to herself, with the realisation that Sòlas would be the only place she could stay. At least she was smart enough to acknowledge that Brón wasn't an option.

The rest of the journey was completed in silence. I caught myself gazing out at the fields with Lorian: they contained wheat, corn, flowers and a small scattering of livestock. The animals had obviously moved pastures as they normally resided on the western side of the town.

As we approached the town, the atmosphere changed. Well, the atmosphere around Lorian did: she got tense, with small beads of sweat forming on her upper lip. It was as if she was drawing into herself more, like a turtle moving further into the darkest parts of its shell. Her eyes were huge, her body stiff and still. What could have made her like that?

The town was quite beautiful that day: the tall stone buildings with carved faces, their tops looking like pointed witch's hats. Some were joined with flat roofs and pointed turrets at each end. Smaller stone houses were dotted around further out behind the large buildings.

I couldn't see what was making Lorian so upset. Hopefully, once she was inside the town, she would see its beauty.

"Honestly, it isn't that bad," I said, trying to ease her tension. "You will see how beautiful it can be, even without colour, once we are further in. There is a market on today and it sells all kinds of fruit. Actually, it is coming up to Samhain…"

"No, no, I'm fine, honestly. If you drop me just here, I will make my own way," she spluttered, cutting me off.

Lorian was gathering up her skirt and looked as though she was going to jump off the wagon before I could bring it to a stop. Tugging on the reins, I managed an abrupt halt, feeling sorry for Mum's old mare, Saffi. Not waiting for me to go round to help her down – the automatic gesture Mum had ingrained in me making a sudden appearance – Lorian hopped off the wagon. A slight squelch of mud from the wet track was her only sound, before she strode to the side of the road putting at least three metres between her and the now-stationary wagon.

"Thank you for the lift, Mister Maverick, it was much appreciated. I—I will make my own way from here." Her voice cracked as if she was forcing the words out.

"But we are still a mile away from the town, and you don't have any shoes on. I don't mind taking you in, I'm going to

20

the market anyway," I blurted.

What was wrong with me? I normally wouldn't care about someone like this. Why her? I think I knew why: she looked so vulnerable, so confused, and I felt protective. I wanted to make sure she would be okay –I guess having a younger sister did that to you.

"No, honestly, I don't want to bother you. I've, uh, got to meet someone anyway."

I knew she wasn't telling the truth. Who could she be meeting if she didn't even know about the curse and thought she was in some land called Temford? Sighing, I knew I couldn't make her come with me.

Reluctantly, I nodded. "Well just go carefully. Don't go to the east side of the town, okay? Nothing good comes from venturing out there."

With that, I shook the reins for Saffi to walk on. I'd keep an eye out for her that's for sure, making sure she was okay anyway I could. I just hoped she wouldn't venture to the east side … that could end in trouble.

Lorian

It was strange, as I stood there on the side of the muddy road, the growing sense of being alone. It began to creep up on me, like a snake slithering out of its dark corner, wrapping itself slowly around me, nestling close. And I greeted it, greeted it as I had so many times before, times when my only friends were Elijah and Maria. Well, Elijah, Maria and dancing.

Gathering myself together, I headed the same way Maverick had gone. Why hadn't I gone with him? Why had I been so stubborn? I knew why: I had begun to feel suffocated by all the information gathering against me, telling me I was somewhere unknown, that I was once again, alone.

As I walked with stones pressing and tearing into my feet, I grizzled to myself. I could have just let Maverick take me into the market then left. At least I would have been able to find somewhere to get shoes. *And with what money would I buy those shoes?* I scoffed to myself.

"Ugh!" Throwing my hands over my face, I collapsed into a

sitting position on the side of the road, dirtying my already filthy skirt. "Why does everything have to be so complicated?" I moaned to myself.

Why did talking to people have to be so difficult? It would have been easy to say, *'Yes please, a lift to the market would be lovely, thank you.'* Why did I have to be so socially inept, pushing people away with the few words I did say or simply not saying anything at all?

Sitting there in a ball of misery that I had often adopted when I was younger, tears began to form in the corners of my eyes. How could I be so alone? Why was I always so alone? How was I going to get back to the people I cared about, who cared about me? If anyone truly had... What was this curse Maverick spoke of? And why were there no cars or the electricity I was so accustomed to seeing everywhere?

As I sat there and allowed the indulgence of self-pity and loneliness consume me, a small slither of hope crept in. What if I took control? Surely someone would know what had happened to me. I couldn't get back unless I got help from someone who might know about this kind of thing. Someone with magic.

Clambering to my feet I straightened my plain, rough, now-muddy cotton skirt. As I shuffled my way along the dirt road towards the town, I tried to formulate a plan of how I would get back home, to my era, or whatever I should call it. Surely there would be someone who would understand what had happened to me in this place full of magic?

"Yes, that's what I'll do. I'll find someone that will help me get back to where I belong, then I will be able to see Elijah again!" I declared with renewed excitement. "I'll be back to what I know and what I can deal with in no time."

Turning my slow meander into an excitable jog, I sped off to the imposing town of grey that spread before me.

Maverick

Making my way into the town, I navigated the crowded streets to try and find Mum at our flower stall, a nervous tug pulling at my stomach. I hoped Lorian would be okay.

I weaved in and out of the mass of people and stalls that littered the streets – now that the rain had finally subsided – selling all manner of things from candles and incense to furniture, all handcrafted, beautiful masterpieces. But if you looked closely, it didn't seem as though many people could see the beauty. Yes they looked happy to be at the market preparing for Samhain, but if you really looked – which after my conversation with Lorian I seemed to be doing more acutely than normal – it was all so false. False smiles, false laughs, even false hugs for individuals they had known their whole lives. I felt exhausted with it. Why did it seem as though I was the only one to admire the beauty? No matter how colourless it all was, I knew it was still there.

"Hey, stop! Hey, Maverick, stop!!"

I heard the voice over the hustle and bustle of the crowd, even with the urgency and sadness that made his voice higher, which was odd, I could tell it was Emerys.

"Hey, Emerys. Climb up! I've got to get these flowers to the stall or Mum will clout me round the ear."

He clambered up onto the seat next to me where Lorian had been, making me wonder whether she had made it to the town yet or not. I nudged Saffi to move on. Emerys had been my best friend since I was little. Well, I guess he was more like a brother to me; we'd grown up together, getting into all sorts of trouble over the years, especially when our powers started to manifest a little stronger.

I could feel the smile begin to spread across my face as I remembered all the times we had played a trick on other kids our age, and sometimes the older ones too. But it wasn't all fun and games. Emerys had had a difficult upbringing; his parents never really wanted to bother with him unless they were training him to take over their logging business. I suppose that was why he always stayed with us so much. Well, until Gwilym, his younger brother, was born, then he felt it was his duty to look after him. Emerys always wanted to ensure that Gwilym was able to play and enjoy himself as much as he could, not letting his parents draw him into too many chores.

Focusing my errant thoughts, I reacquainted myself with all the features that made Emerys stand out in our little village. He was a giant: at least six foot ten and built like a house, (but his build was hardly a surprise as his family were woodsmen). Light hair with its darker tones added to his allure to the girls; he always seemed to have someone hanging off him.

"Alright? I was wondering where you were. You must have

26

been getting these," Emerys said, pointing his thumb over his shoulder, his face glum.

"Where's Lila today, then?" I said, shaking the reins for Saffi to walk on. "Emerys, what happened?"

With a barely audible whisper, he said, "She's gone."

"What do you mean 'gone'? Left you?" I burst out laughing. "So you're down because she left you? Well, I hate to break it to you, but you've left plenty of women before, you can't go around sulking because one of them left you."

"No, you don't understand – she hasn't left me, she's gone, disappeared. She's not even been seen by her family for two days."

"What? And you're only just telling me now?"

Moving through the crowd, I finally noticed that the hustle and bustle of the market wasn't the same as normal. Everyone was looking over their shoulders, specifically at Emerys. Noticing that I was looking their way, many of them turned back to what they were doing or hurried off in another direction.

"Emerys, what actually happened? Why is everyone looking at you oddly?"

"Because they think I took Lila," Emerys mumbled, his head hanging low and his shoulders hunched. The dark circles under his eyes indicated that he hadn't been sleeping well the past few nights, and the shadow round his jaw showed that he hadn't been worrying about how he looked, which was definitely off for Emerys.

"How could they think you had something to do with it? You wouldn't hurt anyone," I protested, pulling to a stop in front of my family's market stall.

Jumping off the cart, I moved around the back to unload

the flowers. Emerys followed silently, lifting huge bundles at a time. "Well, not anyone that wouldn't deserve it anyway. And go careful – Mum will kill you if they are all crushed. You know she needs these desperately as the stock has been disappearing lately." I nodded towards his overloaded arms and clenched fists on the stems.

"Maybe that would do me a favour. I wouldn't have to be looked at like I am some beast that would go on a rampage and kill them all…" he grunted back.

"We'll sort it, okay? I promise you we will find Lila and show to everyone you had nothing to do with her disappearing." Putting my hand on his arm, I sent him all the reassuring feelings I could.

Emerys slowly began to relax, easing his grip on the flowers and loosening his shoulders. "Thanks, Mav. Now I'd best go and apologise to your mum."

"What for?" I was sure the puzzlement I felt was written all over my face.

"For two things: firstly, for keeping you on one of the busiest market days and secondly," he looked down at the mangled goldenrod stems, "for crushing the stems of her flowers. You know she is going to go nuts at me for that."

"Em, have you ever heard of cars? Or electricity?" I asked, before he could make his way over to the back of the stall.

"No. What are they?"

"I'm not really too sure, exactly," I muttered. Right, best take those round."

Sighing, and with the slightest of smiles on his face, Emerys moved around the back of the stall and walked up to a woman in a simple, long, fitted cotton dress with her hair tied up in a loose bun: Mum.

I could hear Emerys muttering his apologies to Mum but what she did shocked me. She pulled him into a tight hug, saying all that needed to be said without uttering a word – we didn't suspect him. Which was true of course, but was I the only one that hadn't heard anything about it?

Annoyance closed in on me. Annoyance at my family for not telling me sooner that my best friend was in trouble and annoyance that I couldn't do anything to help him.

Or could I?

Lorian

As I wander into the town on sore feet, I was engulfed by the crowd. I couldn't remember the last time people had gathered in the streets of Temford for a market like this. There were people everywhere, moving in and out of shops, pushing past one another to get to the small wooden stalls that lined the streets.

One of the last times I had seen this many people in one place was during my last dance performance, and then people were only in the room together because they had to be. Then the sickness tore through the town, consuming everything it touched. The streets became a ghost town, with no one wanting to mingle in case they caught it.

This town, Sòlas, was full of chattering happy people, moving from one stall to the next, discovering new and interesting things. I really couldn't see how Maverick could call these people unhappy.

I made my way over to the stalls to get a closer look. They bore all sorts of things: fruit, fabric, silverware, and a vast assortment of candles I couldn't imagine people would feel the need for.

Moving down the streets and mingling between the crowd and the stalls, I came to an abrupt stop. Books, a stall was full of books. I pushed my way through the remaining people that blocked me from this magnificent sight. I could feel my spirits rise. The books were all so beautiful, such a variety of shapes and sizes. Nervously moving my hand towards a small dark-covered volume, I jumped as a knobbly, grey hand clasped around my wrist.

"No touching unless you're going to buy."

Looking up, I met the eyes of a skinny, gaunt-looking man. His wide-brimmed hat was threadbare and his clothes weren't much better, with holes in the elbows of his checked shirt and on the knees of his dark cotton trousers. "You don't look like the sort of girl that would be interested in hexes, do you now?" he wheezed out, narrowing his eyes at me.

"Hexes?" I squeaked, his grip beginning to cause my hand to go numb.

"Yes, hexes," he mocked. "That book is full of them, you see." He gestured with his head towards the little book I had been about to pick up, all the while his vice-like grip never easing. "So, are you going to buy or are you just wasting my time?"

"Oh, I have no money, sir, sorry," I whispered. Would this man ever let me go? I was sure there was going to be a bruise once he did.

"Then what are you doing touching my merchandise? If you're not going to buy, then away with you. You'll get in the way of real customers."

Releasing my hand, he pushed me away from his table and back into the gathering crowd. After that encounter, I didn't think I wanted to look at another stall for a very long while.

Pushing my way through the crowd I tried to get out of the hustle and bustle, all the while rubbing my wrist. And then the thought dawned on me: *where am I going to stay tonight?* As I had told that creepy old man, I didn't have any money. Tears swelled in my eyes, I tried to blink them away the best I could, but they spilt over and ran down my cheeks, causing passers-by to stare.

I shuffled my way further through the crowd, which now felt imposing and not at all as joyful as it had felt only a few moments ago. I needed to find a way out of the crowd. People shouted at me as I tried to squeeze past them without getting in their way.

I caught sight of a little clearing and the smell of flowers danced to me on the wind. They swirled around me, stopping me in my pursuit of a quiet place. Taking another deep breath I tried to decipher the smell, but I couldn't. It infuriated me, as I loved telling the groundskeeper at home which flowers were which and helping him plant the garden.

As though my body had a mind of its own, I changed course; pushing past the last of the crowd, I caught sight of a sturdy wooden table. It was right there with an array of flowers spread out in front of me, none of them bunched, as if they were waiting to be sorted, for someone special.

Moving closer to the stall, I stared at the variety of flowers before me: roses, tulips, lavender, iris, sweet William and more. How there was this variety in autumn, I just couldn't understand. I got as close to the table as I could, itching to pick one up but I forced myself to keep my hands by my sides, afraid the experience of the last stall would be repeated. Instead, I closed my eyes and inhaled deeply. The scents flooded my nose and began to flow around my body – the calmness of the lavender, the sweetness of the rose, all of them so familiar, so comforting I felt safe, just for an instant.

"Calming, aren't they?"

The soft voice broke my dream-like state like a misstep broke a dance routine. Opening my eyes, I was met by a woman. She did not look any older than thirty, but it was the knowing, intelligent look in her eyes that gave away her true age. Her features were strong, she had sharp, high cheekbones, a petite but muscular figure – she could have been a dancer or a warrior for all I knew. I was mesmerised. There was something about her that was familiar, but I didn't know what. How could she be familiar when I had never been there before?

"Don't you think?"

I hadn't realised she had asked me a question, and my embarrassment rose in an instant. I had been so busy staring at her I hadn't known she had been talking to me.

"Pardon me, I am sorry. I should go, I am in the way."

I began to move off, but her words brought me to a stop.

"You are not in the way, my bird. I was asking if you found the flowers calming. See, I find them very calming."

A smile played at her lips and I could swear there was a blush of colour in her cheeks but there couldn't have been. Maverick said colour had been gone for hundreds of years. Something else nagged at me, at the edge of my memory – the pet name she called me so freely seemed somewhat familiar too.

"Oh, um, yes I do. I'd best be going," I whispered, turning away from the lovely lady again.

As I began to walk off, a lovely small spray of flowers

appeared in front of me, a mixture of lavender and pale iris. I looked up at the lady's smiling face, her eyes filled with kindness.

"I have no money," I blurted, not knowing what else to say.

"That's okay. I am giving these to you, they are a gift."

"Really? I couldn't. They are your livelihood."

"They are only a small spray of what I have, they do not cost much." She smiled. "Plus seeing the joy they bring can be another form of payment."

"Surely you must lose a lot of income if you do this? Though I understand you might enjoy seeing flowers bringing joy to another person."

I didn't know what was wrong with me. I never talked this much, not even to close friends, let alone strangers, and this had happened twice in one day. But I knew how I had loved seeing Maria, my maid and dear friend, beaming at me when I brought her flowers and the swell of happiness it brought me.

"I don't see the joy in others often these days. Normally only children." Her voice had grown colder. It was only for an instant, but I was sure it had. "Anyway, here, take them and if you still feel as though you need to pay me, you can come and help at the stall tomorrow if you like?"

She began to turn away when I called after her: "I would love to! I don't know how good I will be but I would love to help."

"Something tells me you will do just fine," she replied over her shoulder, and I could swear her hair took on a slight shinier sheen.

Shrugging off the confusion, I wandered back into the crowd and away from the flower stall, a smile playing at the corner of my lips. *Maybe this won't be all bad, maybe I will be able to help at the flower stall and earn a little money*, I thought.

Putting the beautiful small spray of flowers to my nose I inhaled their delicious scent and carried on through the crowded streets, pondering my biggest challenge: finding somewhere to sleep.

Maverick

After taking Emerys home on Mum's orders – she didn't want him on the streets just in case anyone took the far-fetched accusations to a whole new level – Mum seemed to be in a better mood. She was almost happy and I could swear there was almost a slight brightness to her skin. "Hey, what has made you so happy? I wasn't gone that long!" I asked her.

"Oh, just a nice girl in the street. Never seen her before, but maybe she is just passing through."

She smiled at me, one of her rare bright smiles. She didn't smiled often after my father left. She could see the puzzled look on my face as she spoke.

"Right, you, stop looking at me like that and go and get your sister from Grandma Wren's. She should be done with her studies now." Mum turned back to the stall and started to trim the stems of the flowers Emerys and I had just dropped off.

"Ugh! Alright, but you know I hate going to Grandma

Wren's."

"Oh, hush now, Mav." Mum cut me off by the wave of her hand before I could say anything else.

Turning back towards the cart, I was just about to climb back up when Mum's voice stopped me. "Now you leave Saffi be. You've had her out all day, let her rest for a while. Plus the walk will do you good – clear your head before the festival tomorrow night."

"Fine," I replied, sighing.

I really didn't want to have to go to Grandma Wren's place to pick up Connie, let alone go on foot and have no real excuse to get away. It wasn't that Grandma Wren was a bad person – actually, she was one of our elders and led most of the festivals along with the other elders throughout the year. It was just that she was ancient ... literally. None of us understood how it was possible, but Grandma Wren remembered the time before the colour disappeared, which made her over three hundred years old. But it was more than her practices being old, she liked to retell stories of what she called the 'better time', a time when all the fruits were different colours, and different again as they ripened. She always described the flowers and how they brought her such joy – all different varieties mixed together to make a room brighter. It could all be so interesting and completely unimaginable, but hard to get away once she started. And after finishing my lessons two years ago, being sent there at the age of five for fourteen years, I think I had heard most of the stories.

Striding out of the busy market area I slowed to a walk as I entered the quieter streets. As I wound round the twisting alleys a thought occurred to me: maybe Grandma Wren would know about cars and electricity and how someone could come up with such unusual inventions. As I walked through the town, I tried to imagine how it was when my Grandma was young. The centre of Sólas was built inside an old fortress. There was a large wall circling the outside, with larger buildings nearer the centre, along with our grassed festival area which had a few ancient trees in it. The smaller stone and wooden houses were set at the outer edges of the wall.

Then there was Grandma Wren's. She lived outside the town wall and towards the woodland on the southern side. Her small, well-kept wooden cottage stood out from everything else within the town. Instead of the dark panelling that adorned the other wooden houses, hers was bare, just the small seams where the wood joined one another. The only decorations were the small flower beds beneath her windowsills. And where the others had tiled roofs, hers was thatched. She didn't have any close family, well, she did once, but her direct family had died. Now she had only her descendants from them: me, Connie and Mum.

The rest of the town was surrounded by fields: to the north a variety of crop fields, in the west, livestock, and to the east, the fields were infertile and abandoned, merging into a skeletal forest that twisted round into the woodland behind Grandma Wren's. No one knew why, but since colour disappeared, that side of the town seemed to suffer the most.

As I made my way out of the southern gate, I was met by some of the other siblings, most a few years younger than me, tasked with picking up their younger brothers and sisters.

"Bit late today aren't we, Mav?"

"Oh, shut up, Feren, you know I have to help Mum!" I shouted back laughing.

38

Feren was in mine and Emerys' class. We had a temperamental relationship at best, always getting into fights and then suddenly being friends again. He had just picked up his younger brother and was striding back towards the town, the poor little tike having to skip to keep up.

"Yeah, well, you'd better hurry up or Grandma Wren will be having a cup of tea with Connie and then you'll never get away."

"Damn, you're right! Thanks."

"No problem, just do the same for me next time I'm late."

Running on ahead, I got to the little wooden cottage just a few minutes later. The fire was obviously lit as there was a little stream of smoke escaping into the night, the flickering of the candles in the windows indicating that they were in the living room at the front of Grandma Wren's home. Slowing to a walk to catch my breath before I got to the door, I crossed the last few feet of the stone path to a low, wooden door.

Knocking, I waited until either Connie or Grandma Wren answered. It had never felt right to just walk in like I did in at Emerys', even though Grandma Wren was family.

The sound of footsteps sounded from behind the door, and I rushed to think of an excuse to leave, which I should have prepared before I'd knocked. Too late, the door swung open but it wasn't Grandma Wren – it was one of the other elders, Grandpa O'Riley, a small, wiry, old man that liked to look down his crooked nose at everyone. Before I could talk, he spoke in a very flat, matter-of-fact tone, as if I had interrupted him doing something important.

"Yes? What do you need?"

"Uh, I'm here to pick up Connie. She had a lesson with Grandma Wren today," I blurted, wishing it was Connie answering the door; she knew I would come to pick her up.

"There is no one else here, Maverick. She must have gone home with the others." He didn't even wait for me to respond before slamming the door in my face.

"Gone home? She wouldn't go off on her own, she would have waited for me knowing Mum would have sent me to get her," I muttered to myself annoyed.

Turning around, I wandered back towards the town. She was going to get a mouthful when I got back, and Feren for not telling me she had already left. He had even made it seem as though she was still there.

Quickening my pace, I headed for the town wall and home to a vegetable stew.

Lorian

Wandering through the market had been eye-opening, even enjoyable, if I didn't venture too close to the stalls. Meeting the lovely flower-stall lady, whose name I didn't know, made it all the better. Even without colour, I could really get a sense of the beauty of the products the different vendors were selling. But now my true challenge awaited – I had put it off as long as I could. I had to try and find somewhere to spend the night, and somewhere that wouldn't put people out of pocket to keep me.

Maybe I could stay in one of the barns on the outskirts of town? I thought. No one would notice and I wouldn't be in the way of anyone. But how would I get there? Maybe Maverick could take me if I could find him, or maybe someone else could give me a lift. Maverick had said it was roughly ten miles from where he had found me, so I knew I wouldn't be able to make it back there before nightfall without help.

As I wound my way through the streets it slowly got darker. I wished Maverick had been wrong when he'd said there was no electricity. The buildings got more run down and dilapidated the further I walked. The chill in the air clung to my damp, muddy clothes like dead leaves clung to a tree, and the smell, a pungent smell of wood rot, hung in the air like a dense smog cloud.

I found myself outside a small church that looked similar to the Welmshire Chapel in Temford, but somehow more sinister. The stonework had gone black and vines trailed over its once-sturdy roof, breaking apart the solid slate. I don't know how I stumbled into this place from the market square that I had been in for hours, but it was giving me the creeps. A chill chased down my spine the longer I looked at it.

Shaking off the feeling, I turned to try and retrace my steps back to the market, but as I did so, I came a hair's breadth away from a man's chest. Glancing up into a grubby face, I quickly averted my eyes back to the ground. "I'm sorry, I didn't mean to bump into you." I made to walk around him but he side-stepped, blocking my path.

"No worries. Where are you heading?"

His gruff voice sent goose-pimples across my skin, there was something in the tone that made me feel uneasy. I don't know why – maybe it was because I was never allowed to wander the streets alone – but I just knew I needed to get away.

"Um…" I hesitated.

What could I say to this man so I could get past him?

"Just back home to my … my betrothed," I stammered, hoping that he would let me go if I said I had someone waiting for me. An increased sense of urgency was forming in the pit of my stomach. My body had never had such a violent reaction to someone's presence before. Not even the gaunt old man had warranted such a response, but I just knew deep in my soul I should heed it.

"You ain't old enough to have a betrothed – you're just a little girl. Bet you ain't even laid with a man have you?"

The cruel curl of his mouth made my stomach feel sick, my mind racing with all the possibilities of what he was thinking. I tried to slowly move away, putting distance between us. He continued talking, his words dripping with longing and what I believed was some deranged sense of lust.

"How about I change that for you, aye? How about we go somewhere quiet?"

He was moving towards me, closing the space I'd made too quickly. Feeling as though it was my last chance to try and get away, I tried to push past him and run back the way I came but he was too fast, his strong rough hand enclosing around my small wrist so hard I felt it click.

"No! Stop!" I shouted, hoping my voice didn't falter as it had so many times before, silencing me when I needed it.

"Shh, there's no need to shout. How about we go somewhere a little quieter?"

He pulled me into him so I was now with my back against his chest, his lips so close to my ear I could feel the brush of his stagnant breath against my cheek.

He dragged me backwards, my bare feet trying fruitlessly to run. I couldn't see where I was going but it was getting darker as the buildings began to swallow us into their shadows. Taking a deep breath, I let out the most ear-piercing scream I could, hoping against all hope that someone would hear me.

His rough hand collided with my mouth, stifling my attempt to be heard, his pace quickening, plunging us deeper into the shadows.

"Now stop doing that," he whispered, his breath starting to come faster now; I could feel his sweat soaking through my cotton blouse, "and you won't get hurt."

He threw me further down the alleyway, my knees colliding with the hard moist stones. I scrambled to move away from him. I turned quickly, shuffling backwards, my bare feet tearing on the uneven ground. I didn't want him close to me, I had to keep as much distance from him as I could. I scrabbled fast and faster as he moved closer.

A thud.

The back of my head sang as it found the dark, wet and mossy surface of the back of the alley. *This is it,* I thought, *I have nowhere to go.* Tears began to stream down my face, my vision blurring from the contact with the wall. Without so much as a second of hesitation, he pulled me back up and pushed me hard into the wall again. My vision hadn't cleared from the first time I had hit my head, but now it pulsed in and out, and the blackness threatened to consume me. The only reason I stayed upright was due to his hand against my throat, his breath misting over my face as he began to pull up my skirt, making his intentions clear. A sickening feeling churned in my stomach.

"No, please, stop," I sobbed, tears still pouring as my vision became increasingly narrowed, a dark mist closing in from every side. My eyes were too unfocused to see the back of his hand swing until it made contact with the right side of my face with a loud clap.

"Shut it, girl."

His voice had lost all its seductive, enticing tone; now all I could hear was his hunger for me. I tried to thrash with my legs and arms, hoping, praying I would land one shot and he would release me, but his grip just grew tighter on my throat, restricting my breathing. My laboured sobs tried to escape as I squirmed. I knew then, that no matter how hard I fought, I wouldn't get away. No one was coming to help, and no one cared enough to help me, they never had. So I did the only thing I knew how to do, I retreated into myself, hiding away so deep I hoped the outside world would never touch me again.

And then a figure loomed over the man on top of me, who was fumbling with his clothes. I slid down to the floor as I heard a thunderous crash. My attacker had hit the wall opposite.

"Get off her, you dirty bastard!" the stranger shouted.

The deep hatred that laced his voice was so intense it made me cower further, even if it wasn't directed at me. I curled myself into the tightest ball I could in the corner of the dark alley, hoping I would not be seen. My vision was still out of focus but no matter how much I willed it to take me, the darkness stayed just out of my reach.

My attacker snarled at him: "This is none of your business, laddie. Just go home to your little family and leave me be."

"Ha, no chance of that. Does it make you feel big, attacking young girls? Makes you feel in control, does it?" the stranger mocked.

I didn't think it was a good idea to bait my attacker, he seemed like he would stop at nothing to get what he wanted. The temperature in the alley dropped further as the two men squared off to each other.

"You don't want to do this, boy – it won't end well for you," my attacker murmured coldly, fists clenched at his sides.

The next thing I knew, he had swung a punch at the stranger, who dodged it easily and landed one of his own to the side of the attacker's face. He went down but turned his focus back on me, grabbing at my ankles he began to pull me towards him. I kicked out, hoping against all hope that I could kick myself free but he caught my feet easily, pushing against the bruised flesh and making me cry out in pain.

Hoisting us both up into a kneeling position, he held me in front of him like a shield. He placed his hand back on my throat and the other clenched my thigh. I knew from the strength of his grip that I would bruise, his nails dug in pinching my tender flesh.

"I will carry on then, and you can just stand there." My attacker squeezed my throat again and I gagged, clawing at his hands.

The stranger, whom I could only see as a silhouette, backlit from the light at the end of the alley, took a step towards us.

"Ah, ah, ah. I wouldn't if I were you." My attacker squeezed my throat even more and began to pull my skirt up, pinching my now-bare thigh. My tears were coming thick and heavy.

A warm spray suddenly hit my cheek and neck, as my attacker went rigid and his hands slowly released me. It wasn't until I looked round that I saw a large gash in his neck and that a knife had clattered to the ground beside me. I brought my hands down to touch my face and a dark thick liquid coated them. Blood. The realisation of what had happened made me heave but I had nothing to bring up.

"Hey, are you okay? You are safe now. I'm sorry – don't look – I didn't know what else to do."

He spoke in such a soft voice my mind swum with confusion. Glancing over my shoulder, I could see my attacker's lifeless body. The stranger now in front of me didn't act like he had just killed someone. He was so calm.

My body began to quake as fear replaced the surge of adrenaline.

Why? Why me? Why did it have to happen to me?

"It's okay, can you stand? I have somewhere that will be safe."

The stranger was like someone I had never seen before, he was a giant. The darkness still pulsed at the edges of my vision but I could see the worry in his pale eyes.

I tried to get up, but my legs just wouldn't support me, I was shaking too much. My legs crumpled from the small effort I made and I slumped back onto the floor, back into the blood that trickled around me. The stranger put his arms out to catch me. Flinching at the sudden contact, I made myself still, but his firm and gentle grip on my arms was in stark contrast to what had just happened. I felt myself stiffen as he held me steady.

"Here, let me help you. Do you mind if I pick you up?"

Looking into the stranger's eyes, I did all I could do to plead with him to leave me, to not hurt me, as once again I was trapped in silence, screaming on the inside but never out loud.

"Don't worry, I won't hurt you. I know it's hard, but trust me. I just want to take you somewhere safe. I know this lady in the town – she owns the flower stall. She knows how to take really good care of people, and she is an excellent healer."

He spoke softly but reassuringly to me. *He can't be talking about the lady I saw earlier today, can he?* I did the only thing I could to try and ask the question. I still clung to the flowers the lady had given me earlier – although crumpled, I held them out towards him.

Looking down, he caught sight of the little bunch and a

small smile grew across his face.

"So you've met her. She will take care of you I promise. Can I take you to her?"

I nodded my agreement tentatively. As he began to lift me into his arms I stiffened, all too aware that my skirt and blouse had been torn by the brute of a man lying not five feet away from us, dead.

"It's okay, I won't hurt you, and I'll get you somewhere safe. My name is Emerys, what's yours?"

I just looked at him, unable to make myself say my name. Bundled in the arms of this huge man I felt small and fragile.

Slowly my vision began to finally narrow and I couldn't make out what he looked like as we emerged into the gloomy light. I only remember seeing streaks in his hair and large pale eyes. His voice had begun to fade, but I managed to hear him say,

"Don't go to sleep! You hit your head pretty hard. I've got to get you back quickly. Hold on, it won't be long, okay?"

Hit my head? But when did do that?

Emerys

The young girl was still out cold as I hurried through the streets. My white shirt was covered in the blood she had landed in when she fell and her feet were dirty. Where were her shoes?

Holding her firmly in my arms I tried to quicken my pace back to Neave. She would know what to do. It wasn't much further and luckily the girl was light, so I could move swiftly.

The girl felt so fragile in my arms, and so cold. She was so cold. Her skirt and blouse had been ripped during her scuffle with her attacker. I tried my best to keep her covered, but it was hard when most of her clothes had been torn. It was also hard not to stare at the lattice of scars on the top part of her breasts. I could not bear to think about what could have caused them.

Quickening my pace, I all but ran through the now-deserted streets of Sòlas. It started to rain, making the town look bleak. Finally turning into the street I needed, I hurried the last few metres to Neave's door.

"Neave! Connie! Mav!" I shouted. Someone had to hear me, someone had to be home to help. I sent a silent prayer up to the Goddess begging for someone to be there. There wasn't anyone else in this town that would help without something being in it for them.

"Anybody there?! Help!" I shouted again, but there wasn't an answer.

Just as I was about to give up hope, the door swung open. Mav and Neave both stood in the doorway, bleary-eyed from sleep, but once they caught sight of the girl I was holding, I could see a sense of alertness wash over them.

"Get in here, now!" ordered Neave. "Put her over there on the rug, by the fire. Not too close or she will get chilblains…"

I did as instructed, placing the girl gently on the rug, ensuring that her clothes covered her before I stood up.

Turning around, the look on Mav's face was unexpected. I had never seen him look so furious. There was also something else in his expression that was hard to place. Hopelessness? Pity? No – blame. But who was he blaming? Surely it wasn't her? She hadn't asked for this to happen, she was just in the wrong part of the town.

"What happened?"

The growl erupted from Mav so fiercely it made me jump, even though I was looking at him. I had never seen him like this, never seen him so worked up about a stranger before.

"She was attacked. I found her on the east side of the town. And not a moment too soon, I would say."

"Not soon enough, by the looks of it. And what were you doing over there? You know you shouldn't be there, especially not at night."

"I was looking for Lila, alright? I thought she might have

got into trouble over there. And anyway, it was lucky I was, otherwise this girl wouldn't have been so lucky."

"Her name is Lorian."

He said her name in such a gentle way, as if caressing it. His face looked slightly crestfallen and he didn't avert his gaze from her, guilt radiating off him in intense waves.

"You know her? How?" I looked at him questioningly.

"I met her earlier today. I gave her a lift into town, or at least most of the way. I did warn her not to go to the east side." Maverick sighed, defeated. "This shouldn't have happened. I should have brought her into the town and explained where not to go."

"Surely she knows the town? There isn't another town for miles – well, apart from Brón but no one goes there. And anyway, you only met her today – how could you know she would wander over there?"

Maverick's response was cut short by his mum, Neave, coming back into the room. But the anger burning in his dark eyes was something he couldn't mask as his brow furrowed.

"Enough of the talk, we need to somehow get this tonic down her to help her distress. Then she can be put to bed," Neave said quickly.

Neave bustled around the girl, cleaning off the dirt and examining her. Turning away, I began to walk into the small adjacent kitchen to get a glass of water as Neave began to remove her ruined clothes and gently pulled a pale cotton nightgown over her.

Hearing Mav suck in a sharp breath I turned around, knowing it was more than a response to seeing her being undressed. Bruises. An array of bruises lined her right thigh and throat. As Neave was clearing off the grime they stood out on her pale skin.

"Enough gawping, go and get a hot water bottle ready for her, would you, Maverick? And Emerys, get some blankets from the cupboard." Neave barked at us, shielding the girl with her body.

Catching hold of Mav's arm, I dragged him the rest of the way into the kitchen.

"How? How could someone do that?" snarled Maverick.

"I don't know, Mav, I really don't."

I moved off into the hall the other side of the kitchen to retrieve the blankets Neave had instructed me to get. I had spent so much time at Maverick's house when I was younger, I knew it better than my own.

"You killed him, right?"

"Hey Mav, come on. Calm down…"

Depositing my armload of blankets onto the small kitchen table I glanced up at him. Maverick still hadn't moved from the edge of the doorway, taking small glances back into the sitting room where Neave spoke quietly to the frightened girl. She had come to after Neave had dressed her and applied a salve to her bruises.

"No, I won't calm down! You killed him, didn't you?"

Maverick's temper was rising and along with his voice. But that wasn't what worried me. I knew that Maverick's magic was on a tight leash at the best of times, but when he was angry that leash seemed to quiver with barely contained excitement.

"I did. He wouldn't leave her when I tried to intervene. You need to calm down, Mav. You know what could happen if you don't…"

"Good. And don't coddle me, I'm not a child."

Maverick snarled again but took a deep calming breath,

knowing I spoke the truth. I knew he still fought his inner fire as I watched him tuck the small strands of hair that escaped from behind his ears back into place. This is what he did when he was uncomfortable.

Neave called for us to come back into the sitting room, and as we entered I saw Lorian was sitting up, propped against a chair. Panic washed over Lorian as she looked at us; it was as if she was painted with it. She shuffled back as far away from us as she could, pulling at her nightgown.

Realising her distress, Neave moved closer, whispering quickly and softly, trying to take her focus away from us. Lorian was now crying, tears streaming down her face.

"Maverick, it's best you leave as I think you are upsetting her. Emerys, you stay. She has asked for you. Did you say her name is Lorian?"

Maverick nodded, pain and worry written on his face, as he retreated back into the kitchen. I couldn't believe that it would be Maverick causing Lorian so much distress but sure enough, once he left, she stopped pulling at her nightgown and her small sobs reduced to barely audible hiccups. Now it seemed her attention was solely on me. The panic that had etched her face just moments before, was now replaced with calm, quiet understanding as she sipped a tonic Neave had given her.

"Emerys," Neave said gently. Turning to her, I saw her take one of the girl's hands. "Would you help Lorian to her room, please?"

Confusion flickered through me but I tried to ensure it didn't show, schooling my face into neutrality and gentleness as I moved through the dimly lit room towards the pair. I knew Lorian would be frightened if she saw my misunderstanding, but Neave had obviously noticed as she answered my unasked question.

"I need to check on Maverick and get Lorian a hot-water bottle. She will be staying in Maverick's room and he will sleep out here. Please show her the way."

Moving the last few steps closer to Lorian, I took her small hand from Neave and put my other under her elbow to steady her. She was still unbalanced on her feet but was better than before. My large hand seemed to engulf hers; it felt as if I would break the small bones if I held on too tight.

Going down the hallway out of the living room, we passed the other side of the kitchen. Muffled voices, along with the sweet smell of lavender, drifted out. Mav sounded angrier than I had heard him be in a long time. Neave seemed to be fighting the losing battle to calm him.

I could feel Lorian squeezing my hand tightly, or as tightly as she could around my large paw, drawing my attention back to her. Her eyes were big and she was beginning to tremble again.

"It's okay, you're safe, I promise. You will stay in Maverick's room and don't worry, he will be staying out here," I said, trying to ease her already-frayed nerves.

I pushed on the creaky wooden door to Maverick's room. The sheets were tousled where he'd thrown them off, but I quickly pulled them together so she could gently lie down. Lorian glanced around her temporary sleeping quarters, she seemed so tense and uneasy but there was nothing I could do to ease her. She would feel better after Neave's tonic started to work.

"Goodnight, Lorian, try to get some sleep. No one will hurt you now, I promise."

Closing the door gently behind me, I waited a few moments to make sure she didn't try to get up out of bed, worried the blow to her head and the tonic would make her woozy. I heard her soft sniffles. With a sigh, I went to join Maverick and Neave in the kitchen. Inevitably there would be a round of questions.

Maverick

I don't think I'd ever felt so angry. I wanted to tear
something apart. Some *scum* put their hands on someone
like that?! I had so many questions to ask Emerys, about
what happened and why he thought Lila, his most recent
girlfriend, would be over the east side of the town. I hadn't
realised I had been pacing until Mum spoke.

"Oh, sit down, Maverick, you're putting me on edge."

Begrudgingly, I sat down in the chair across from her as she
continued to talk, all the while I fidgeted restlessly in my seat,
willing Emerys to hurry up and get back from helping Lorian.
It wasn't like we had a big house or anything. I didn't know
what could be taking him so long.

Mum's voice pulled my full focus back to her. She was upset,
looking at her hands.

"I met her today, you know – in the market. The flowers
she was clutching when she came in – I gave her those and
then offered her work as payment. She was going to refuse
them because she had no money. I should have realised then

that she couldn't afford anywhere to stay." Mum looked more distressed than I had ever seen her.

"I should have known as well. I met her in the north fields. She didn't have any shoes and she didn't even know where she was, or even that colour had disappeared."

"What do you mean she didn't know colour had gone?" Mum asked, bewilderment etched deeply on her normally lineless face. "She is obviously lying. No one could not know about the curse."

"I don't know... She just didn't know where she was, she thought she was in some place called Temford and talked about something called electricity. She seemed so disorientated but she was stubborn, adamant that she wanted to walk in to town by herself."

"Wait, wait, you said she was stubborn? She seemed very quiet and a bit timid when I spoke to her today. Are you sure it's the same person? And Temford... I think I need to talk with her in the morning, and if I'm right, I will need to see Grandma Wren."

"Yes, I am a hundred percent sure that it's her, Mum. What's so important about Temford that you would need to talk to Grandma Wren?"

"Not now, Maverick, we have more important things to worry about. For one, where is your sister?"

"Is she not home yet? I went to Grandma Wren's but she wasn't there."

Mum seemed so preoccupied with what I had said about Temford and Lorian not knowing there wasn't any colour, that she didn't seem to take any notice of me, so I sat and waited for Emerys. As he walked into the kitchen, my anger resurfaced. I wanted to launch at him and beat out the answers

I so desired, my sense of protectiveness running on overdrive. I hadn't realised I had been staring at him until he began to fidget and cleared his throat.

"Hey, I'm sorry, you know? I don't know why she acted like that when she saw you. Maybe she's just a little freaked after … well, you know, what happened…" Emerys shrugged.

I had never seen him so deflated. He always had a joke to crack or a sarcastic comment to make, and for an instant, I didn't feel angry. I just felt sad, very sad.

Slumping in the chair, my shoulders hunched, I sighed. "I know it isn't your fault, Emerys, I just don't understand how it could have happened. I only saw her this morning. I feel like I should have done more, I knew she was alone and didn't know the town. I should have helped her."

Emerys moved to sit in the chair next to me, placing his elbows on the table and his head in his hands. "I don't think anyone could have known what was going to happen. Yeah, maybe you could have done something to help her out, but honestly, you don't know what people are like and you only met her this morning. She wouldn't have made it as far as she did without your help and you did try to warn her. You know, with all the strange stuff happening, I don't blame you for not being more helpful; I wouldn't have been. I'm just glad I turned up when I did."

Emerys was right, with all the strange disappearances and people's market stock going missing you couldn't be too careful.

"That's enough for this evening," Mum said. "I don't know where your good-for-nothing sister is, but with everything going on she should be home. We just have to hope she gets here soon. Emerys, you can stay in the lounge with Maverick.

The fire is lit so it will keep you warm enough and there are more blankets and spare pillows in the cupboard in the hallway if you haven't pulled enough out already."

Mum eyed the pile that we had she seemed oblivious to a moment ago. I hadn't even realised she had been listening, she was so engrossed in thought about seeing Grandma Wren. But I could now see the worry on her face about Connie.

"I am sure she is okay. Good night, Mum!" I called after her as she began to gather herself up to leave. "Thank you for helping tonight."

"That's okay. You know too many people turn others away when they need help, and you know that I would never do that." She sighed. "But I will say one thing, we don't know this girl and so we should approach this situation with caution, you hear me?"

"We will. Thank you again. Sleep well."

Getting up from the table I grabbed a bundle of blankets and moved into the living room with Emerys on my heels.

"You know, I think she is going to be okay," Emerys said, causing me to jump.

He stood so close to me with his arms laden with yet more blankets from the cupboard. Throwing my armload down in front of the fire, I began to move some of the furniture to the side so we would have enough room to set up our camp beds. Emerys just stood there watching me, with not even the slightest intention of helping. "How do you know, though? And can you give me a hand with this table? If I scratch it or the floor, Mum will kill me."

Emerys responded to my second question with a grunt, dumping his blankets next to my pile and grabbing the other end of the coffee table. The front door suddenly let out a loud snick as Connie closed it behind her. There was a question in her eyes as she took one look at us moving furniture, but she thought better of asking it and tried to skulk off to bed.

"Where the hell have you been? I went to Grandma Wren's to collect you and you weren't there. Mum is worried…" I hissed at her before she could leave.

"I was out…" was all she said, raising her eyebrows. Her tone was cold and challenging, but I couldn't be bothered to argue.

"Well, you'd best think of a better excuse before you see Mum tomorrow. You know about the disappearances, Connie – now isn't the time for pulling your stunts." Turning away from Connie, I pushed Emerys for an answer: "Well?"

"Well, what?" Emerys seemed so distant all of a sudden.

"Well, how do you know Lorian will be okay? You never answered. And what's wrong? You suddenly seem like you're in another world."

"Oh, she is a fighter. I heard her screaming to get attention and trying to kick the guy off before I got to her. I think she'll be okay. And… oh never mind, let's set this up. I get the fire this time, I am not freezing my butt off as you soak up all the heat."

He tried, but was unsuccessful, to cover the pain on his face with humour. Putting the table down next to the door, Emerys moved back over to the blankets and started setting up his bed.

"What is it? What's wrong?" I wasn't going to let this go. Whatever was eating away at Emerys would be better dealt with at that moment.

I was in the middle of the room which now looked a lot larger with all the furniture pushed to the sides. We hadn't cleared it like this since the last circle was held here a few months ago. The ashy-white remnant of chalk still peeking out from the sides of the rug was the only tell-tale sign that this room had been used for anything other than family gatherings. The chalk circle had been drawn so many times that the only way it could be got rid of was painting over the floorboards.

Sighing, Emerys finally answered my question: "Hmph… It's just… Do you think something like that happened to Lila? And if so, do you think she would fight as hard as Lorian did or would she be too scared to?"

Placing my hand on his shoulder, I tried my hardest to calm him. "I don't think that would have happened to her, but if it did, I know she would fight like hell. I know I joke about all the girls that hang around you as there always seems to be a new one…"

"Don't, Mav, just don't…" The anger in Emerys' voice was thick.

"No, no, listen. You and Lila seem different – she gets all your jokes and doesn't mind hanging out with me either."

Emerys' shoulders relaxed. "I feel different, Mav. Yeah, I would have looked after all the others but it's making me crazy that she's gone and that I can't find her."

"I know… How about we both look again tomorrow?" I suggested as we climbed into our makeshift beds.

"But what about Samhain? And won't you want to help to look after Lorian? There is obviously something going on there, even though she seems a little freaked out. You evidently feel a little bit protective."

"We will be back in time for Samhain and by the looks of it, Lorian doesn't want to see me, so I think it would be best for her if Mum looked after her alone. Anyway, let's get to sleep

– we will be able to think better in the morning."

I ignored his statement suggesting there was something going on between me and Lorian. I knew I felt interested in her, she was just so different. Putting the thought out of my head I rolled over.

"Night," Emerys muttered.

"Night," I responded.

It was the same ritual we had used for years: we'd talk about our concerns but never actually make any headway in finding solutions.

Sighing, I waited for the fire to dim. I knew I wouldn't be able to sleep for a long while. As the clock ticked by the hours, I knew we were both just lying there awake, lost in our own thoughts.

Lorian

I lay there most of the night, my eyes heavy, cheeks damp, and throat sore from suppressing sobs until the dark night turned a light grey. Numb, that's what I felt; completely hollow as if nothing good could ever warm me again. There were only two other times I had felt like this: the first was when my father had died when I was eight. The second and last time was when I was twelve, the night my life changed forever.

It had been a weird night, one of release but also devastation. It was the night my mother and stepfather died. And that wasn't the worst of it. Oh no, the worst thing was that I had helped bring about their deaths. Afterwards, I had to live with my uncle who used my brother, Hugh, and I as charity cases, parading us in front of his friends, talking about how he had to look after us and how we really should have been in an orphanage. He was just *too kind* to let that happen…

Memories flitted through my mind. *A locked door. A sly calculating glance. A large tree overhanging the garden wall.*

I watched as the memories unfolded unbidden, but I was helpless to do anything to stop them. They were not in a coherent sequence, but random images flashing in rapid succession in the dark. The boy who brought me into town made an appearance, but before I could remember his name he was gone, replaced by the dark damp smell of an alleyway.

I could feel my pulse rising. Something wasn't right.

I shouldn't be here.

How am I here – I was just in bed?

A large hand gripped my shoulder, spun me around, and rancid stale breath crept into my nose. I expected to see my attacker but the scene snapped and changed again, churning my stomach at the ferocity of it.

Hugh was looming over me with a cruel snarl on his face. He raised his hand as he had so many times before, but before it made contact, I was thrust back into the alley, sliding along the moss-slicked ground. Hands grabbed at my legs as I kicked with all my might to get away.

I was thrust into a small living room with a wave of nausea, the warmth of the fire near burning against my cold body. When had I got up? My mind wouldn't let me dwell on such idle thoughts as images continued swimming in and out of my mind's eye. A kind-looking woman hovered close by, snapping instructions at two looming figures that hovered at the edge of my consciousness. I couldn't let them see me, not like this. Not so exposed.

Commanding my legs, I pushed myself a few steps forward, the scene swayed and changed once more. I was now running, running as fast I could, mud enveloping my feet as I pushed through the manicured borders of my uncle's estate. Loud voices approached quickly, accompanied by the sound of crunching leaves as I tried to conceal myself amongst the plants.

"It is okay, my bird. No need to panic, you are safe..."

The consoling words drifted around my head as I threw myself out from behind the plants, my feet colliding with hard uneven stone instead of the soft grass of my uncle's lawn, my vision hazy. Pushing my legs faster, I ran, but still the voice drifted to me:

"Where are you going, my bird?"

That saying... What was it about that saying that I recognised? A face flashed before me, causing me to stumble as I ran but it was gone too quickly for me to see who it was.

Pounding rang out behind me... They were coming, coming to take me away. Hands gripped my throat, hot putrid breath at my ear, a spray of blood coating my skin. Bile rose in my mouth, but nothing would come; my stomach was empty, but still it heaved; my body shook to rid itself of the smell, the feeling of their hands.

My legs trembled from the running, but still my feet hammered on the uneven ground as it turned soft. A strange smell of water drifted up to my nose; the visions were fading, blurring at the edges. A face flashed before me, guiding me back from the darkness, from the oblivion of the nightmares that tormented me.

"It does not do one well to dwell, for it only holds them back from what is in front of them."

A smiling face came further into view and my heart swelled at the sight of it. Maria, my old maid and cook. As if my brain finally caught up with itself, the fog dissipated. Maria, it was the name she always insisted I use. But one image, one memory remained. Like a whisper against my mind, consoling it from all the pain, like lavender soothes the soul.

"Remember my bird, do not dwell, you need to be strong now..."

Her voice tumbled into me like the melody of a dance piece would, lifting my soul with it. Then everything went black.

Slowly the light managed to creep back in, but with it so did sound.

Maverick

Thundering footsteps sounded along the hall, coming closer. Rubbing my eyes, I looked up to see Lorian standing in the narrow mouth of the hallway. Horror creased her forehead and in the next instant she was running.

"Lorian!" I shouted as I jumped up off the floor where mine and Emerys' makeshift beds had been put together. She had taken off so quickly that none of us had even been able to get up quickly enough before she was out of the door.

"What is happening? Maverick, why are you shouting?" Mum stormed out of her room, wrapping a dressing gown around herself.

"It's Lorian, she just left. I don't know what is wrong with her, but something isn't right. She looked upset…" I rambled, quickly pulling my clothes on. Emerys was doing the same beside me.

Before Mum could say another word, Emerys pushed past me and was out of the door. I was close behind him. Looking up the street, we could see Lorian's small form weaving around the cobbled road. She looked drunk, and she would catch her death from the cold in the thin nightdress she wore.

Running as fast as we could up the road, it quickly became apparent that she was too far out of our reach to catch as she disappeared into the maze of alleyways.

"I will get Xaviran. It will be faster to follow her on horseback and who knows what state she will be in when we find her."

I turned back towards my home, glancing up at the sky I worked out the time: five-thirty in the morning. It was still early and late-autumn weather could be unpredictable. Picking up my pace, I made my way towards the stables where mine and Mum's horses were kept, and where Emerys had put his horse earlier.

"I'll follow you on Garnet," he added.

"No, go to Mum, tell her what's happened. I'll bring Lorian back here."

"Fine, but if you're not back soon I will follow," he said stubbornly, turning into the house as I ran the last few yards to the stables behind.

Throwing open the door of the small barn I strode over to Xaviran's stable. My large loyal horse was there, waiting, as if he had known I would need him this morning.

Guiding him outside, I hoisted myself onto him without tack. Xaviran always preferred to be ridden bareback and would not even consider letting me put a saddle on. I stroked his side, inhaling his familiar scent, savouring the easing in my chest I always felt when we were about to go out and ride. I took a final deep breath, sending a silent prayer to the God and Goddess that I would not be too late.

"Run, Xaviran, run! We have to make sure she is okay…" I

whispered to my loyal horse, digging my heels into his sides as we tried to retrace Lorian's steps.

Lorian

My head pounded as I blinked my eyes clear of their heaviness, pulling myself up into a sitting position from where I had ended up lying on the ground. The place I found myself in looked derelict, like no one had lived there for years. Memories of the night before in the abandoned alley flooded me and my panic rose higher. Glancing around I tried to get my bearings. The buildings were wooden but I was sure if a heavy gust of wind blew they would just disintegrate into dust and be no more, forgotten, with all the people in them, if there were any.

A heavy dusty smell lingered in the air with undertones of rot, both from vegetation and something else I couldn't quite place. I didn't want to begin to think about what it could have been, decay was something I had never known until I had run away into the lower classes of Temford. Trying to retrace my steps through the soggy streets, I could only hope what I was walking through was water and mud and not something worse. The smell seemed to grow stronger the more I moved, confirming to my horror that it was something foul. Pushing away the thoughts of what was floating round my feet, I tried to remember which way I had come, but everything looked so similar. How could I not have realised I was heading into this disgusting place? I knew why – the memories had been coming so quickly, so vividly I hadn't seen where I had been running.

That was when I felt it, that feeling, a slight tickle that creeps up, as though something is watching me, the feeling I had always felt as I roamed the gardens at home. I knew when I turned that I wouldn't see Mother or my uncle standing at the tall town house windows, and that made the hairs on the back of my neck stand up just a little bit more.

An animalistic snarl that could only have come from a starving beast erupted from the darkness of the buildings behind me. I turned to face the sound as it tore through the air again. I had only ever been told about such things by my brother in the stories he used to tell to scare me, but nothing, not even the most horrific and terrifying of my brother's stories, could prepare me for what came next.

There was a human tone amidst the creature's snarl that had me wanting to run as fast as I could. But it was as though my mind and body were at odds – I could not move other than to tremble. The beast chattered and clicked to itself, as if assessing me. Instead of running as I so wanted to do, I forced myself to turn and face what must be a monster. I would not be afraid of fragments of my imagination any more.

As I turned, I realised my mistake. I blinked my eyes to be sure, that this was not a fragment of my imagination. I could not have come up with the beast that stood before me. The sight of it was far more disturbing than the voice that accompanied it. Every inch of its skin was covered in welts. Its one open eye blazed wildly and the other was crusted shut. The creature before me was bent and crooked, with limbs that seemed to twist in ways that shouldn't be possible. Its yellow elongated teeth didn't fit behind the shredded flaps of skin that were supposed to pass for lips. I didn't know whether to be sick, turn and run, or buckle under the sorrow of what I could see – it was clear that what was now a monster, was once a person.

I stood there, eyes widening with shock as the creature clicked its tongue a few more times and then began to speak.

"Oooh, what a lovely specimen we have here," groaned the mutilated being, clicking again.

As it moved closer it was as though the morning sky darkened in its presence. I tried to take in every detail as if my eyes were still deceiving me, all the while slowly edging away on my weak, wobbly legs, hoping that I could find my way back. How had I got here?

"Oh yes, quite exquisite indeed," came a hissing voice from behind me, so close that I could feel its breath on the back of my neck, like my attacker last night.

A shriek exploded from my chest before I could even think. My movements were stiff as fear began to grip me, but I pushed myself to move away faster. As I moved, more creatures appeared out of the shadows of the dilapidated buildings from every direction. They were surrounding me, isolating me from any way of escape.

Why, why had I been so stupid as to run away? Why had I let those memories grip me? I felt as though I was in a zoo, the new prized attraction, and maybe I was. Maybe to these mutilated people I was the first 'normal' person they had seen, if you could call a girl transported to a colourless place 'normal'. I was probably the only normal person they had seen in months, possibly years.

They kept talking, edging closer, looking me over as they would a meal before taking the first mouthful, and so I did the only thing I could. Reverting back to the years of trying to escape from my house, I crouched down, pulling my hands over my head and trying to block out the terrible, rasping sound of their voices. My fatigued body shuddered while the creatures moved closer, sniffing and tormenting me. I waited, waited for them to take me away, to become like them … or worse. All the while I was consumed by the memories of the night before, as they drew closer.

One of the creatures brushed my forearm with its mutilated, taloned hand but as it did, there was a loud bang that rippled through my body. The sudden shock had me clutching my arms over my head even tighter. The monsters that circled me let out an ear-splitting scream and then fell silent. I couldn't hear their rasps any more, and opening my tightly shut eyes I could just make out the feet of the creatures moving a few feet away from me.

I forced myself to look at what had caused the creatures to back away, to pull their starving eyes to something else. The image of the blurred men standing behind the kind-faced woman flashed across my vision, and I remembered at once who he was.

Maverick.

He sat tall and proud, and utterly furious atop a beautiful black horse. Pulling my hands over my head I shielded myself from another blast of the strange thunder that had come moments before. But I would not wait idly by and let myself

be hurt again.
Not this time.

Maverick

I felt sick. It had taken me hours to find Lorian. She had gone deeper into the labyrinth of alleyways than I thought, running for miles and ended up in that rotten place. Although the sky had grown dark I could tell it was now creeping towards seven-thirty. Anger pulsed through me, so much so it was as if my body rippled with the dark fury's power. It consumed me like it hadn't for years, not since I was a child when I had seen a man – the man I believed was my father – lay a hand on my mother so hard,he knocked her unconscious. Even when she came around she didn't quite know where she was. But I'd sorted out that threat. When my magic consumed me then, I ensured he would never harm my mother again.

These deranged things were trying to prey on Lorian, and taunt her when she was so obviously scared. That made the dark fury engulf me once more – fully, utterly, completely.

Sliding off Xaviran, I pulled all that energy to me, I focused on the deformed creatures that were now only a metre away from where she was. Lorian looked terrified but determined as she pulled herself up and reached for a wooden beam to use as a weapon. I knew I had to focus, had to ensure the shock wave went around her. Focusing hard and drawing deeper from the place within myself where I felt my power came from, I threw it out, extending both of my hands before me as I released it into the world. I don't know if I actually let out a shout as I did so or if I just felt as though I did, for the power or the shock let out an earth-thundering boom.

The shock wave cascaded through the mutant creatures, not one ripple touching Lorian. It was evident that she could feel its force though, as she swayed on the spot as the creatures flew.

A clattering of hooves indicated that Emerys hadn't listened to me and had followed anyway. He was obviously as furious as I was as he took in the scene. He slid off his horse, and was hunched forwards, teeth bared to the creatures, practically snarling with rage. Seeing what had crept from their bitter existence within the east slums, I was secretly glad Emerys had come, even if he was a stubborn-headed lout. The deformed creatures gathered themselves up and focused their gaze on us, baring their rotten, broken teeth.

"So you want to play, do you?" one of the creatures taunted, taking a step towards us.

"Want to try your luck to see if you can save the pretty little thing, do you? Want to see if you can best us?"

As the creature finished its last words it stood nose-to-nose with me. Its stagnant breath mixed with mine as it laughed in my face. It was all I could do to not show the shock I felt at how it had moved so quickly, or to move away from the rancid creature. I resorted to what I normally do when confronted.

Drawing energy again from the black mass surrounding me, I pushed my face closer to the creature and whispered so only it could hear: "Do you wish to die today, creature? For I can truly give you a death to fear."

The reaction that the creature gave me was not the one I was expecting. It laughed – the creature full-heartedly laughed in my face showing the extent of its rotten teeth, and its tongue, forked like a snake.

"Oh, you can try, boy. We haven't had this much fun for a long while," it hissed, and then faster than I could track, it moved back towards its restless companions.

Glancing across to Emerys, I realised he'd watched the full exchange and was looking at the creature as it now stood whispering to its companions about what was to come. They all looked intoxicated with the challenge, and hungry, so very hungry.

Turning back to the matter at hand, I looked for Lorian. She was tracing the path that the creature had taken as quick as light but still stood firm, with her plank raised, panic in her gaze. I knew full well Emerys could handle himself as he tensed beside me, but we had to get to her. There was no way through without getting past the creatures first, without having to fight. Emerys had come to the same conclusion, as he let out a small snarl.

"Well, are you ready?" I asked.

Palming the hunting knife that never left his side, a half-smile slid onto Emerys' face. "Always. Let's play…"

With that, he pushed off at a sprint, hurtling himself into the mass before us. Emerys had no innate skill that would benefit himself in a fight other than his sheer size and a whole lot of training, whereas I didn't need to solely rely on my fists.

However, his empath skill could throw his enemy off their game.

The dark fury that flittered around me brushed me with its dark touch, caressing my skin. It wasn't always dark – it took on many forms depending on my mood, just like a storm could, but the darkness was what I knew best and what manifested the most.

Drawing it into myself once more, I ran into the fray of creatures that were now launching themselves at Emerys. Needing no other weapon than my hand, I made contact with the jaw of one of the creatures and sent a shock wave bursting through it, so much so I could hear its jaw snap. The creature flew across the street into the wooden frame holding up a rotten house. As the frame broke, the upper level that it was holding collapsed, sealing the creature's fate. I sent the shock-waves through the creatures over and over again, ensuring that they knew we could not be dealt with lightly. I could hear the thump of Lorian's plank making contact as she swung blindly at those approaching her; she was obviously not going down without a fight.

As I sized up the few remaining creatures, one turned to me. It had obviously been a woman but now its hair, once smooth and straight, was matted and encrusted with remnants of whatever it had for food. Its once-pleasant features were twisted into an expression of hatred and disgust, with sores covering every inch of its features.

But it was the gift this creature possessed that stirred something within me, a memory that I couldn't yet grasp. It started to shimmer before a blinding light erupted out of it, the pressure of the light blasting me off my feet. That was when I knew – dread filling me, and nothing could take it away.

Scrambling to my feet, I created a shield around me. I didn't know how long it would last as I had only recently practised it and it still spluttered out randomly. My dark fury could hold a longer, more stable shield than the girl creature's erratic blast would last.

Looking over to Emerys, I could see the unexpected blast had knocked him off his feet as well, but fortunately from lack of experience the creature had knocked all of the other creatures down as well. I sent my dark fury over to Emerys, letting it wrap itself around him, becoming a second skin, cloaking him from any harm. It was another trick I had recently learned.

"Enough," the glowing one mocked. "Enough of this child's play." Turning to look at the others that were gathered beside it, the girl creature barked orders at them. "Take the girl. There is something about her that is different from the rest. I can smell it."

That was all the encouragement Emerys needed. He lunged back into the fray, battering his way through until he reached Lorian's side. She was now sprawled on the floor, her skin raw from the blast, her eyes blinking, unseeing, as she tried to clear her vision. Emerys began to pull her into his arms as one of the creatures wrapped its claw around his bicep, plunging its talons into him. An agonising scream like an animal caught in a snare bellowed from Emerys as he half-dropped Lorian to bury his hunting knife into the creature. My dark fury should have made him impenetrable, so I focused harder, watching as it shimmered darker against his skin then disappeared.

I could see Emerys concentrating and the creatures beginning to look around at one another, becoming jittery and confused as his power infested their beings. I let out the biggest wave I could muster and threw it out to the creatures. I willed it to blow them away and send them back into the depths of this forsaken place. But it didn't just do that, it threw them into the buildings and walls around us. Walls that weren't rotten or crumbling groaned as the now-irreversibly broken creatures cascaded against them. The ones that weren't thrown into the more solid walls limped off, whining like reprimanded dogs.

Turning to face Emerys, I saw him limping over from where he had managed to scooped up Lorian. He had obviously taken a hit to the knee and he had dirt and claw marks covering his clothes. Blood was seeping onto his trousers and running down his arm where the puncture wounds from the beast's claws oozed. Dirt and blood, both his own and the creatures', was splattered across his face, yet still there was a smile tugging at his lips.

"What?" I asked inquisitively. He was always the only person to try and suppress a smile after a fight. He knew more times than not that smiling after would just land him in more trouble. "I think this is one time you are allowed to smile," I said laughing.

"It isn't that I'm smiling about," he said. I now realised he was trying to suppress a laugh.

"Then what is it?" I exclaimed, starting to become exasperated. I was annoyed that the shield I had sent to him hadn't worked the first time. It had worked all the other times I'd tested it.

"It's the fact that you look like a roasted lobster. You're even starting to blister."

This time he couldn't hold the laughter in. Lorian let out a small laugh of her own as we both stared for a moment at the small sound she had made. Feeling her growing nervousness, Emerys quickly recovered.

"Well, you can't laugh too much, your skin is nearly as bad as his."

Emerys rumbled again with a laugh but it was short-lived; when his body began to tremble he winced from the pain it caused in his arm.

Lorian wriggled out of his arms, proclaiming that she could walk even on her shaky legs. They supported one another as they moved closer.

"I am sorry, Emerys. I tried to send you a cloak shield but it didn't work."

Making a mental note to practice more, I moved to help Lorian from under his arm, but at the small shake of her head they continued to where the horses stood. I followed closely by, concerned for their welfare.

Now that he had mentioned it, my skin did feel prickly and sore. Putting my hand up to touch my cheek I winced when I made contact with a large blister that had formed from the light blast. It was full and malleable under my finger. *Great, I'm going to look like an overcooked piece of meat for Samhain,* I thought. Lorian looked at me and an expression I couldn't place covered her face, but I thought it resembled fear. "I'll just go and get the horses," I muttered.

Letting out a sigh, I walked the short distance to where the horses still stood, leaving the two to make their own way. *I am sure they will be fine,* I grizzled to myself. *From now on I'll just stay away from her, she can look after herself.*

Emerys

"It's okay," I said after seeing the look she gave Maverick. I could tell it had annoyed him. "We'll be okay now. Although that was the most fun I've had in ages."

I didn't know how many times I was going to have to say it, but I knew that I would have to keep trying to reassure Lorian that everything was okay. She was still so jumpy and couldn't remember how she had got to this place, only that she thought she was having a nightmare. I could feel her fear was true and stifling; it was washing through me as though it was my own – one of the curses of being an empath. Something felt off. I could feel that there was another reason for her fear lying just beneath the surface – it was not the creatures or the ogre who attacked her the previous night. I could also see her determination to look after herself, as she brandished that plank against the creatures.

"Will you come back with me to Neave's so we can get you checked over? She will have an ointment to help your skin and would like to know what happened and if you're having nightmares. She can give you a special tea to help ward them off. You can also get ready for Samhain this evening. If you want to go, that is?"

"Y—you're bleeding," Lorian stammered, ignoring my question. "Your arm, and all over your face, there is blood."

"Aye, there is," I replied. "So I'd best ask Neave to help me clean it out before there is an infection."

"Some yarrow would help with the bleeding," she said, matter-of-factly.

I suppressed rolling my eyes and forced a small smile on my face. Lorian obviously knew her herbs, but I couldn't understand why she would then lie about not knowing anything about magic if she was so accustomed to their healing properties. Focusing back on Lorian's face I put this question aside for another time. "Good idea, maybe you can help Neave mix that up for me when we are back in town."

Her tense frame grew slack as we moved around to stand by Garnet's side, my hand clasped in hers to guide her.

"Thank you for helping me again. I am sorry, I truly don't know what happened." Lorian spoke softly so I could only just catch her words, but it wasn't fear that was making her quiet. It was because she was distracted, thinking about something other than what had just happened.

"You're most welcome," I replied." But we'd best get going or we will be late. It took us a while to find you when you ran off this morning. Neave will want you to rest when we are back and she will shut the stall earlier so you won't be working today."

I was still clasping her hand with mine, and I could feel her trembling begin to ease. But her face betrayed her feeling of shame, as she would not be able to help as she had promised.

"Do not worry, Neave will understand," I reassured her.

Maverick was already mounted on his horse and had turned both horses so they faced back to the centre of the town. My horse, Garnet, was as different from Maverick's as we were. Maverick's was built for speed, whereas mine was a heavy Clydesdale, built for pulling ploughs over fields.

Maverick turned to look at us, and the shock that covered his eyes at our clasped hands was not lost on me. Fortunately, I don't think Lorian noticed. Clearing his throat, Maverick threw down my reins. "You take Lorian back to Mum's and I will meet you there. I need to go and speak to Grandma Wren."

Lorian glanced at Maverick, puzzlement clouding her features. Maverick, realising her confusion, explained to her:

"Grandma Wren is one of the elders in our village, I need to confirm to her that something is dwelling in the east side and confirm the sightings of the creatures. She might know what these creatures are and where they originally came from. I think these creatures could have something to do with the disappearances..."

"She is still in shock," I replied quietly to Maverick as, after his explanation, Lorian still seemed confused. It was too much information to take in all at once. "I will take her back to your Mum's and see you in an hour, but I would make sure you are back in enough time so you can put some ointment or something on your face."

Lorian pulled her slight hand free from mine and moving around to Garnet's head, she began to whisper and mutter to him as if only she and he could hear. Garnet's ears twitched as though he was listening intently to what she was saying to him as she stroked his nose. I felt her begin to calm further, the longer she cooed to my horse.

Maverick's attention was fixed on Lorian as he spoke but he addressed me: "We'd better get going – we don't want to be out here long enough for those creatures to regroup. I will see you in an hour."

And with that he nudged Xaviran and disappeared down the street.

"Come here and I will help you up on him," I instructed Lorian, cupping my hands as a foothold for her. "Stand on my hands and I will hoist you up."

Lorian tentatively put her slight foot into my hand – I could feel her reluctance to follow my instructions.

"Unless you want to sit on him backwards, I suggest you use the other foot. Just stand the way he is looking, place your left foot in my hand, hold onto the side of his mane here." I pointed to the lower part of Garnet's mane, towards its base. "And no, you won't pull it out." I had noticed the horror-struck look on her face. "Swing your right leg over."

Following all the instructions precisely, Lorian was sitting astride Garnet a moment later.

"What is his name?" she asked, stroking him on the side of his neck.

"Garnet," I replied as I hauled myself up behind her.

Lifting Lorian and then pulling myself up had broken the wound on my arm. It had only been bleeding at a trickle but it was now a steady flow.

"Now, we must go!"

Nudging Garnet on, I guided us back to the town and Neave's house. Neave was going to give us a mouthful when she heard what had happened, that was for sure.

Lorian

As I thought back on the events of that morning, my stomach felt hollow. I could not remember when I had last eaten – not since I arrived in Sòlas, that was for certain. One minute I was running as fast as I could trying to get away from my uncle and all the other memories, and then I was surrounded by a horde of the most hideous creatures. I remember seeing Emerys and Maverick there, looking ready to fight, but I also remember the images that drove me from my bed into that place. I hoped I had dreamt it all, but as I looked at Emerys' blood-speckled face the snarls came back to me within an instant, along with their mutilated faces and a distinct, rancid scent. I shivered.

"Are you cold?" Emerys asked, tightening one arm around me as we entered the town through the east side's small alleys. I hadn't realised I had gone so far.

"No, I was just thinking about what happened."

I twisted to look up at Emerys' face. "Thank you for what you and Maverick did for me – they were just so awful."

As I looked up into his kind face, I noticed a stark difference to how he had looked earlier. His eyes were distant, as if he couldn't focus, and he looked paler. That was when I noticed my right thigh was damp – it was soaked with blood. "Are you okay?" I exclaimed, my panic rising. "Your wound is bleeding a lot now."

"I will be okay, I just need to get to Neave's – she will know what to do," Emerys replied, but his voice was shaky and weak.

From the amount of blood running down my thigh there was no time to get to Neave's, we needed help right then. Taking hold of the reins in front of Emerys' hands, I pulled us to a stop. Emerys began to slide to the left with his hand still around my waist, pulling me down with him. We landed with a hard thud onto the solid stone track. Pulling myself up, I knelt on my haunches, assessing Emerys' arm and other wounds. His arm was definitely the one causing him the most trouble, the others could wait until later to be tended. As I tried to pull back the torn fabric of his shirt he groaned and tried to cover his wounded arm with his hand.

"Don't touch," I instructed. "You will make it worse. Let me have a look. Lie on your back."

Tentatively, I started to roll the sleeve of his shirt up past the wound, but the fabric began to snag, congealed with the blood and dirt in the wound.

"Use the knife from my belt," Emerys suggested, wincing as he rolled onto his left side and reached for the bone-handled knife that he kept sheathed at his waist.

"Here, let me do it, and don't roll onto your side – you'll get more dirt in the wound."

I leaned across him and unclipped the knife from his belt. As carefully as I could, I began slicing the shirt as I tried to prise it away from the deep wound. Slowly I cut away the fabric that clung to the wound, but as I began to pull away the last of it, a rotten smell rose to my nose. The edges of the opening were blackened. "It is infected. I don't understand how because it only just happened."

I pressed my thumbs gently around the wound and a foul pus-like substance oozed out, coating the rest of Emerys' arm, causing him to wince. "I am sorry, but we have to pack this, then we really need to get you to Neave."

I began searching around us to see if I could find the herbs I so desperately needed, I knew it was frivolous but I just needed something, anything that would help.

"There will be a small pack of clay powder that will help with bleeding in the pouch on my belt. Neave doesn't let me go anywhere without it, just in case," he revealed, in between panting breaths.

"Why didn't you tell me about this before?" I scolded. "Gosh, if only Maria was here, she would be able to staunch it in an instant," I muttered under my breath as I leaned over Emerys and pulled the small pouch off his belt. I pulled out the bentonite clay, contemplating the powdery substance I had only read about. "This will do for now, but you can't use it for long. It can have some bad side effects, but at least it will help with the swelling and some of the infection. Do you have any water so I can mix it to a paste?"

Emerys blinked at me slowly as if just registering what I'd said, before raising his hand to Garnet. I saw that there was a small water container strapped to the side of his saddle. Tugging it off, I moved back to Emerys and took out a small amount of the powder, cupping it in one hand. Carefully to not wash the powder away, I drizzled a small amount of water and began forming the slimy putty substance.

"Who is Maria?" Emerys asked, trying to lift himself but he didn't have the energy and his body slumped back down.

"She was fantastic with herbs and natural remedies." I could see him contemplate my words as I said this, but he was so weak he could barely keep his eyes open.

"You knew her well?" he panted, his voice barely audible.

"Well, yes, even though she was the maid within my mother's household, she was my friend. When I ran away, I stayed with her and her family. She taught me about herbs and how to care for the sick, which we did a lot when the sickness struck Temford," I babbled as I began to pack the herbs into the four long gouges on Emerys' arm. "Anyway, let us just focus on what is happening now, then we need to get you back to Neave's. But you have to help me, I don't know where I am going and I can't move you on my own."

I finished packing the wounds and lifting Emerys' good arm, I tucked myself under him to try and hoist him up. "Please, Emerys, I need your help – I can't do this on my own," I pleaded.

Emerys groaned as he tried to get his legs under him, and with a combined effort we just managed to get him standing upright, even if he did sway slightly.

"Right, we need to get you back on Garnet – it will be far quicker than walking."

"I don't think I will be able to get myself on him – not with one arm – and I don't think I have the strength…"

"Well… Let's try how you got me on him. See if that works," I said determinedly, moving Emerys over next to Garnet. I let him lean against the horse for support. "Lean your shoulder on to him but make sure you don't pull the clay out of your wounds."

Bending over, I cupped my hands just as Emerys had earlier.

"But I am too heavy – you won't be able to lift me," Emerys protested.

"Enough! If we don't try, we won't know, and you won't be strong enough to walk and I certainly don't want to leave you here," I growled.

My temper was rising, mixing with my worry. I would not leave him here injured, not after everything he had done for me.

Again, I bent over and placed my feet firmly on the ground and bent my knees. *Please hold,* I thought to myself. *I just have to get him on the horse.*

Emerys carefully placed his booted foot in my hands and pushed his weight onto them. As soon as he did, I pushed up with all my might so he could heave himself onto Garnet.

"I reckon you leant into him more than normal, am I right?" I smiled up at Emerys who was now slumped over Garnet's neck.

"Well, I couldn't just let you try and push me up – I had to help!"

"I think Garnet is going to need a wash now, you have covered him in blood and other horrible things," I jested, trying my best to lighten his spirits.

His face was drawn from the pain. I knew pulling himself up on Garnet hurt but I knew we wouldn't make it otherwise. "Now come on, which way are we going?"

Leading Garnet on, I walked as fast as I could with Emerys' faint guidance to Neave's.

Maverick

As I walked back from my visit to Grandma Wren's I grumbled to myself about what a waste of time it had been. She had mostly listened to my recount of what had happened, giving nothing away that would help. I tried questioning her as to why Mum would want to see her after she had met Lorian, but she just avoided my questions and asked one of her own. Even though this was something I knew she did to try and get you to work through your own problems, she was hiding something. Something in her eye looked almost … hopeful. But I didn't get the chance to press further before she asked me to leave.

Still thinking about why Grandma Wren wouldn't explain or even talk much about the matter, I walked through the entrance of the city walls and back to Mum's with Xav. I was later than I thought I would have been but I rode slowly, giving me time to think.

As soon as I turned onto my street, I caught a glimpse of Lorian and Emerys moving towards the back of the house towards the stables. Something wasn't right. Lorian wasn't on the horse and Emerys was slumped over Garnet.

Kicking Xav into a trot, I shouted at people to move out of the way. I had to get to them and quickly – a nagging feeling had formed in my gut. When I reached them, I saw that Garnet was covered in blood on both sides, so much so it was slowly trickling off him, leaving a small dark train behind him.

"What's happened?" I shouted. "He was fine when I left!" I couldn't believe my eyes as I brought Xaviran to a stop in the yard.

"His arm is infected and it wouldn't stop bleeding. I have packed it with bentonite clay to staunch the bleeding and help with the swelling and the infection, but I didn't have any echinacea which would have helped, or yarrow would have been the best."

Lorian spoke breathlessly as she moved to the side of the horse, as if she was going to try and catch Emerys as he dismounted. I was shocked by Lorian's confident voice and knew I was staring as a consequence.

Emerys had obviously noticed. "Come on, Mav, close your mouth and give Lorian a hand. I'll squash her if she tries to catch me on her own." Emerys tried shifting his weight as he made to dismount but just ended up grimacing, letting out a small grunt of pain.

Dismounting Xaviran swiftly, I moved to where Lorian stood ready to help Emerys down. He leant forward and held onto Garnet's mane as he lowered himself slowly, his breath hitching as his wound brushed down the saddle. As soon as his feet were on the ground, he let go and collapsed, but he did not hit the floor as Lorian and I caught him under his arms.

"By the Gods! Emerys, you great oaf, stay with me – we've just got to get you inside now. Mum! Mum!" I shouted. We needed to get her to sort him out now, he was boiling hot and there was an awful smell cocooning him.

Mum appeared in the doorway a moment later, shock on her face at how dishevelled we looked.

"Whereby the Goddess have you been?" She swooped in on Emerys, ignoring any response we might have given. "In. Now. What happened? I need to know how to treat it."

Before I could say a word, Lorian spoke up, all of us focusing our full attention on her.

"I got into some trouble with some creatures, after … after my nightmares. Both Maverick and Emerys were there defending me from these … things. I tried to help but wasn't much use against them." Turning to look at Emerys and myself she gave me a small unsure smile before continuing. "Maverick's and my skin was burnt by this strange light, that I think came from one of the creatures, but I can't be sure. One minute I was hitting these creatures with a plank of wood and the next my vision was spotted with light and I was on my back."

She glanced at her feet then back up to meet my eyes as if trying to get confirmation of what had happened. I gave her a small nod, urging her to continue. This was the most she had spoken and I wasn't going to stop her. Seeing her confidence grow stirred an unusual sense of pride in myself. I shook myself and buried the feeling.

"I can see Maverick's wounds need treating – they're not infected. I assume mine is similar. But Emerys' arm is infected – it has come on quickly and he has lost a lot of blood."

Emerys moaned and Lorian shifted her grip on him, trying

to hurry him in through the door. At her sudden change in pace, I lost my grip on Emerys and they both collided with the door frame.

"Ah Mav, you could at least help Lorian," Emerys scolded, lucid enough to berate me. "You know I would crush her in a second if I fell on her."

Regaining my composure, I helped manoeuvre him into a chair in our small kitchen, as Mum bustled to look at Emerys' wound.

"Maverick, go and get the burn salve and apply it thoroughly to your face. It looks like just burns but I will look at again in a minute. I need to deal with Emerys first. Who packed your wound, Emerys?"

"Lorian did." Emerys coughed and I could visibly see the blood draining from his face.

"You did?" Mum briefly paused in her assessment to look at Lorian.

"Yes, I would have used yarrow for both the infection and bleeding, but I only had what you gave Emerys in the pouch."

Lorian had moved to the sink and was filling a bowl with water. "Do you have any calendula I can put in the water to bathe the packing clay out? When I packed it there was a lot of pus."

Lorian moved over to sit by Emerys' right arm and began looking at his wound. How did she know calendula was antiseptic?

Mum was obviously stunned as well, as it took her a moment to respond to Lorian's request. "Right, yes, of course – good deduction and good thinking, using what I had given him. I know it isn't the best, but the clay packs in easier for his line of work. Herbs don't stick as well," Mum answered swiftly, seeing Lorian pulling a face at the clay.

"Use this cloth to clean it with." Mum handed Lorian a cloth out of one of her many herb drawers. "It will aid in the healing. But then you must apply some salve to your skin as well and we will have to talk about what happened this morning."

"How will it help?" Lorian asked quizzically, taking the cloth and examining Emerys' arm.

"I have spelled it with healing properties and infused it with calendula – now get on. He isn't doing well and time is critical before the poison spreads."

With that, Mum went to get the herbs for the stronger infections that she didn't use as often. All the while I had been standing in the door of the kitchen. Lorian had shocked the hell out of me. How did she know all this? And she seemed so confident. Where had the shy girl that could barely get her words out gone?

"Mav, stop staring. Lorian hasn't grown another head," Emerys teased, but he was quickly silenced as Lorian wiped and scraped the wounds on his arm.

"I'm sorry, but I really need to get it out and the clay had to be pushed in deep to help with the bleeding," Lorian mumbled as she concentrated on removing the hardening clay out of Emerys' arm with the soaked cloth. The small kitchen was starting to smell from the pus that slowly oozed out of the wounds now the clay was being removed.

Moving over to get a closer look at Emerys' arm I bent down next to Lorian. Even over the smell of rotting flesh, Lorian smelt musty from where she had been thrown to the ground. As I leant over, as if looking into Emerys' wounds, a slight blush crept up her neck.

"Gods, give her a bit of space will you, Mav? Why are you

acting so oddly? You'll make her lose her concentration and it is already hurting like being hit with one of your waves without you putting her off."

Emerys tried to chuckle but it sounded forced. His eyes had been closed so I didn't realise he knew I was there. *He has obviously sensed me with his touchy-feely powers,* I moaned to myself. Moving away from Lorian, I pushed my hair behind my ears and tried to school myself. What was I doing?

"W—w—would you like a cup of tea?" I stuttered like a fool.

I didn't know what had come over me. And why was I stuttering? I never stuttered. She had thrown me off. It was as though she was a different person to the one that we rescued earlier in the day.

"No," Emerys hissed.

Glancing back over my shoulder I could see Emerys watching what Lorian was doing as she sat in front of him. The pain was etched deeply on his face as she removed the clay, scraping deeply. The other wounds on his chest and shoulders weren't bleeding as much, just small scrapes in comparison to the one on his arm.

"I am sorry, Emerys, I truly am. I have nearly got it all out now. Yes please, Maverick. I would love a tea – cinnamon if you have it."

"Right, okay, did you not go to market today, Mum?" I called through to her, wanting to try and ease some tension while I pulled things from the cupboard.

It seemed odd to me: someone who had come from an entirely different background, an entirely different world, knew the different types of tea and herbs. As I filled the kettle and put it over the fire, Mum walked back into the tiny kitchen, suddenly making it very crowded. Striking a match, I lit the aga and began to excuse myself. It would take so long for the kettle to grow hot enough that Mum would be done before it even began to whistle.

"No, I thought after everything that's happened I wouldn't attend market today. Everyone will have all they need by now and if they don't then that is their fault," Mum answered quickly before turning back to Lorian. "Lorian, I will take over now. Thank you for your quick thinking. I do believe you saved his life."

Mum took the cloth from Lorian and switched places with her. "If you wouldn't mind, would you be able to tend to Maverick's burns? He never does put the salve on when I tell him. Also, could you bathe them with lavender which will aid the healing? I have put it all on the little coffee table in the lounge. Would you mind?"

"Certainly, I am just glad I could help."

Feeling annoyed that I had to be tended to, I turned to go into the lounge. But as I did, I saw Lorian squeeze Emerys' hand and the little smile that she gave him, and my anger rose. I tried to damp it down as quickly as possible – it had no reason to be there. Why did I even feel that way? It was nothing to do with me that Lorian had taken a shine to Emerys – didn't every girl take a shine to him? Nevertheless, it was annoying. Emerys didn't even have to try and even when I tried it never seemed to be enough to catch a girl.

Moving swiftly out of the room, I went to sit on the floor in front of the blazing fire that crackled in the lounge, which Mum had managed to rearrange after Emerys and I slept in there the night before. Sitting that close to the heat made my skin start to prickle, but I just couldn't get over what I had seen. Even the small gesture infuriated me, knowing it would lead to more: both of them together at some point. The prickly pain was a welcome distraction.

Being engulfed within my own thoughts, I hadn't realised Lorian had entered the cosy little room as I sat in front of the fire twiddling my hair. The room always seemed small and overfull even though we only had a small plaid armchair and a sofa that could barely fit two people centred around the fireplace. A few wooden coffee tables clustered the edges of the seating area and a large, low wooden coffee table occupied the centre. The rest of the surrounding walls were covered with bookcases or trunks full of equipment, but at that moment it felt oppressive.

Lorian moved to the small coffee table and picked up the bowl and salve that Mum had laid out for her. "Do you mind if we sit a little further away from the fire? I don't think I will be able to stand the heat. Also, it will make your skin sting more. I can see it starting to get prickly from here. And I can feel mine doing the same." She gave me a small smile.

Clearing my throat, I stood and made my way over to her and sat down. "Yes sure, sorry – I wasn't thinking."

"I am sorry to interrupt your thoughts, your mum wanted me to tend to your burns, if you don't mind…"

She spoke so softly and so formally that it seemed as if the person that she was in the kitchen never existed. Glancing up at her I could see that she was nervous again – she was shuffling the cloth between her forefinger and her thumb and looking down at the bowl as if it would give her the answers to whatever she asked. It was so infuriating that she felt uncomfortable around me yet confident around Emerys – she had only known us both for a day. Why was it so different? But also, why did I care so much?

"Sure, whatever you think is best."

"You mind if I sit? It won't take me long and I will be out of your way."

"Just sit and get on with it will you?" I snapped, the temper that I had tried to keep at bay exploding out of me in an instant, like an animal let loose after being kept in captivity.

Lorian cowered from my outburst. Why couldn't I control my temper? *Another way I've scared her off,* I thought. But for a flicker of a moment, I thought I saw her jaw tighten in annoyance.

Lorian knelt in front of me and placed the bowl beside her, soaking the cloth in the ointment. She started with my hands and bathed the sores that had formed from the blast. She wouldn't make eye contact with me and so I took the moment to look at her properly. Her burns weren't as bad as mine as she had been further away from the culprit; hers had just shadowed whereas mine had blistered. I focused on her delicate features: high cheekbones and a strong nose that had a small scattering of freckles across it, and full lips. However, it was her eyes that were intriguing. She had this wistful look as if she was in another place most of the time, or constantly playing out another turn of events. But they were also calculating; she seemed to take in everything around her. I don't know how she had managed to get Emerys onto his horse – that hadn't come up in conversation yet, but she must have had trouble. There was obviously more to her than I originally thought.

"Do you mind if I start on your face now? It may take me a while as it seems to be a lot worse than your hands."

Her voice made me jump as she spoke. She rinsed out the cloth and brought it to my face without waiting for me to respond. "Was this just from the light? Both yours and Emerys' wounds are so irregular, I haven't seen anything like them before."

But I wasn't concentrating on what she was saying to me; her touch made me feel so calm, my temper all but disappeared. I felt as though I was falling into a trance as she cleansed my blisters.

"Are you okay?" Lorian paused in her task, rinsing the cloth once again. "Your eyes are closed. Does it hurt? I am trying to be as careful as I can, but I need to clear out all the dirt and grime from that place."

My eyes had drifted shut on their own. I had been so caught up in my own thoughts that I hadn't even felt Lorian stop until she had spoken to me.

"Oh no, I was just thinking. You aren't hurting me at all. In fact, I haven't felt a thing. The ointment seems to be helping," I commented, trying to ease her concern.

"Yes, it seems as though it is taking some of the swellings away which is good as you have the festival to go to tonight, I believe. What time does it start?"

"Well, the festivities start at six, but the circle starts at a quarter to twelve. It is still early yet so we should have some time to rest before."

"It is a long night then. What's the time?" Lorian asked. "I haven't seen a clock to tell it by."

"What's a clock? And it is about ten – it took us a while to get home."

"Oh, it is a small device that tells you the time. Do you not have them? How do you tell the time?" she asked puzzled, fiddling with the ointment pot.

"By how the sun or moon sits in the sky."

Pausing, I let the silence draw out as I tried to gather my thoughts.

"What happened earlier, Lorian? Why did you run off?" I asked carefully.

"I don't know really… I thought I was just having a nightmare." Lorian seemed to drift into thought and I could see a small crease form in between her eyebrows.

"What? What are you thinking?"

My question startled her out of her daydream as she began to apply the salve to my face. "I think I should try to find somewhere else to stay, is all I was thinking," she confessed after a sigh. "I cannot put you out of your room again and get in your mother's way, though your hospitality has been graciously appreciated." Resealing the small tin she sighed again. "There, all done. I am going to check on Emerys and wash my hands and then I will leave you to get ready for your festival."

And with that she rose and began to walk out of the room.

As quickly as I could I stood in front of her, blocking her path to the kitchen, and took the bowl she was holding. "You must stay longer. Where will you go other than here? Mum doesn't mind, and after showing her your tending skills she is bound to want your help and have questions about who taught you…" I blurted.

I couldn't let her leave just yet, not after all the trouble she had got into in the past two days. What would happen if she got into trouble and no one was there to help her? I was certain no one else in this soulless town would help her, that was for sure.

Lorian's cheeks turned darker, like they had in the kitchen. She was blushing again. "Well, maybe. I must wash my hands, please excuse me."

With that, she sidestepped around me and disappeared into the kitchen just as the kettle began to whistle.

Lorian

◦⸝⸌◦

A s I walked quietly into the kitchen to wash up the bowl, I removed the whistling kettle from the stove. I had gone off the idea of tea, my stomach clenching as the adrenaline left me leaving me feeling slightly sick.

Placing the kettle on the cooling rack beside the stove, I glanced round the small room. It was just big enough to have four small cupboards, a sink, and an aga. There was also a large pantry set into the wall next to the aga that allowed for additional storage. The table was pushed against the only spare wall, giving the inhabitants just enough room to stand by the sink when someone was sitting. There were drying herbs hanging from the ceiling and small debris littered the floor. Mother would never have allowed it at home, but it made me feel more at home than I had living in that town house.

As I moved to the sink, I had the distinct feeling I was being watched, that creeping prickly feeling on the back of my neck. Glancing back over my shoulder I saw, not Maverick as I suspected, but Connie, Maverick's younger sister. Neave had mentioned her when she tended to me last night, watching me from the small hallway leading down to the bedrooms.

"Hello!"

My attempt to befriend her was cut short as Neave re-entered the room. "How are Maverick's burns now?" I could see a slight flush to her cheeks that I'd never seen anyone have since I had been in this town, only the odd occasion I had seen a place with colour. But Maverick had said there wasn't any colour now, so surely it was just my imagination?

"I think the swelling is going down, the salve and ointment seem to be helping. What is in the salve? I have never seen burns heal so fast before."

I just couldn't get over this strange world that I found myself in. It didn't have colour. I still felt as if this could all be some strange lucid dream that I had been swept up in due to a fever.

I always had an overactive imagination. As a child, I would pretend that I was part of a fairy family out in the garden and build little villages within the flowerbeds for the fairy population to settle into. That was until my brother found out and destroyed them, along with the majority of our groundskeepers, Mr Wren's, flowerbeds. I had spent hours crying into Maria's apron about him destroying the fairies' homes. When Mother found out about it she just said that I should stop concentrating on mindless fantasies and focus on my lessons. But I clutched on to what Maria always said: *"Children are more susceptible to the magic that the world offers; adults become shielded by the fickle musings of what they deem to be important."*

Wringing out the cloth, I turned back to Neave. She had moved over to one of her cupboards and was shuffling a variety of herbs that had been hung to dry and stored in jars.

"The salve is made of aloe vera, lavender and echinacea," she said. "You need to apply some to help your skin as well. I believe you saved Emerys by using the clay that he had on him. I make him carry it because of his work – he is a woodsman, you know, and it can be dangerous work. I don't think he realised how serious it was until I told him; either that or he was just trying to put on a brave face in front of you. Now, why don't you tell me what happened this morning?"

It took me a moment to respond – she had changed subjects so quickly and I had to scramble to gather my thoughts. "I am just glad I could help, but I hope he wasn't trying to keep it to himself if he thought it was serious because of me. I know I seem a little nervous at times."

I slumped into the small wooden chair that was still pulled out from the table. "Honestly, I don't know what happened, I thought I was just having a nightmare. And I am sorry I made you miss the market…"

"Well, I haven't seen them – him or Maverick, I mean – like this before. Hmm … maybe it was just a nightmare, but I want you to put two drops of this under your tongue before bed." Neave pulled several pots from a crowded cupboard. "Oh, don't look so concerned – it is only limeflower. It will help keep the night terrors away. But I also want you to take ashwagandha before bed. Just add a small spoonful of the powder to your tea and give it a good stir – this will help you to respond to stress better."

She handed me a small vial with a pipette inside, and another small pot with a white powder and a tiny metal spatula. "Anyway, enough of that. Who taught you about the properties of herbs? You seemed to know what you needed and what you were looking for, and yet Maverick says you claim to have no knowledge about magic?"

"I know nothing of magic – I learnt long ago that it does not exist. As I mentioned before, I learnt about herbs from my old maid at the house. She was the gardener's wife and they both taught me. I used to play in the gardens a lot when I was younger," I explained as I applied the ointment to my tingling skin.

"Ah, what were their names?"

"Wren, Maria and Ivan Wren. They were so dear to me. I just wish I knew how I got here."

Neave stood looking at me for a moment before she answered, but it was long enough for me to see the understanding and worry in her eyes. "We will figure that out what happened today and how you got here, do not worry. That is enough for today, we will talk again tomorrow. For now, I want you to pop some limeflower under your tongue and head to bed and then we will get ready for the festivities later. You need to rest. You are more than welcome to stay with us. Also, a little warning, Lorian. Be careful at the festivities – cruelty runs deep here."

Neave turned towards the doorway and drifted out, as though what she had just said was casual conversation and not a warning.

Maybe I would stay a little longer, but I couldn't put Neave and Maverick out for too long, I'd have to find somewhere to live. I just couldn't understand how Maverick, Emerys and Neave seemed so pleasant when I'd been told everyone in Sòlas was cruel. From the townsfolk I had met so far they seemed so different. However, from the look in her eyes when she saw me, Connie seemed to be as dire as they were said to be.

Sitting down at the small wooden kitchen table, I looked at the herbs Maverick's mother had hung above it. There were so many different varieties: lavender, sage, angelica, basil, bay leaves – all sorts in various different stages of the drying process. It was fascinating to see them all strung above me. Something about them felt comforting, more homely than anything I was used to. But there was no denying this place was strange.

Carefully and quietly, I walked down the hall and back to Maverick's room where I would be staying for a while longer and lay down to rest, remembering just in time to put a few drops of the strong, sweet-tasting limeflower under my tongue before I drifted off into a blissful sleep, which surprised even me after everything that had happened.

Once awake, I tiptoed to the kitchen to wait for the others to get up. Again, I was comforted by the sight of the array of herbs and the aromatic smell that seemed to infuse every nook and cranny of the room. Closing my eyes, I inhaled deeply and felt some of the lingering tension ease from my stiff joints.

I heard heavy footfall from down the hallway and turned, expecting to see Neave come in. But Connie entered the kitchen and stood staring at me as she leaned on the door frame, with a disgusted look on her face. Connie was a small girl with a face in a perpetual scowl.

"Sorry, did you need something?" I asked. I didn't know why she was just standing there staring at me but it made me feel as though I shouldn't be there. Unfortunately, I had nowhere else to go.

"Funny, being asked if I want anything in my own home..."

Connie spat back. "Mother wants you – it seems you are her favourite now. Honestly, I can't see why." The venom in her voice cut deep, and for a moment I hadn't heard that she had said Neave wanted me.

Standing, I shuffled around the small girl into the little hallway. I tiptoed to what Maverick had said was Neave's bedroom. The door was closed so I knocked on the dark wood and waited for an answer. There was a rustling and the slamming of drawers before the door opened and Neave filled the doorway. She was now wearing a loose, silk dress with three-quarter-length sleeves. A small tinge of pink still covered her cheeks as she smiled at me. Curious.

"Connie said you wanted to see me?"

I felt nervous standing in the hallway, waiting to know why Neave wanted me. Mother only ever asked me to come to her room when she wanted to tell me what I had done wrong and that I was a disappointment to her, or to wonder aloud why I couldn't be more like Hugh. Standing here in the small dark corridor, in a house with a family I didn't know, in this colourless, miserable world that I didn't understand was starting to bring back nauseatingly horrible memories.

"Oh yes," Neave blazed, with a cheerful smile. "I have an old dress for you to wear tonight to the festival."

She handed me a black silk gown, hardly different from the one she was wearing, other than the fact that it was smaller. The hem was slightly frayed but otherwise it looked new.

"Oh, um," I stammered. How was I going to put it without being rude? "I wasn't going to come to the festival tonight – I don't want to intrude on your traditions."

"Nonsense, you have to come. Now slip into the dress and pop the ballet slippers on that Connie will bring down and we shall be ready to leave. Emerys and Maverick should be ready now. I think Emerys is well enough to come tonight, as long as he doesn't move his arm too much and tear the stitches. The clay saved him a world of trouble, and what I have dressed it with will heal it and provide him with enough strength for tonight."

Neave looked down at a small pair of threadbare slippers, that had been left by the side of the door, the sole nearly falling away from the uppers and holes in the toes.

"Oh that useless girl… She will be sorry. She is playing a game, giving you a ruined pair of shoes when she works for a man that damn well makes shoes daily." She looked up at me and put on a mock-cheerful tone. "Don't worry – I will get you another pair. We don't wear shoes for the festival itself, but you will want something to walk down in with your bruised feet. Now wait here, I have to go and check on Connie."

She left the room but not before I saw a frown take over her pretty features and a sneer curl her top lip. In that moment, she looked more like Connie than I'd seen her look within the time that I had spent in the house. I was glad that she had left; I didn't want anyone seeing me undress – I didn't even want to see myself.

I stripped off the nightdress I was still wearing and put the silk gown on as quickly as possible, avoiding looking in the mirror. The gown was close-fitting and 'left little to the imagination', as my mother would have said, but I felt completely uncomfortable in it, especially after yesterday's incident.

Folding up the nightdress, I placed it on the end of Neave's bed and perched next to it. My gaze drifted around the room. Furniture-wise it was pretty bare: just a small chest of drawers and a wardrobe, a small table with a china washbasin, accompanied by a tall jug and small cotton cloth. Neave's bed filled the majority of the open space, but it was what was on the floor and furniture that fascinated me. There were hundreds of books piled all around the room – at least a hundred and fifty, possibly more. I couldn't tell what they were, as the spines were old and weathered; I could just make out the indentations where the book titles had been embossed.

As I sat waiting for Neave to come back, I could hear raised, muffled voices coming from one of the rooms further down the corridor. I could tell it was Neave and Connie talking, from the pitch of their voices, but I couldn't tell what they were saying. And honestly, I didn't want to know.

The look on Neave's face when she left the room had frightened me. I thought Maverick had been kidding when he said that everyone was bitter and joyless underneath in Sòlas. And when I met Neave, she had seemed so happy and truly content with who she was. It was only when she saw the shoes Connie left me that she changed completely.

I don't know how long I sat and waited, not daring to move for fear of being told off for venturing into another part of her house, but in the end it wasn't Neave or Maverick that came for me, but Emerys.

"Can I come in?" he asked, knocking and waiting for me to murmur my confirmation. He poked his head around the door. "Are you nearly ready?"

"Yes, but do you think Neave would mind if I wore a different dress? I think this one is a little small…" I tried to pull the hem of the skirt down a little more over my knees. I was not used to showing this much flesh, not since I was a little girl – or unless I was in a dance recital wearing tights as

Lorian

well. And after last night I didn't want to show any more skin than I needed to.

Opening the door fully and striding into the room – ensuring he ducked to miss the door frame – Emerys stood in front of me, wearing silk trousers and a long-sleeved, loose-fitting shirt.

"Nonsense, it fits you just fine. Stand up and let me see."

He put out his hand and then I noticed his other hand carrying a different pair of ballet slippers than the ones I'd seen earlier. Taking his hand, I rose, trying to pull the skirt down as I did.

"See? It's fine. All the other girls wear the same dresses. The only difference is that older women wear a longer one to the floor."

"Why can't I wear a longer one? I would feel much more comfortable. And I am classed as a woman now I am eighteen," I pleaded, taking the small ballet slippers he offered and slipping them on.

"Eighteen? I thought you were younger…" Emerys commented, his brow furrowing. "Normally a woman is classed when she is tested at twenty-one, but I will ask Neave if she will allow you to wear a longer dress." He smiled and let go of my hand. "Come, if she does not allow it, we will have to leave now or we will be late. Maverick and Connie are waiting in the lounge. You go in there and I will ask Neave."

Striding the short distance to the door, he looked back over his shoulder and realised I hadn't moved from where I was standing. "Oh come on. And you don't need to stand like that – you look fine in the dress." There was a tiny edge to his voice; maybe it was the pain. But Neave's warning once again drifted into my mind.

111

Cruelty runs deep.

Looking up into Emerys' kind face – even though I now knew that even the kindest of faces could transform into a cruel snarl when you thought it not possible – I tried to smile.

I couldn't hear any talking as I approached the lounge, sighing with relief that I might be alone for a little longer before I had to bear Connie's cruel comments and Maverick's scrutinizing stares. However, it looked as though my luck was out, as Connie sat in the small armchair fiddling with something on her lap and Maverick stood watching the colourless fire dance around the hearth.

On my approach, they both looked up from what they were doing. I could see Maverick's eyes slightly widen as he quickly tucked his hair behind his ears. Those eyes still unsettled me; something about them was so familiar. Even more disturbing was the slight smile that adorned Connie's lips. Why would she be smiling at me? She had taken an instant dislike to me, even though I had only met her when I brought Emerys in.

As if on cue, she got up and announced that she was leaving. Maverick ignored her, still gazing into the fire, but just before she left the room, she turned back and threw something in my direction. I have never been good at catching, so I was expecting to drop it, but it was as if it was attracted to my hands. To my surprise, I caught the small square parcel. Inside it was a small plant with long, thin stalks, and small flowers. Connie had definitely used magic to deliver it to me.

I tried to catch Maverick's attention to see if he had noticed anything, but his gaze was still fixed on the fire. I couldn't fathom why his sister would have thrown the plant at me, so I placed it on the table. I didn't think anything more of it. There was no need to keep anything Connie had given me, especially after the unsettling look she gave me.

Emerys' voice startled me as I gazed at the small plant.

"You are still too young to be in a long dress. It is a tradition that Neave upholds, I'm afraid. Now, we'd best go."

Turning to face him, I was confronted with a solid chest clad in pale grey. Taking a step back, I looked up into Emerys' face and his eyes... They couldn't be brown eyes, could they? "Thank you for asking."

Maverick

I couldn't think straight, I didn't know what was wrong with me. I had only met this god-damn girl yesterday, but I felt this strange attraction to her. I became like an overprotective fool when she was in trouble and even around Emerys – it needed to stop. I would have to look in the spell books to see if there was something that would stop me feeling that way. Even though she claimed to know nothing of this world, I felt as though I recognised her from somewhere. But I knew everyone in our small town and I had never ventured anywhere beyond the forest on the south side of the town and the northern croplands.

"I will see you at the festival!" I shouted to Mum as I stomped off down the cobbled street towards the festivities for the evening. Maybe it would be good if Lorian found somewhere else to stay; I wouldn't have to see her and then I could forget about her, as I had the other girls who had never seemed to notice me.

"Maverick!" Mum shouted after me, but I was already

running down the road away from their small talk.

The streets on the outer side of the town were quiet, with only a few people still wandering towards the green. Most of the others must already be there. Looking at the sky, I checked the time. Half-past six. Yes, almost everyone would be there now. There wasn't a festival of this size often. There would be the usual circle, a meeting and a ritual performed, but on Samhain there would be a variety of extra events, from pumpkin-carving to dancing, all leading up to a circle at midnight.

Slowing my pace, knowing that it would take Mum, Emerys and Lorian a while to catch up, I took in the decorated streets as I approached the town centre. The oil street-lights flickered, illuminating the small walkways with a haunting but mesmerising glow, sending shadows dancing across the walls of the opposite houses. The lamps themselves were decorated with fragrant potpourri strips.

Doorways were lined with offerings – the traditional Sabbat Cake and a cup of wine – to the spirits that would be roaming the streets on this fated night. I would have to remind Mum to put out our offering before bed – we did not want the spirits that visited us to become malevolent due to there being no cake. They would become a nuisance very fast.

The music from the festivities flooded my ears. How I hadn't heard it from further out of the town I didn't know. It seemed so loud now I was in the centre at the large grassy green, surrounded by trees and benches where people sat and stalls were erected.

I stood, quieting my internal grumbles and just looked for a moment. This time of year was one of the most celebrated, everyone hoping to hear from a lost loved one. But there was no one I wished to hear from. Everyone seemed to be having a good time, or they were making out that they were. I always wonder what bitter things went on in other folk's hearts, for what went on in mine was truly vicious.

I moved towards my favourite area of the Samhain festival: the apple-bobbing, where around twenty cauldrons were filled with water and apples, surrounded by people dunking their heads, trying to catch an apple in their mouths.

As I approached, I could see Feren watching another boy dunk his head. There was a cruel smile on his lips, suggesting that he didn't intend to lose this match against whomever was unlucky enough to have challenged him.

Quickening my pace, I weaved in and out of the other revellers to the place where he leaned over the boy in the cauldron, holding him there. I called out to him.

"You know, Feren, it is enough to win. We don't have to test how long he can hold his breath for."

Feren looked around and the sheer pleasure he was getting out of holding the boy there was visible in his eyes. I hated how cruel these people I called friends could be, but what was worse was that I knew I wasn't much better.

"Oh well, where's the fun in that?" Feren smirked as he released the boy that was no older than fifteen. "Want to challenge me, do you?"

"Aye, I do. You haven't used that luck spell have you?"

Feren believed he was the only one that knew he spelled himself to win but I had caught him doing it once before a training tournament when we were being taught defensive and attacking spells, and I had teased him ever since.

Trying to maintain his nonchalant appearance, Feren turned and refilled the cauldron with water so that the apples bobbed just under the brim. I saw the flicker of annoyance in his eyes and I relished it.

"Well, what would be the fun in that? But for your knowledge, I don't use that spell any longer, I am simply better than those around me now," Feren sniggered.

"We shall see. How about you go first and see how many apples you get in a minute?" I smiled mischievously at him.

I was sure he would have used the spell as he wouldn't have given up on something that had served him well for so long, but nevertheless, a test to see if he really had could never hurt. Bobbing for apples was always harder than it looked; the apples always seemed to float free just when you thought you would get them.

"What are the stakes?" he smirked. I should have guessed he never would go into something without getting something out of it.

"What do you want?" I asked, but I knew what it would be before he said it. It would be what he always wanted: fame.

"You have to duel me in a tournament and show everyone I am better than you."

Rolling my eyes, I sighed. In other words, he wanted me to go easy on him to let him win. Although he would never say that.

"Fine."

Kneeling down by the cauldron, Feren looked up at me. "You don't know what you've let yourself in for."

"Sure, whatever you say, Fer – just get on with it, will you? Ready, go!"

Feren plunged head first into the cauldron, spilling what seemed like half the water, along with a few apples in the process. He had his hands behind his back to ensure that he didn't use them to aid himself in any way.

Feren had always been the one to watch when it came to cheating but Emerys and I had got used to having him around when we were younger. As we grew up, Feren's tricks and sense of superiority got tiresome and we let him know they were wearing thin. We didn't mean to get so rough with him, but we had and so his mum forbade him to see us other than at full community circles. Now he was a bit older he could hold his own, and I was able to control myself and my powers more to ensure no one got irreversibly hurt. But now he had challenged me, I knew we would be back fighting soon. Maybe sooner than he thought.

Once Feren was done, achieving a good number of four apples out of the cauldron, it was my turn. Plunging my head into the cold water, I fished around for an apple. Apple-bobbing, unless you had help from a spell, was quite difficult. It wasn't finding the apple that was the hardest bit, it was trying to get your mouth around the thing and to bite into it without having anything to push it against.

Finding an apple, I pushed and clamped my jaw shut around it as best I could but the thing wasn't having any of it, slipping nimbly out of my mouth. Wary of the time, and at least wanting to get one apple out, I tried again. I repeated this over and over again until by the end of my minute I had two apples out.

"You liar! You have been using that spell!" I shouted. "There is no way you would have been able to get four apples out in that time." Even though I knew this was just a game, and I had suspected he had used the spell, it infuriated me that he would cheat.

Turning to look at me, he had a disgusted but amused look

on his face. "What? Just because you have to show everyone how much better I am than you at the tournament now… " he jeered back, taking a few steps closer. It was as if the atmosphere around us became darker when our tempers flared.

"You heard, you cheating scumbag." I was losing control of my short-leashed anger, days' worth of annoyance coming to a head, my dark fury growing.

That was it. No more words were exchanged, and before I realised what was happening, Feren charged at me and tackled, slamming his shoulder into my stomach and lifting me off the ground.

I reined in my anger the best I could, but the release of the pent-up frustration that I had tried to conceal was addictive. As we tackled and hit one another, we were drawing such a crowd, and pushing their way through from the back were Mum, Emerys and Lorian.

As they got to the front, I could see the death stare Mum was giving me; I had truly messed up this time. Even though everyone was sour and cold-hearted in Sòlas, fighting was still frowned upon – and fighting at a festival was a disgrace. I could also see the embarrassment that Mum was feeling as it was her son involved in such a disruption of the festivities.

Emerys, on the other hand, was trying to fight back laughter. He was straining to keep his face serious, but his eyes betrayed his amusement. Lorian looked terrified, as though she had never seen anyone get in a scuffle before. But there was something else in her eyes that I could not place; an expression that I had never seen her wear before. Disappointment, if I had to take a guess. I knew I shouldn't care, but my stomach lurched at the thought. I reminded myself that she was nothing to me. I had to ensure that she realised this. I didn't know what stupid feelings I had been harbouring over the last day or so but they were sure to not last.

Standing, I gave Feren one last shove. I had a cut lip and what would be a swollen black eye, but I fared better than him. He had broken his nose and most likely his wrist, and what was more disturbing was that I felt nothing for what I had just done – no guilt or anger, only annoyance. I could not control the fury's power that burned so close to the surface.

As I looked up, Mum was coming towards us. However, instead of walking over to me, she walked past me and over to Feren, assessing the damage to his wrist and nose.

"Go home, Maverick. You have already had enough of the festivities. Only come back for the circle later tonight." She spoke in a low growl over her shoulder.

I had never missed a festival before, so I knew I had really messed up this time. Mum continued talking but I couldn't respond, the shock consumed me. I knew I had never got into a fight at a festival but I had been in many fights before this. I didn't think Mum would make me miss Samhain.

"You are lucky the circle tonight is about new beginnings, because you'd better hope the consequences of this don't get more serious." She glowered at me. "Go now, tend to your own wounds for your stupid actions." She dismissed me with a turn of her head.

Walking towards Emerys and Lorian, I spoke directly to Emerys. "I will be back for the circle tonight but don't bother keeping me a place – I will find somewhere else to stand."

I was annoyed. If it hadn't been for my feelings and Feren and his stupid cheating, I wouldn't have done what I did. I would have been fine. Well, maybe I would have done it but not on a festival day – I would have waited until afterwards.

As I made my way home, my face was starting to sting as the scabs that had formed over the burns pulled away. I had almost forgotten that they covered my face. I knew I was going to look like a mess with a black eye and cut lip to accompany them.

Lorian

Emerys, Neave and myself wove ourselves back into the festival from where Maverick had been fighting. Shaking the nervousness the fight had left in my stomach, I distracted myself with the scene around me. There were decorations everywhere – although there were no colours, I could imagine what they would have been like at this time of year: all the blazing oranges and reds accompanied by lush earthy tones. A cool autumn breeze brushed past me, awakening my senses. Pumpkins both carved and uncarved were strewn around in what seemed to be a haphazard way but I quickly realised that they were placed to guide people to the different stalls and activities on the green.

There were what seemed like hundreds of people bustling about, more than I had thought this little town contained. Many were making small talk or buying products from various stall vendors. The stall wares ranged widely from what seemed to be apples covered in a shiny liquid, to some sort of pie, but I had to ask Emerys what was covering the

122

apples as I couldn't quite place the smell. It was spicy sweet and oh so delicious, making my mouth water. There were also other products that seemed out of place, but they were probably part of the evening's celebrations: necklaces, stones, lace and silk garments.

My awestruck face must have betrayed me as Emerys turned to me with a large grin on his face. "Quite the sight, isn't it? Do you have festivals like this where you're from?"

"N—no," I stammered.

For once it wasn't my nerves causing me to stammer but the beautiful scene on the green that lay before me. How could a people supposedly so cruel create and organise something like this? Maybe deep down they weren't truly awful, I pondered.

"We had more garden parties of sorts, but they always seemed more formal with games such as croquet and badminton. Or we would have people over in the evenings for drinks and canapés."

"What?" Emerys asked, looking at me quizzically.

I racked my brain for the best way to describe the evenings my stepfather and mother, and later my uncle, would put on. "Well, the garden parties often included small sandwiches, tea and lemonade, and then everyone would watch the games and converse. The evening parties were more formal, where people would come over and talk, sometimes about business, which was mostly the men. Or gossip, which mostly the women took part in, as well as standing around, showing off their clothes. Or at least that was how it was in my household."

"Sounds rather boring."

Emerys' attention was wavering as he looked around the stalls to find something more interesting. Not wanting to stop the easy conversation that I so rarely made, I quickly changed the subject to what was drawing his eye. "It is so beautiful, don't you think? What is this festival for? I can almost see all the colours."

As soon as the words left my lips, I regretted them. What an idiotic thing to say to someone who has never seen colour. I doubt he would have even known what a specific colour would be called. However, the reaction Emerys gave me was totally unexpected – his face was full of surprise and wonder.

"Well, this festival is to celebrate our ancestors. It is also a time when the veil between the two worlds: our world and the afterlife, is at its thinnest. So, this is a time when our ancestors and other spirits can walk among us again. You always have to be careful about malevolent spirits. You know the offering on the doorsteps you saw?"

I nod, I had seen the small tokens on the doorsteps but hadn't understood their importance

"Well, they are to keep the malevolent spirits at bay. If you do not put them out, they will come and cause havoc in your household. Anyway, can you tell me what are colours are like? What does it feel like to see them?"

I hadn't ever really thought about how I would describe colours to someone, or how they made me feel. And I hadn't ever thought that the colours I saw every day might no longer be there. "Well, umm…" I stumbled, trying to come up with the best way to explain colours to someone who had never experienced them before. Luckily, I was saved from the trouble when a young boy of roughly eight years of age came running up to us.

"Emerys!" he shouted, skidding to a stop in front of us, "Mum says you have to look after me as she has some things to do."

Sighing, Emerys bent down in front of what appeared to be his younger brother, ruffling the small boy's hair. "Gwilym, you have to behave if you are with me, okay?" Emerys looked up at me. "This is Lorian, and Lorian – this is Gwilym. He is my younger half-brother."

"Nice to meet you, Gwilym," I responded with a smile.

"What is wrong with her eyes? They aren't like ours. Also, I want a toffee apple. Let's get a toffee apple," he said in one quick blur of speech.

Tugging on Emerys' hand, Gwilym led us over to the stall with apples covered in the sweet-smelling substance that had caught my nose earlier. I was still contemplating what the young boy had said about my eyes as we approached. What could be wrong with my eyes? But I couldn't focus on that now, so putting the thought aside, I followed Emerys and Gwilym, standing a short distance away from where they huddled around the stall.

I watched as people made their way closer; they were pushing and shoving one another to get to the front, the complete opposite to the stores Mother would drag me to. No one seemed to have any regard for those around them, they just thought of themselves and what they wanted. Even Emerys pushed his way to the front without a care for those that had been there longer than him. He even nearly knocked someone to the floor.

Shaking myself, I turned my gaze to the small stall. It was wooden and had a small, checked-cloth roof. There were two pots on it, one full of apples and the other full of the deliciously sweet-smelling liquid that caused my stomach to rumble. This pot was placed over a small flame, keeping it soft. The vendor completed his ritual to create the sweet treats, first sticking the apple on a thin cylindrical stick and then dunking it in the clear liquid. He would then twist the apple carefully to break the runny stream, not wasting a drop. The vendor would then allow the apple to stand and the liquid to harden before giving them to his patrons. The delicious smell of the sweet alluring spiced sugar wafted closer, drawing me to the stall.

"If only I had some money," I said wistfully to myself as I gazed upon one individual trying as hard as they could to get through the crystallised outer shell.

"No need!" Emerys' voice made me jump as he had returned with his young brother. Gwilym was chomping happily on his apple, covering his lips and cheeks in the sticky residue. *He must have teeth of stone to make it through the tough shell*, I thought, smiling to myself.

Looking back to Emerys, I realised he had two shiny coated apples in his hands. "Here," he said, handing me one. "But I wouldn't leave it too long, the toffee gets too hard," he chuckled.

"Toffee?" I asked in puzzlement, taking the apple.

"Yes, that's what it is covered in. What did you think it was?" he asked, taking a large bite.

"Just some sort of syrup." Poking the toffee, I could feel it hardening in places already.

"Ah no, it's toffee and you'd best eat it quickly, or you will be like that poor man over there, nearly breaking his teeth to eat it."

Ah, that was the key. Eat quickly.

I thanked him quickly, taking the apple. Looking back over at Gwilym, I realised something I had missed before. The young boy's hair was a sandy blonde colour and he had a faint scattering of brown freckles covering his nose.

Curious, I wondered why I would see colour on one individual and not another? I thought I had seen colour a few times in the last day but only very pale hints and I was certain that they were a mind trick. But here it was as plain as the toffee on the apple that young Gwilym's hair was a sandy blonde.

Turning to Emerys, I asked him if he saw anything different about his brother's hair and freckles, for surely he would know if there was something different about someone he saw each day?

"What do you mean? His hair has always been that colour. And he always had paler freckles on his nose than the other kids."

Emerys looked at me in puzzlement as we strolled over to a patch of grass in between the trees. Gwilym was wandering around nearby, talking to a few people and munching on his toffee apple, not caring where we were or if he'd wandered too far. After seeing his sandy hair and light freckles a small bloom of hope blossomed. At that moment I knew how I could explain colour to Emerys, or at least I thought I could.

Settling on the ground, my legs tucked beside me, I looked at the tree above. A light rustling passed through its branches and you could hear the faint ringing of small bells that hung from the nearby trees in decoration. It was a big maple tree, the leaves all different shades of grey. I couldn't get over seeing everything in greyscale; I had to really look to see the difference within the tones, at how the veins shaded the leaf differently to the one next to it.

After we sat down, I noticed Emerys' eyes searching through the crowds frantically.

"Do you mind watching Gwilym for a while? I won't be long. The festival starts soon but I just need to check something before it does? And I did get you a toffee apple, so you owe me."

"Umm... Okay, sure. You don't think he will mind, do you?" I asked nervously, looking towards the small boy that was playing in the tree's scattered leaves.

My stomach gave a nervous twist, I didn't like how Emerys had said I owed him for a gesture I hadn't even asked for.

"No, he won't mind at all. To be honest, he probably won't notice. He is used to playing by himself."

He got up and strode off into the crowded stalls without even a look back

Emerys

Pushing my way through the crowd, I could feel my heart racing in my chest. How had I forgotten to look for Lila? How could I not have thought to look here, where everyone was gathered in one place? Surely she would come. She had to. She never missed a festival, especially not one like this.

But I knew why I hadn't been looking this past day. It was because of Lorian, because of her helplessness, her stupidity going to the east side of the city, for her complete lack of understanding where she was. I could feel my temper rising as I pushed past the elderly and young alike, all making their way to the festival green. What if something had actually happened to Lila and I'd been looking after someone I didn't even know?

I shoved someone in front of me out of the way, but with the mist of rage starting to descend upon me, I pushed them to the ground.

"Hey!" shouted the young boy. "What are you doing? You've

made me cut my leg – you are nasty."

The young boy looked up at me and tears begin to pool in his eyes. At the sight, some of my rage faded, slowly receding with the guilt of what I had done. I could feel everything the little boy was feeling, the pain in his leg and slight fear in his veins.

"I'm sorry, I didn't see you there. Are you okay? Let me have a look." I leaned closer, reaching out to his injured leg.

"Oliver, there you are. Come, now. We have to make our way to the circle, it is about to start." A woman pushed through the crowd to the little boy on the ground. "What have you done now?" She glared at him.

"It isn't my fault, Mama. It's his!" he said, pointing at me.

"You did this, did you?" The woman rounded on me. I think she was one of the foragers for the stall but I couldn't be certain. Everyone knew everyone in this town but it didn't mean we all knew each other well.

"It was an accident. I wasn't looking where I was going. I am sorry." I ground out, my anger still close to the surface.

"You are in enough trouble as it is, by the sounds of it," the woman spat, a cruel snarl on her face as she scooped up her boy. "Oh yes, for what you've done with your pretty little girlfriend I think you are in a whole lot of trouble. Now stay away from my boy. If anything happens to him, I will know who to come to."

I was stunned. I knew people suspected me but I didn't realise they had already condemned me. Before I could respond, the lady turned, merging back into the crowd, taking the last of my anger with her.

Sighing, I looked around at the remaining faces making their way to the green. All glanced at me with suspicion, and none were the face I was looking for. Turning, I let the flow sweep me up and guide me back to Lorian and Gwilym.

I'll find you, Lila. By the God and Goddess I'll find you.

Lorian

I sat there watching Gwilym laugh and giggle to himself as he kicked through the leaves. He would pile them up and collapse on top of them, setting them sailing into the air around him. But what captivated me the most was when he sent one sailing over to me on a little gust of wind.

"How did you manage to do that?" I giggled, grasping the huge maple leaf right out of the air.

"It's my power, although I'm not very good at it yet. I can only lift light things. But the elders say I'll be able to do lots more as I get older and stronger," he explained excitedly, as he flexed his arm muscles.

"But that's a long way off yet, squirt."

Emerys emerged from behind me, ruffling his brother's hair with a laugh.

"Hey, stop that!" shouted Gwilym as he sent a flurry of leaves directly at Emerys. "Or this means war…"

"Oh you are on, little man. Show me what you've got."

Emerys charged forward and went to catch Gwilym round

the waist, but the little boy was fast. Dodging out of his big brother's grip and diving into a pile of leaves, he created an impressive wall between them. He sent over little leaf missiles on a small intense gust of wind at such a rapid rate that Emerys could not deflect them fast enough.

"Okay, okay I surrender," Emerys chuckled, collapsing on the ground as his brother shot out from behind the wall of leaves and stood atop his chest, claiming victory. "You've got pretty good, little man. Now you head off to the circle – it is going to start soon."

"Okay, see you later. Bye, Lorian!" He waved as he hopped off Emerys and darted towards the green.

"He has quite the spirit," I giggled, standing and stretching, knowing Emerys would want to leave. "Did you find what you were looking for?" I asked, glancing up into his face.

"No, not yet," he sighed, and although I could see the humour still playing in his features a shadow passed over his eyes. "Come, we don't want to be late."

He waited till I was by his side to start walking towards the green. I could still see the shadow lingering over his eyes.

Searching for something to change the subject and take his thoughts away from whatever was eating at him, I went back to the conversation we'd been having earlier. "I can answer your question, now I've had time to think. Colour makes everything seem bright, more alive. There are so many different tones of colour, as there are greys, blacks, and whites within your world. However, imagine you could see someone with a completely different colour hair to anything you've seen. Imagine they had hair the colour of flames."

Emerys was looking puzzled. "What is the colour of a flame? We only have white-hot…"

I thought about this for a minute before speaking. "There is a different colour – red – for many things in my world. You know when you see someone blush and you see their skin changes to a darker shade?" Emerys nodded, his gaze fixed on me as he hung on each word I spoke. "Well, if there was colour, they would turn a slight shade of red. Red is bright and alluring but can also mean something is dangerous. We have brown – the leaves on the trees turn to brown in the autumn, brown as the soil that is under our feet, so rich and full of life you just want to hold it and run your fingers through it while planting something. We also have the cleansing colour of a light yellow, so bright and vibrant it would remind you of spring sunshine."

I was beginning to talk quickly, recalling all the images of the different colours I had seen. I couldn't explain what exactly colours were, for how could you?

Doing my best to slow down, I took a breath, trying to give Emerys a basic understanding. "Colours allow you to differentiate between things, not just by tone but by the feeling they give you. Someone may associate different colours with different things, allowing them to feel joy, sadness, anger … well, anything really. Oh, I wish I could explain it so much better than I have, Emerys."

I looked at him, pleading for him to understand that I was trying my best to explain, but colour was something so magical that it was nearly impossible to put it into words.

"I think I get it. Colours, even though I haven't seen any, can make you feel certain things: happiness, sadness, or anything, depending on what they are. I just wish I could see them so I know what it is you see when you look around."

"Well, you have seen colour, Emerys." He looked at me with

the same bewilderment in his eyes as he had a minute ago. "Your brother's hair isn't the same as everyone else's is it? Nor his freckles." Emerys shook his head. I smiled. "That's because they are a colour – his hair is sandy blonde, which is a shade of yellow, and his freckles are a pale brown."

Emerys looked at me awestruck. Searching for his brother who was a little way ahead of us, a small smile spread across his face.

Weaving through the last of the crowd, I looked quizzically at the salt laid out on the ground in an almost-complete circle.

"It is a protection circle," Emerys said. "We have to enter through the opening. It is used in every circle to control the energy cast and to protect those inside from outside influence. I'll explain everything but we need to get in first."

Slipping off our shoes and placing them with everyone else's, we passed through the gap in the circle and over to Neave on the other side of it.

Maverick

I had tended to my cut lip and black eye the best I could,
but it wasn't anything like Mum's treatment. She would
have ensured that there was no swelling and helped
my lip to close up so much faster. The discomfort they
were giving me, alongside the burns now that the salve and
ointments were wearing off, was numbingly painful. They
were also excruciatingly itchy. The prickling sensation that
covered my face and neck just added to my frustration.

After six hours of boredom at home, only grooming and
grizzling at Xaviran for company, I made my way back to
the festival, with nothing but the question over why Mum
had a piece of rue herb in the living room to keep my restless
thoughts at bay.

As I passed the now-quiet stalls, a feeling of anticipation
washed over me. I couldn't wait to get the rush of energy
that would come as the circle was cast. Festival circles always
allowed for a more significant amount of energy to be drawn
due to the number of people that were casting one at once.

However, it also allowed everyone within that hour of the circle-casting to be joined, which could be both problematic and exhilarating.

Being joined to everyone within the circle allowed us all to feel what the others were feeling, especially someone like Emerys. His empath magic was affected by the circle more. Most people within this forsaken town preyed on the vulnerable, so trying to hide feelings within the circle was a priority, if not fully possible. No matter how much you tried, everyone would know something about you at the end. I always ensured that I projected a strong feeling and pushed all thoughts and previous frustrations out of my head when I entered the centre of a circle.

It was coming up for quarter to midnight and the circle was due to start five minutes to the hour. However, as always, trying to get everyone in the circle on time was difficult, with many believing they could enter just before, not thinking of the protection salt having to be closed and everyone in place before the hour.

Joining the last few people that were walking over, I could see the circle of salt. It would only be closed after everyone was inside. I tried to find Mum and Emerys so I could stand near them. No matter the argument we'd had, I knew I would feel happier having their energy closer to me. It took me a moment to find them within the large crowd. Normally covens didn't deal in whole communities but smaller groups, normally of thirteen. However, ours had been brought together by the three elders and held up by our laws. The elders dealt with any conflicts within the society, overseeing issues if they became too disruptive.

I could make out Emerys standing above almost everyone

else. He looked happy and animated, more so than I had seen him before. His eyes actually looked alight with whatever he was talking about. Then I realised it was Lorian that was standing beside him, a hint of nervousness in her eyes as she stood between him and Mum in her black, fitted silk dress. The dress accentuated her small frame; her hair was loose and fell just to her shoulders. She looked the picture of beauty. She stood with purpose, with a poise that I hadn't often seen within the town and in a circle she couldn't begin to understand.

Instead of seeking out the comfort of the energies I knew so well, I decided it was best if I didn't join them as I could not play to their happiness. Squeezing in on the other side of the circle, I watched a small number of the young children within the community get out small willow brooms and sweep their way around the perimeter, casting out the negative energy from the day. *They would have to sweep pretty hard by me,* I thought miserably.

I saw Connie shuffling into place late. That was unusual for her. Normally she was there early with Mum. Now everyone was in place, we turned to the middle, waiting to be given the instruction to face the elements after the ceremonial greetings.

"Welcome," announced one of the three elders in our community, Grandma McLadbrooke.

The elders would start the invoking of the circle and also attend to disputes between the community. Grandma McLadbrooke was tall, in her early seventies, with her grey hair in a tight bun. She always wore a dark plaid skirt and white blouse, but tonight donned the traditional silk dress. She was the youngest of the three elders and gave most of the speeches within the community. "We are gathered here on the night of Samhain to give thanks and good fortune to those that have passed, but also to welcome a new beginning for the new year ahead."

On the night of Samhain, it was common for all three of the elders to give a speech. Grandpa Riley spoke next.

"Tonight is to remember the last year's trials and proceed into the new one with an open mind and to strive for better things," he said. He was in his late eighties, very frail with his spine curved and a lame leg. His crooked nose always reminded me of peeled bark with its dents and open pores. His ragged clothes hung off him as if he was living a hard life, which he most certainly wasn't, for the elders were well-looked after and respected. I didn't know how much of what they said they believed or whether they just said it because it was a tradition, for every year was the same.

Grandma Wren, the eldest of the elders, was the next. "This time is to remember those that we have lost and to give thanks to the lessons that they have taught us. You just have to be willing to open your eyes and see."

As Grandma Wren spoke, I could see Lorian from across the circle freeze, her face falling as tears began to stream down it. She was just about to take a step forward when Emerys grabbed her arm and shook his head. Lorian's slight nod confirmed that she would not move but I could see she was torn, looking down at her feet.

"And now turn west and welcome the ancestors from the past into our realm, and learn of the encounter of death and rebirth so we are not afraid."

Grandpa O'Riley spoke in a clear voice, which was still surprisingly strong for his age. Everyone turned and quietened in apprehension as the rite was about to start.

Grandma Wren was the first to start, followed by Grandpa O'Riley and Grandma McLadbrooke, and then the rest of the community. After each chant, the community would then turn to the next element and direction: north for earth, east for air, south for fire and west for water.

O Protector of the Summerlands
  Lift the veil that covers us
  Allow our Ancestors one night and day
  O Goddess of Shadows
  Show them the way
  Let them commune and revel
  O Lady of Death
  Show us the Summerlands
  The cycle of Death.

As everyone's voices rose in the chant, so did the power. I could tell everyone was feeling it from the look in their eyes as it rose within them too; the shock of the immense force the community cast together.

The wind rose around us as the spell reached its peak. It was almost as if you could feel the veil drop; a chill passed through the air as the spirits entered our world. Everyone's emotions crashed into me, knocking the wind from my lungs: jealousy, exhilaration, greed, longing, pain and malice. All the cruelty and ill-will that everyone in Sòlas always felt, swirled in a mass of pure loathing for one another. Everyone's desires were laid bare. I knew Emerys would be feeling this even stronger than I was with his empathy.

The feelings rose as the wind did, but in amongst it all

there was a slither of something I so rarely felt. Normally it was from a child and flitted away before the thread could be followed, but it was there, bright and full.

Hope.

I followed along that thread, my eyes scanning the crowd to see who it was from, and I could tell many were doing the same thing. It was like a drug; the closer you followed the thread, the stronger the feeling.

There. I chased the invisible tie till I landed on the one person it came from and the one thing they hoped for: a home.

Lorian.

Her eyes were wide, her hair whipping around her face as the wind blew. I didn't think she really knew how to react as she glanced from side to side, trying to see something that wasn't there. I realised she must be trying to see the spirits that were dancing around her as they fed off her warm energy to sustain themselves for their night ahead. The spirits had to have something to keep them whole enough to be spoken to, but we had to be careful on the night of Samhain as some not-so-kindly spirits could also enter through the dropped veil.

As I glanced further round the circle, I could see that others were feeling the chill. That was when Grandma Wren spoke, her eyes darting to where Lorian stood.

"Now we close this circle and ask our ancestors to spend the day amongst us. At midnight tomorrow night, the veil will close and they will return to the Summerlands. Make the most of it my dears, but don't forget to be careful; the other realm can be fruitless, so tread carefully."

I heard people sigh at her warning, but I knew she meant

well. It wasn't just the clamourings of an old woman, as many thought.

"Now we thank the elements for this circle and bid you goodnight."

Moving around the circle to each of the 'corners', starting with east and ending with north, Grandma Wren thanked the elements that had aided us in our magic.

As the circle closed, everyone brushed their foot behind them, distorting part of the salt circle that was behind them. Once the outline had been fully dissolved, everyone began to mill about, heading back to the festival stalls and dancing. I made my way over to Grandma Wren to ask about the festival rite. She had seemed distracted – almost upset – afterwards which was at odds with everyone else. I had never seen her so down. In fact, she was about the only villager that seemed to always be genuinely happy, never saying anything cruel without need. It was as though she had disappeared. I could not find her, pushing my way through the crowd to where she and the other elders had stood.

"Grandpa O'Riley!" I called. He turned and I could see the annoyance already in his eyes for having been disturbed now his duties had been completed. Grandpa O'Riley had always been one of my least-favourite elders. Always making anyone feel uneducated and small at any chance he could, Mum said that before he became an elder, which was before I had been born, he never used to be like that.

"What is it, Maverick?" He only knew my name because I was related to Grandma Wren directly, from her daughter's line, all those years before.

"Have you seen Grandma Wren? I am looking for her and I thought she would be here with you."

"Why would she be here with me? The circle has been cast and closed. She walked off towards your mother, that meddling friend of yours and the young girl." Grandpa O'Riley dismissed me with a quick turn and strode off towards the dancing, no doubt to try and gain attention from the younger women.

Looking across the circle to where Mum and Emerys stood, I caught sight of them with Grandma Wren and Lorian. Grandma Wren had her arm looped through Lorian's and they were in deep chatter, trudging up the crisp grassy hill. Lorian looked completely shaken, shock written deeply across her face but there was also a strange glint I hadn't seen there before.

Could it be happiness?

Lorian

⟨ornament⟩

I couldn't believe it. Maria, my dear friend and former maid, was here. I wasn't alone. But how?

We wound our way up a steep hill and were walking towards an imposing-looking forest. I supposed it might have looked quite beautiful if it was light, but in the middle of the night, it just looked ominous, like one of those in the horror tales Hugh would tell me. Emerys and Neave were walking behind us, now accompanied by Maverick, giving me and Maria time to talk.

"Maria, what has happened? How is it that we have been sent to this other world that is three-hundred years later? And why is there is no colour? Why are there no cars or electricity?" I turned to look at my dear friend. "Why us? Why were you standing in the centre of the circle at the festival?"

I was asking so many questions, it was lucky Maria had always been so patient with me.

"I will tell you in due course, Miss Lorian. All in good time." Maria wheezed again as we climbed the last of the hill towards her now-visible little wooden cottage. As it came into view, I felt my feet stop, my arm falling from where it nestled in the crook of her arm. It was the same, exactly the same as the house that we used to live in after I ran away from home, except it was wooden.

"How?" I breathed. "How is it here? There are no other buildings that look like this here." I turned to Maria, my eyes wide.

"I had it built after the other was destroyed. I loved this house. It reminded me of my family, all of them, including you, Miss Lorian." A small whisper of a smile played at her lips and the ghost of memories appeared in her eyes. "Now come, we have to get inside and I can try to answer your questions, but only when we are inside."

She began shuffling up the track towards her home. It felt as though I was walking in a dream, I couldn't get my head around Maria being here and then the house – no, the home that I had always felt comfortable in. I had a place here.

I had obviously been standing staring for a while as Maria cracked open the familiar wooden door and entered into the glow coming from within.

"Come on, Lorian." Emerys rested his arm around my shoulder and guided me up the path.

As we approached the open door, the smell from inside wafted out on a small breeze and I all but ran across the threshold.

"Eager now, are we?" Emerys joked, following in behind.

Yes I was eager. The pinewood-and-crushed-herbs smell that clung to everything within the place was a sanctuary, the very things that I tried to surround myself with in the garden of my parent's town house.

"Come, sit, all of you." Maria beckoned from where she had situated herself in a comfy, soft armchair by the fire.

I sat in the closest seat to her. The cottage reminded me of the one I lived in with the Wren family for the short time before I got ill. From where I sat, I could see the small kitchen that was situated just off the lounge with an open doorway, allowing full view of the small wooden worktops and ceramic sink. The shelves above it were littered with all manner of herb bottles and ointments.

In the living room, I noticed a bookshelf at one end that held old bound books, similar to those I had seen in Neave's bedroom. The rest of the small room was pretty sparse, just a few trunks against another wall. The majority of the room was taken up with two large sofas and Maria's comfy armchair.

"Miss Lorian, what was it you wanted to know?" Maria panted, bringing my wandering eye back to look upon her from my inventory of the room. Before I could answer, she spoke to Maverick from where he lingered by the door. "Maverick, could you get everyone some camomile tea, please?"

Maverick gave a curt nod, but before he turned away he cast me a funny look, as though I was in the way.

"So let me try and explain what has happened, Miss. First of all, within this village, I am classed as an elder. Basically, just one really old coot that has been here longer than most. Along with the other elders that were standing with me, we conduct the festival rites and are here for teaching and advice on all things magic."

She looked older than when I last saw her, she must be in her mid-seventies, with a slight curve to her spine, wrinkles framing her eyes and mouth.

"There is no need to call me miss, Maria. You have always

146

been my friend and I wish you would treat me as such. I always hated Mother insisting on people addressing us like that. Why are we here? Why have I suddenly been brought into a world like this? Where is Temford? Is this just a fever dream?" I reeled off a mountain of questions that had been pressing on me since I saw her.

"Of course, I am sorry – old habits. But let me warn you there are only certain things that I am able to explain at the moment, but I can assure you this is not a fever dream, Lorian. This is very real. I believe Maverick has told you some of the story when you first met. Oh yes, dear, he told me he met someone who knew nothing of magic and I did wonder if the time had come.

"First of all, let me explain more about Temford and Sòlas. When the Stravaig, a dark witch, cursed this land three hundred years ago, Sòlas stood roughly where Temford was. My cottage is where your family home would have been and your family's estate would have extended into the forest behind us. But the Stravaig didn't just curse the land with no colour or joy, he destroyed as much of Temford as he could, and its people along with it. That is why there is no electricity or cars. We have basically regressed." Maria smiled as if trying to reassure me.

"You see, we are here due to mine and Ivan's powers. My power of timekeeping means I can manipulate time and Ivan can preserve things. We were able to preserve you as the fever took you away from us, then bring you back to us now. I was able to use my own powers as a timekeeper to stay until I saw you again. We changed the name to Sòlas after the destruction of Temford and the majority of its non-magical residents. It became a beacon to those who did possess magic. That is how our community was built."

As Maria ended her story, her eyes snapped to Maverick and her tone grew stern. "Oh Maverick, stop looking at Lorian like that. I told you I used to work as a maid when I was much younger. Lorian here was my mistress' daughter."

Everyone's gaze seemed to pierce me, inspecting me in a new way. Not just some girl, unknown to them, but someone who once employed a respected member of their community.

"W—w—what? So you used to work for Lorian's mother?"

Maverick stuttered, his thoughts seeming to stumble over themselves for a moment, but that didn't last long and he quickly rounded on me with a hate blazing in his eyes that I had never seen anyone possess before. "So you and your family caused Grandma and Grandpa Wren all that grief, and treated them as if they were animals?"

Maverick moved quickly, dropping the tray he was holding with a clatter, towering over me and filling my vision. The room seemed to get darker at the corners, as if the light from the fire was being suppressed and snuffed out.

"Maverick, enough!" Neave stood up from where she had perched on the opposite sofa, forcing herself between us, shielding me. "Stop, Maverick. You know what damage releasing your powers would have in here."

"Come on, Mav, you have to stop. You are going to end up hurting everyone, not just Lorian." Emerys loomed behind Maverick, causing his attention to falter and focus on him.

"But wouldn't you want to do the same if it was your family, Emerys? You know the stories, you were here when Grandma Wren told them."

"Yeah, I do and I would feel the same, but do you want to hurt Grandma Wren and your Mum in the process?"

"Enough!"

The single word was so loud and so unexpected, it took all of us in the room a moment to realise where it had come from. Maria was now striding the short distance over to Maverick, anger in her eyes.

"Now you can calm down, shut up and listen or you can leave, boy. No one enters my home and disrespects my guests, no matter who they are to me."

She was considerably smaller than Maverick, but I could feel the power that radiated off her and clearly, so could he. Even though it would seem he could have harmed her easily, he recoiled, as if he had been struck.

"Do you understand me? Being my grandson gives you no authority over anyone else, do you hear?" Maria spoke in such a soft voice it slithered over your skin with its menace.

"Y—y—yes, I'm sorry," Maverick stammered once again.

Even though I hadn't been there long, I didn't think Maverick had seemed the type to have been reduced to apologising for any reason. And that was it, as quickly as the event had occurred, it was over. Everyone retook their seats, Maverick cleaned up the broken china, and the room grew deathly silent for the next few minutes. You could feel the tension in the air and hear the deep breaths as everyone was trying to calm themselves.

Maria was the first to speak. "In answer to your unasked question, Maverick, yes I did work for Miss." She looked towards me briefly. "I mean, Lorian's family." She smiled, quieting my frayed, quivering nerves, and then looked back towards where Maverick crouched. "You see, what I told you was specifically about Lorian's parents or mother and stepfather for that matter, and then her uncle. They were the cruel people I told you about, always shouting and complaining, never seeming to have enough time for the children. Well, apart from Hugh, but he was another thing entirely: beyond cruel. When their parents died they lived with their uncle for a time before … well let's just say, before Lorian came to stay with me and Ivan."

Everyone's focus seemed to briefly rest on me, as my past began to reveal itself. I could feel the unseen blush start to creep into my cheeks. I suppose that was one good thing about there not being colour – no one would see me blush, or at least not as prominently.

"You see," Maria went on, "Lorian was different from the rest of her family. She seemed to appreciate the less-obvious things, whether it was a peacock butterfly searching out a thistle or learning about a new herb in her garden." Maria smiled.

These were all the things that we used to like to do together, hidden away in the vast expanse of my parent's town house estate. The brief history that Maria shared, explaining that I hadn't mistreated her as my parents had done to all their staff, seemed to calm the whole atmosphere. I took this opportunity to ask the question that I really wanted to ask.

"How am I here, Maria? I know you said your powers brought me here, but I don't understand. If you are here, does that mean Elijah is here as well?"

I didn't call her Grandma Wren as the others had; she wasn't that for me. She was always my friend, more like the mother I had always wished for. Though the years had aged her, she still looked the same strong woman to me.

"Well, as I explained before, Ivan and I had to make a decision and this was the best outcome, we thought." Maria looked down at her hands twisting in her lap.

What did she mean, the best decision? The best decision for whom? But I didn't need to ask, it was as if she knew what I was about to say, and she launched into a horrific story, one that I remembered but only roughly, for I was only lucid a handful of times.

"You see, the fever was getting worse. We were lucky if you were lucid for an hour a day at the end"

The end. Those simple words that sounded so ominous, so final.

"There was nothing we could do, no spell could cure what you had. We didn't and still don't know to this day what it was. It was nothing like the sickness sweeping the town." Guilt and helplessness were written all over Maria's face.

I came to kneel in front of her, and I could feel the heat of the fire blaze through the thin silk dress that I wore. "You couldn't do anything, Maria. I knew that, and so did you. That is one thing I remember: I had said my goodbyes, I understood."

A small tear ran down her cheek. Tenderly, I brushed it away with the pad of my thumb as she had done many times for me. "You have nothing to blame yourself for, nor Ivan, Elijah or young Gwen." Speaking of Elijah, my dear friend and Maria and Ivan's son, and young Gwen, their daughter, brought tears to my eyes.

"We made a choice though, Lorian – Ivan and I. You see, we used our magic and it has brought you to me now. I am just saddened that Ivan could not be here to see it."

"But how do I not have it now? How am I still not ill?"

I thought back through the last forty-eight hours since I'd woken up and I couldn't recall feeling ill once. Scared, yes, at least every second I had spent in this new place I had been terrified until I saw Maria, but no fever.

"When we did the spell, it caused you to freeze. I believe it would have killed the virus that was ailing you. As a matter of fact, you died, Lorian, so even if it wasn't a virus and something more … sinister, it would have been fulfilled." Maria looked at me plainly in the face. "We reversed death, and so have killed the virus or fulfilled the curse. And in answer to your previous question, I am afraid he is not, not our Elijah."

Even though I was grateful that Maria was here, I was still saddened Elijah wasn't, my dear friend. My mind whirled with all the information, the fact that I had died and come back to life. I still felt as though I should be in a fever dream, but I believed Maria when she said I wasn't. I couldn't come up with this world even if I tried.

There was a gasp behind me, which reminded me that Maria and I weren't the only ones in the room. Looking over my shoulder, horror was etched on Neave's face.

"What about the threefold law?"

"What is the threefold law?" I asked. I really didn't understand anything in this new world; it was as if everyone spoke a new unknown language.

"The threefold law is that if you do harm to anyone it will come back on you three times as bad. It is to keep the natural balance of things. It has gone a bit awry since the curse, but it is still there in extreme events," Neave told me. "Grandma Wren – did it occur or was there no consequence?"

"Oh there was a consequence… Ivan was the consequence."

The silence was almost deafening in response. My life had been spared at the cost of Ivan's, dear Ivan, who had taught me nearly all I knew about herbs. The tears that I had managed to contain before spilled over.

Maria visibly shook off the memories and the chill that seemed to enclose the room. Tentatively, I asked about the only other people I had been close to. "Maria, what happened to Elijah and Gwen?"

"Gwen died giving birth to a little boy, Lucas. Neave and Maverick follow her line. And Elijah… He drifted too far to be reached."

The pain lacing her voice was enough to cut through the toughest of skin. She had loved her family deeply. Clearing her throat she eased herself out of her chair. "Now, the night is getting late and we should get to bed. You are all staying here tonight."

I felt relief at being able to stay in this familiar house, but the others were shocked.

"But why, Grandma Wren? The festival is still going on. Can't we go back and join in?" Emerys spoke in a gentle voice.

"No, the chant has been changed too much and the incantation is too loose. A number of malicious spirits could be wandering with any number of agendas. And the disappearances are too frequent. We elders are looking into it, but we haven't any answers yet."

"Was that why Grandpa Ladbrooke was here the other day?" Maverick asked.

Maria nodded, a visible weight on her shoulders. Reaching out I grasped her familiar hand in mine. A sense of ease washed over me at knowing she was there.

"What do you mean the chant has changed? It has always been done that way, always with the same words, and nothing has come of it before," Neave asked.

"That was when we didn't have an additional person within

our circle. Now, Maverick. Please put out the offering I left in the kitchen, then to bed."

She left us in the living room to get ready for bed, giving my hand a reassuring squeeze before she let go.

Maverick

I couldn't believe we were all being forced to stay in Grandma Wren's tiny house. There were three spare rooms but only one was big enough for two people: Grandma Wren's. Mum and Lorian took the two smaller rooms, meaning that Emerys and I would have to stay in the lounge, again. Grandma Wren mentioned that the protection spells and the offering of wine and Sabbat cake would keep the spirits content for the night. We would have to decide what we could do tomorrow when the spirits were walking the earth. I didn't know why she was worrying so much; it was no different from the other years, apart from Lorian being with us.

"I am worried about Connie," Mum said walking into the room holding some blankets and spare pillows in her arms. A deep frown settled itself between her brows as she began to make up the two large sofas for me and Emerys to sleep on.

"She will be okay, Mum, she knows to stay indoors and to leave an offering; she will be fine." I tried to console her, pulling her into a hug. I always forgot how much shorter she was than me; her head rested just below my shoulder. "I promise she will be fine, she is probably tucked up in bed as we speak."

"You are right, I am being silly, but I am so used to having to make sure she is okay. I'm always at home with her. If it was you, I know you and Emerys would be sensible enough. I just can't help this niggling feeling that something is wrong."

"Go to bed, Mum, the night will be chased away quicker with sleep," I reminded her.

It was something she always told me when I was a child and had a night terror. She would always say that it was my imagination, that sleep would chase away the night quickly, and that the sun would rise and brighten the thoughts that troubled me.

Letting go, Mum turned to head into the dim glow coming from the room she had chosen for the night. Picking one of the now made-up sofas, I began to undress and get ready for bed. I was exhausted after the events of the day and I was ready for a long, dreamless sleep. I could hear the tap running as Emerys washed the cups we'd used for the tea.

The wooden door opened to the small room Lorian had chosen to sleep in, creaking slightly. The door was engraved with a small bird. Grandma Wren never used to let anyone into that room, but now we knew why. It was Lorian's old room and she had kept it exactly how Lorian had it in Grandma Wren's original house. I managed to catch a glimpse inside when the Lorian left the door open but there wasn't much to it, just a small bed, wardrobe and side table. The rest of it was pretty bare, but I could see a small trunk with leather straps under the bed where most of her possessions would have been kept.

I knew how much it meant to Lorian by the look on her face when Grandma Wren had shown her to where she'd be staying. Her eyes were so alight I swear they practically glowed as she threw her arms around Grandma Wren. No one was that informal with an elder in Sòlas, not even their family.

As Lorian tiptoed to the kitchen to fill her water jug up, she caught sight of me. Dropping her eyes to the floor she turned to go back into her room. "I'm sorry, I didn't mean to intrude…"

"What is it?"

The words pushed their way out of my mouth before my mind could catch up and I realized my tone was sharper than I'd intended it to be.

"I'm sorry, I didn't mean to sound harsh. I thought you'd gone to bed, you just, um, startled me. Did you need something?"

"Well… I came to fill the water jug but I wanted to thank you for all you have done for me today." She could not bring her eyes to look at mine – it was as if she had never seen a man shirtless before. "You and Emerys have been there when I really needed someone and I thank you for it. I don't know what I would have done if you hadn't—"

"There is no need, we are happy to help. I am sorry for what I said to you earlier. Are you able to talk about what Grandma Wren told you? It is just I saw how upset you looked when she was talking."

"The memories are hard, but maybe someday." Saying this, Lorian looked up and gave me a small smile, the light reflecting off her eyes giving them an otherworldly glow. "I just didn't know the sacrifices Ivan and Maria had made…" She dropped her eyes as sorrow clouded them.

Before I could think, my feet guided me in front of her, as her gaze drew back up, craning her neck to look up at me so she wasn't looking directly at my chest.

"What is so different about your eyes?" I whispered. "Why are they so much more unusual than anyone else's?"

I was transfixed by her eyes, all thoughts from before forgotten. Though duller than they were a moment ago, her eyes still glowed.

"What do you mean?" she whispered back, looking directly at me, her eyes caught by my own.

"Come, look, there is something different about them." I moved her over to the mirror that hung just above the mantelpiece surrounding the fireplace. She stood just in front of me looking into the intricately framed oval. I was captivated by her reflection. "See, they are not like mine." I indicated to my eyes and then hers, hoping she would see the difference.

Lorian let out a small gasp, touching her face around her eyes. "No, they are not, and that is because they are not grey, they are… they are green. Not as dark as they used to be, but they are green," The excitement in her voice was infectious, she was grinning a full-faced grin that I hadn't seen before.

"What is green?" I asked, smiling back. Honestly, in the space of twenty-four hours of knowing her, Lorian had caused and been in more trouble than I had ever known, but she also intrigued me.

Moving closer to the mirror she gazed at herself for a moment longer, as if she couldn't really believe that there was something different about herself.

"It is a colour; the grass, spring leaves, vegetables – most of these things are green," she said.

"Careful…"

Putting my arm around her waist I pulled her back from the hearth as her dress floated in the breeze her legs had created. In her surprise and excitement she seemed to forget that the fire was just in front of her.

"You would have caught alight if you'd gone any closer."

"Th—thank you," she stammered, shocked how close she had come to nearly going up in flames.

I didn't realise that I still had my arm around her until I heard the clearing of a throat and Emerys speaking from the doorway.

"Interrupting, am I?" I could hear the humour in his voice.

At his words, Lorian wriggled away and began to retreat back to her room.

I wasn't meaning you had to leave!" Emerys called after her, his voice losing humour as he sensed he had embarrassed her.

"It's okay, I should be off to bed. Goodnight," she replied stiltedly, and shut the door behind her.

Moving closer to the sofa I climbed into the makeshift bed, looking up at the ceiling. It was wooden but it had a special whitewash on it to seal the wood.

"I didn't mean to interrupt you and Lorian," Emerys said with a smug smile and humour back in his voice. I knew what he was getting at as he turned away from me, trying to suppress a small chuckle.

"Oh shut it, nothing happened. She just got too close to the fire and I pulled her back. Have you ever noticed anything different about her eyes?" I asked, trying to change the subject.

"I see what you're doing there, but in answer to your question, no – I haven't, but Gwilym said something about her eyes earlier."

"She said they are green. I don't know what that is but she said it is a colour, the colour of grass and spring leaves."

Emerys answered my unspoken question as if anticipating it. "She said Gwilym's hair and freckles were a colour also. What do you think is happening? There has been nothing like this before, or Grandma Wren would have said something. Why now?"

"I don't know, but I think we should mention it tomorrow. Grandma Wren will know but we shouldn't wake her now."

"You're right, what was it your mum would say? '*Sleep chases the night away.*' I think we should hope for that anyway. We have a lot to talk about in the morning. It feels like something is happening. Goodnight, Mav."

The room fell into a heavy silence, the only sound the crackle of the fire. I could feel the heaviness of sleep but it eluded me each time I thought I was about to drift off. I lay awake looking around the dimly lit room. Lorian's water jug was left, forgotten, on a small wooden end table. I just couldn't get my mind to settle, to stop asking why strange occurrences were happening ever since she'd shown up … or was that something to do with the spirits entering the living world tonight?

I had just begun to drift off to sleep when I was woken by an ear-piercing scream. The scream was coming in short bursts, broken by chest-racking sobs. They were coming from Lorian's room.

"By the Goddess, what is happening, Mav?" Emerys grumbled across from me as he sat up, rubbing his eyes.

"I don't know, but I think it is coming from Lorian's room."

Emerys moved towards the door as Mum and Grandma Wren rushed out of their rooms.

"Let me, Emerys."

Grandma Wren's voice was strong but thick with sleep. Entering the small dark room, she knelt by the low wooden bed. Maverick could just make out a thrashing mound under the sheets. Another ear-piercing scream erupted from Lorian as if it had been ripped from deep within her.

"Enough now, child, enough. It is just a nightmare. You need to wake up and all will be well."

"Did she not take the limeflower and ashwagandha?" I muttered from the doorway as Lorian let out another ear-piercing scream.

"It burns, why does it burn so much! Make it stop, oh please make it stop." Lorian's pleas tore through the silent cottage.

Maverick could see the glimmer of restless spirits outside the window, being drawn to the noise. It was not good, that type of noise was best avoided on a night like Samhain.

"It seems as though she must have forgotten. What burns, Lorian? You need to open your eyes and tell me," Grandma Wren coaxed.

"Everywhere, all under my skin." Lorian pried her scrunched-up eyes open, causing Grandma Wren to inhale sharply.

I pushed past Mum and Emerys and crouched behind Grandma Wren. Lorian's eyes were milky white; I could just make out a pale grey pupil in the centre.

"Hexed!" Grandma Wren spat suddenly. "Neave, we need to draw her a bath. Make sure you squeeze lemons and limes in the water. Hurry! She is going to keep transitioning into her worst memories if we are not careful. And make sure you leave the rinds in the water."

Mum dashed from the room and started cutting up lemons

161

and limes, while Emerys filled a small metal bathtub with hot water in the lounge.

"What is happening, Grandma Wren? Would the limeflower and ashwagandha not help?"

"No, they would have no effect on a hex. And at the moment, Maverick, I believe she is reliving when she had the fever that killed her. She was given ginger by a doctor she took herself to, to try and burn off the fever. It could have helped if she wasn't allergic to ginger, but he hadn't bothered to ask; the stupid man didn't know what he was doing, but her memories will keep getting worse and more twisted if we don't reverse it soon."

Lorian was continuously muttering and whimpering to herself. Mum came back in after what seemed like forever, but the clock said it had only been a matter of minutes.

"The bath is ready. Maverick, please lift her and take her into the lounge," Mum instructed. Swapping places with Grandma Wren and moving to Lorian's side, I hoisted her small frame from the bed and carefully moved her into the lounge where Emerys was adding more water to the tub. Large lemons and smaller, darker limes bobbed on the surface and I could smell their juices mixing with the steam.

"Neave, help me undress her and then we will lower her into the bath. She can't have anything on that the hex might cling to."

Grandma Wren bustled beside me as I hurried to the tub. I perched on the edge of the sofa lowing Lorian gently onto it as Mum and Grandma Wren swiftly undressed her. Her small body was so tiny under her oversized nightwear, the bruises caused by her encounter with her attacker visible on her pale skin. Just seeing them caused my anger to flare but I clamped it down as quickly as possible.

Lifting her I adjusted my grip and lowered her into the small metal tub, supporting her neck to make sure she didn't slide underneath. As soon as she touched the water, I could hear her sigh and within the next few minutes of soaking, she opened her eyes.

"What is happening?" Lorian looked about her and then realised she was sitting in a warm bath whilst Mum rubbed her skin with lemons. As soon as she realised where she was, she tried to cover herself.

"Shhh… it's okay, Lorian. The boys will sit far enough away so they won't see anything and Neave is a practiced healer so you don't have to cover yourself. Let her do her work."

Grandma Wren rubbed Lorian's back where she was hunched over, attempting to cover herself. "You were hexed, little bird, but it is all better now. Emerys, please get a bay leaf from the kitchen." Grandma Wren spoke softly and patiently as she explained what happened to Lorian. "Now chew this, don't swallow! It will help us understand what happened, or how it was caused."

Emerys and I moved as far away from the tub, giving Lorian as much space as we could. I wouldn't tell her that I had placed her in the bath or initially started to rub the hex away with the lemons. I wouldn't embarrass her like that.

"It is quite a good hex, really," Mum said as we waited for the bay leaf to take effect.

But before Mum could say any more, Grandma Wren gave her a piercing stare. "An awful one, you mean. Don't succumb to the bitterness the curse brings, Neave. Luckily, it is easily removed."

Lorian chewed the bay leaf, her eyes getting wider the longer it was in her mouth. "I see Neave's home and a little wrapped parcel on an end table. I think I caught something like it when Connie threw it to me earlier today," she said tentatively, knowing by saying so, she was casting blame.

"It was rue; I saw it when I went home," I interrupted. "I wondered why it was there. I didn't notice Connie passing anything to Lorian earlier. I was ... distracted," I said, casting my eyes to Lorian and quickly looking away, knowing that if I had noticed I might have prevented this. Another failure.

"Right, we will deal with this tomorrow. Now off to bed everyone. Lorian, just get into bed damp – it is best to dry naturally. Don't worry, it is all over now," Grandma Wren commanded. She tried to keep her voice light but I could see the annoyance on her face and the sharp edge to her tone.

Mum helped Lorian climb out of the slippery tub, shielding her with her body from me and Emerys, and draped a light blanket over her. As she helped her back into her room, a small trail of water followed in her wake.

"She will sleep now as her body adjusts to its normal pattern. Now back to bed, we shouldn't linger." Grandma Wren eased herself up and began to shuffle out of the room.

"Is that it? But that didn't seem to be very much considering what was happening to her?" I challenged.

"It was a simple but effective hex, Maverick. We need to find out why this happened, but that is a task for tomorrow. To bed."

After everyone got themselves settled again and began to fall asleep, I replayed everything that had happened that day. I still couldn't sleep and I couldn't even begin to drift this time, too much had happened and Grandma Wren seemed too calm. I saw all the long hours and heard all the spirits dance until the sky began to lighten and the birds began to sing.

Lorian

I felt drained when I woke up the next morning; my body screamed at me as I tried to ease myself out of bed. The dreams came back in a sudden rush as though they were imprinted on the backs of my eyelids, playing on repeat. They had felt so real; it was as though I was living the incidents all over again. The most prominent was my recent attack, I knew that would forever haunt me. I was sure I wasn't up too late but as I walked urging my stiff muscles to ease out of my small room and into the light kitchen to make tea, it was apparent everyone was up and about already.

"What time is it?" My voice was thick from sleep. I needed a hot cup of tea to soothe my sore throat.

"Just before seven. Don't worry, you aren't late." Maria was already filling a large teapot with boiling water and there was freshly baked bread and cheese on the table. "I know how you hate being up late."

"I thought everyone would have slept in longer after last night!" I commented whilst slicing the still-steaming bread into a large wedge. Looking at Maria when she didn't respond, I noticed the look of concern in her eye. "What is it, Maria? I know you want to ask me something."

"What do you remember from last night?" she asked as she drew a strange-looking pocket watch out of her skirt and flicked open the lid. Her hands moved behind the metal lid but I couldn't see what she was doing. In the next instance it was snapped closed.

"Well, the nightmares – is that what you mean?" Maria nodded. "I also remember you waking me whilst I was in some sort of bath. What is going on, Maria? Please tell me."

"It wasn't just a bad dream – you had been hexed, Lorian. I am sorry, I know this is all new to you and I can see you are scared, but trust me we have reversed it and are looking into how it happened."

"But I had taken the medicine Neave said would help…"

"But if you were hexed, my bird, it wouldn't have helped. I am sorry that it happened, but I promise we will find out why. We had to bathe the hex off you; that's why you woke up in the bath." Maria answered my unspoken question as she had so many times before. "This world isn't just full of magic that helps people and creatures, there is evil here. You have seen it manifest in the form of those creatures and now, unfortunately, you have experienced it personally. Over the last three hundred years, things have grown a little more unstable. People more unstable, willing to harm one another without much thought."

Hexed? But who would want to do that? We swiftly changed the subject as everyone filtered in from outside to have some breakfast and Neave left to set up the stall. Emerys and Maverick offered to take me into the town centre for the day of festivities which I was, surprisingly, quite excited about. But I could feel a lingering anxiousness in the pit of my stomach.

Neave was setting up her flower stall as I arrived with Emerys and Maverick in the square an hour or so later. She was making a few small flower wreaths for decorating doors at night.

"As a farewell to the spirits," Emerys explained.

"Neave, would you like some help?" I offered, as we approached her.

I was eager to help. I loved spending time amidst the smell of the flowers and it would give me something to occupy my mind other than worry about what happened last night.

I could see from the tiredness in Neave's eyes that it would be beneficial for her too. She had been worried about Connie the night before, and we hadn't seen her this morning yet. Not that I was complaining; Connie was as spiteful as you could get it seemed.

"That would be a great help, Lorian, but only for the morning as you should really see the festival events. Just be wary of fighting or thievery, which we tend to have most years. Apart from those things, it is quite spectacular." I was shocked by her interest in others misfortune, but before I could think, my arms were laden with cut flowers and I began to help set up the stall.

"Yes, as long as it isn't on the day of the circle, it is quite fantastic," Maverick said bitterly.

He had been more distant this morning, ensuring he turned away each time I caught him looking at me.

Half an hour later, the stall was full of all sorts of blooms. There was only a small workspace for myself and Neave to create the bouquets and other items she sold on either end of the bench.

"We are going to look at the duelling," Maverick huffed, but before even Neave could answer he was walking off. Emerys bid us farewell and followed behind his friend.

"I will never understand that boy," Neave exclaimed exasperatedly, picking up the shears Emerys had just put down and trimming the ends off flowers.

"What do you mean?" I had only met Maverick a few days ago and he had always seemed aloof and rude.

"Never you mind. Right, do you think you can identify all the flowers if I ask you to get them?"

Looking at the arrangements of flowers in front of me, I realised it would be harder than I originally thought. It had taken a while to set up the stall and I mostly just handed the flowers to Neave for her to place. Without their colour, certain flowers looked the same as the one next to them, such as anemones and poppies.

"Here, let me run through it with you."

Neave patiently went through the varieties of flowers and explained how to easily identify each of them, using leaf texture and length as well as the flower shape itself.

A while after we'd opened up for business, Connie stopped by, so I made sure I stayed down at the other end of the stall, out of harm's way. I tried to busy myself with creating a small spray for a customer. But nothing could have drowned out the argument that was quickly in full swing.

"Where have you been, Connie? And what was this little hex game of yours?" Neave spat, her face again contorted into a cruel snarl that I had only seen briefly before the festival a few nights ago.

"What's it to you where I am? You don't really care do you,

Mum? You've got a new plaything to amuse you," Connie retorted, her eyes drifting to me.

Quickly, I turned back to the stall and tried to resume arranging the small spray of veronica and snowberries.

"Don't you dare. With everything going on and now Lila disappearing, you need to come home, Connie. I thought being as it was Lila, you would have been more careful."

"Oh, don't pretend you care, Mum," Connie shouted.

Even though I didn't see it, I heard the almighty slap that Neave dealt in response. Looking out the corner of my eye, I could see Connie clutching her cheek as Neave leaned in and whispered something to her. In the next instant, Connie turned and disappeared into the crowd.

Straightening, Neave looked around at the customers turned onlookers. "What are you all looking at? Haven't you got anything else to do with your time?"

She turned and fumbled in the back of the cart. All those still standing around gawking began skulking back to wherever they needed to go, realising the drama had now finished.

"I'm sorry, Lorian, that was not pleasant to hear." Neave sighed. "But let's try not to dwell and let it ruin the rest of our day."

The day consisted of a steady stream of patrons buying a vast variety of flowers for various different purposes. They were going to be used for spells, dried for ointments or simply eaten. I didn't know that you could eat flowers but apparently, you could eat certain types, like violets. I would have to ask Maria if she had some paper to write it all down, or I was certain to forget it.

Come mid-afternoon, the stream of customers slowed and the sun, which had been low but bright in the cold autumn sky, began to set.

"Oh, I am so sorry, Lorian. I didn't mean to keep you all day. Please go and see the last few events around the festival – I believe the dancing will still be on."

Hurrying to tidy up, Neave took over from where I was gathering up all the cut stem ends.

"Won't you need help?" I protested. I hated to think that I would be leaving her to do it all on her own.

"No, no, Connie will come by soon, I'm sure and she will help me. You go and have fun."

It was the first time Neave had mentioned Connie since that morning, but the constant worry had lingered in the tightness around her mouth. Connie had stopped by early in the morning to let Neave know she was okay, but Neave seemed little concerned with her wellbeing, sending Connie off into the market without so much as a smile. We hadn't seen hide nor hair of her since then, not that I was complaining.

I did feel eager to go and see the dancing, I couldn't wait for the music to fill me as it once did. As I hurried over to the musical area, I could see that the dancing wasn't like the ballet or ballroom I was used to, but an odd style that had people swapping partners and dancing on their own, with no one step the same. Although there was one thing that stayed the same: I just couldn't stay still when I heard music.

As I stood watching the dancers, I could feel the music begin to wash over me, ignite me, however, this was one of the only times that I felt too nervous to join in. I didn't understand what the steps were and I couldn't seem to remember them when I watched. I had always been able to pick up the steps to a dance so easily; I could pretty much watch the first few and then follow on. But there didn't seem to be a logical pattern or sequence that the dancers went through here.

"Would you like to dance?"

The voice was unknown to me but as I turned, I recognized the face. However, I did not know a name to go with it.

"I, uh, don't know the routine," I mumbled. I didn't know what to say to this stranger, I didn't even know what his name was. All I knew was that he was the person Maverick had been fighting last night.

"Well, there isn't one. Have you never danced before?"

I could see humour playing within his pale eyes – so pale that it seemed as though his whole eye, other than the pupil, was white. He was tall, but not as tall as Maverick or Emerys, but still a good five inches taller than me. His hair would have had a curl to it if it had not been cropped so short against his head, emphasizing the scar that travelled his hairline, from the centre of his forehead to his right ear. It could have made him look menacing, were it not for the easy-going smile and the humour that seemed to be fixed in his eye.

"I used to dance a lot, but never like this. It seems as though there is no structure or set to it. Do they just make it up as they go?" I asked, puzzled, my eyes wandering back to the dancers. The music still had its calming effect on me and I was fixated once again on watching the dancers move around a circle made of spectators.

"That they do. Would you like to give it a go?" he asked, holding his hand out towards me.

I looked down at it. I could see that he obviously worked with his hands, a blacksmith maybe. The calluses and dirt that were ground into his outstretched palm suggested that it was hard labour, whatever he did.

"Sure," I said, steeling myself against the rise of embarrassment and nervousness I felt bubbling under the surface. I was itching to have a go, and maybe as there were no steps to learn, it would be more fun. "My name is Lorian," I said, taking his hand we both walked into the mass of people. Almost instantly the music took over me. I nearly didn't hear his name, Feren. Funny name, but he seemed nice.

We danced for what seemed like hours. It took me a while to get into the rhythm, but before long I began to let go, not worrying if I looked silly or not.

I became joyful and free.

Maverick

The day had seemed to be going pretty well. I managed to leave Lorian and Mum to the flower stall quickly, so keeping my distance was working out to be pretty easy. Emerys had a few questions as to why I was so anxious to leave, especially as he had taken to thinking something was going on between me and Lorian.

"I do find her interesting, but if there's something there, I'll back off, Mav. Just say the word," he repeated again, for what seemed like the hundredth time that day, just when I thought he had given up.

"You know what, if you don't shut up, I'll make it so you can't talk for a week. You remember that little spell we used, don't you? Shut it. Nothing happened last night, she was getting too close to the fire so I pulled her away. Anyway, shouldn't you be thinking about Lila?"

My patience was beginning to wear thin and I knew my reply was harsh but if he didn't shut his mouth soon I would end up sealing his vocal cords off for the next week, just for a bit of peace and quiet.

I remembered the last time I had cast that curse; it was Connie that took the brunt that time. When we were younger – she must have been about four – and had a fever, she wouldn't stop crying for a solid three days. Mum went mental when she found out that I had figured out a spell to shut her up. I could see that Mum was a little relieved that the crying had stopped but nevertheless I got a lecture on the threefold law to go along with it:

"Never use a spell against anyone, Maverick, not unless it is to help them. Never harm, or it will come back on you threefold, no matter how mundane the spell is."

I could recite Mum's speech word for word, having heard it so many times. Luckily, nothing happened to me and just confirmed my thinking that the threefold law was just there to scare young children into behaving.

We wound our way through the crowds of people mingling around the last of the Samhain festivities, still bickering as we so often did. Only on the rare occasion did it get out of hand and end up coming to blows. But even if it did, after a few hours everything would be back to normal.

Queueing up for another, and probably our last toffee apple, I asked Emerys the question that had been playing on my mind since the night he'd brought Lorian to my house. He had seemed quite taken with her and even though my earlier comment was just a quip, I still wondered what that meant for him and Lila.

"Are you still going to look for Lila?" I asked tentatively. "One toffee apple, please." I looked towards Emerys. "You having one, or are you having pie?"

"Huh?" Emerys looked puzzled for a minute then seemed

to realise that he needed to order. "Oh uh, a toffee apple as well."

The vendor, whose name I could never remember, grunted his acknowledgement as he started preparing our last sweet treats. He was a short man with a large belly, about sixty-five at a guess, but in all the years he had sold apples I had never seen him smile. He always looked miserable and lost, as though he was just drifting through his life, existing, not living a single day. *My worst nightmare.* I thought of all the fights I had when the discontent took me, just to feel something, to know I was alive.

Bringing my attention back to the topic that I had raised, I took the two toffee apples that had been propped in the small wooden stand and handed one to Emerys.

"Well, of course, I am going to still look," he said. "I just haven't been able to leave the past few days, with Lorian turning up, and honestly, I don't know where to start. You know, since the day she disappeared I think I have scoured this side of the town about a dozen times and the east side at least half of that. I tried looking in the festival yesterday but didn't see anything."

"Have you checked the forest behind Grandma Wren's?"

"Why would she have gone there? And surely she would have been back by now, we all know the woods out that way," Emerys countered but he was considering the idea.

"I don't know, and she might have gone in too deep and got lost. I just thought you might have given up on Lila by now – you haven't talked about her in a good few days and you don't seem as concerned about her."

Emerys turned angry-looking eyes on me. Feigning disinterest, I bit into my apple and began chomping into the sugary

176

goodness that came just once a year. Emerys ignored my statement and we walked on in silence, both in quiet contemplation. We walked through the various stalls, uninterested in what they were selling, but it allowed us to be part of the festivities for a little longer.

Soon the night began to draw in and twilight started to descend. Considering the spirits were meant to walk among us, it had been a rather boring and uneventful day. No one had had a mischievous or angry spirit chasing after them this year. Thinking upon it, I had barely seen anyone talking to any of their lost relatives. Maybe this year they were more subdued, had fewer things to say. I most certainly hadn't heard from any of mine, anyway. There was only one I looked for every year, just to see if my wishes had come true, but maybe that meant he – my dad – was still alive somewhere. What a shame.

As we drew closer to the dancing, Emerys' voice surprised me. I had almost forgotten he was there. As he spoke, I could hear the tentativeness in his voice, as if he didn't know how I would react. He'd never seemed to worry about how I would react to something before.

"Would you help me look in the woods behind Grandma Wren's tomorrow? Once you've set the stall up. I don't have to be at work until the afternoon."

I considered his words, wondering if I would have time to get back to finish some projects I'd just started carving. Carving was always a good way for me to de-stress; focusing on the work at hand and bringing something beautiful to life out of wood always made me feel at peace.

"Sure, we will go as soon as I'm done," I finally called across the distance between us as we criss-crossed through the dancing crowd. I saw him nod in acknowledgement.

"Oi, what are you doing?" Emerys exclaimed, recovering quickly after nearly barrelling into me as I came to an abrupt stop. He picked the last of his toffee apple up from the ground where he had dropped it.

"Look, that scumbag Feren is he…? No he can't be." I was looking straight at Lorian. I didn't think she would dance, she seemed too timid, not wanting to draw attention to herself all the time. And yet here she was dancing, and dancing well, in front of at least fifty different strangers with Feren. It wasn't just the sight of her dancing that was so unusual, something about the sight of her moving so freely caused a tickle of a memory to form in my mind. It was something I knew I should remember easily but it just wouldn't come.

Her feet were moving fast but in time with the music; her body was fluid as it swayed and twisted. The pair danced sometimes together, sometimes apart, but to me it seemed as though everyone was watching Lorian, captivated by her.

"He is. Lorian is dancing with Feren, and she's pretty good as well!" said Emerys.

"Does she seem familiar to you?"

"I suppose something about seeing her makes me remember that glade we used to go to in the forest when we were younger. You know, the one with the statue?"

That was when I realised; as she danced, memories came back to me, memories of all the times Emerys and I had gone to that glade to escape. The times I had poured my frustration to that nameless face, and cried in front of it as my powers grew and I had no idea how to control them. That face was not nameless any more.

"Hey, her eyes are really looking weird now, as if they have a strange light in them … and what is that on her cheeks?"

Emerys drew me out of my stare, but instead of responding to his question, I turned and walked away.

I lost it, I couldn't help it. The light-heartedness of the dance threw me. But what threw me more was the way Feren was looking at Lorian. I honestly didn't know what it was about him, but there was something not right. And after everything I had done to help Lorian, she seemed more comfortable with him than me. I know I had snapped a few times but still, surely she could see I had helped her? I could understand why she was more comfortable around Emerys with his touchy-feely empath skills, even though sometimes he didn't listen to them. But mere novices in the world of feelings had to go around blind. It frustrated me that couldn't I understand it like Emerys.

I kicked a leftover cup and whatever debris from the festival was lying around as I made my way back to the house. I just had to get away. The spirits would be gone and the days would go back to normal; Lorian was going to stay with Grandma Wren now they'd been reunited.

Earlier that morning I had seen Grandma Wren give Lorian an old leather-bound book. It was one I had never seen before, which was odd as I must have gone through all her books at least twice. She always let her family read her book of shadows and learn from the experiences she had gone through, but I had never seen that one. I just couldn't take my mind off of what it could be, and why she would give it to someone that knows nothing about magic. I was stuck on the idea that I should just ask Grandma Wren. I just wanted to make sure nothing was going to happen to my family and that our secrets were safe.

Changing direction, I started to trek back up the hill towards Grandma Wren's house. I had a few questions that I needed to be answered, I needed to talk to Grandma Wren.

I needed that book.

Emerys

I had honestly never seen anything so mesmerising. I was drawn to her; the smile on her face made me smile too. She was captivating as she moved around the small area that had opened up around them in the crowd. Lorian and Feren continued to dance for several songs. It was odd to think of Lorian's similarity to the statue, now that Maverick had linked her to it. I hadn't seen the old pile of stone for years, so he could be wrong.

Maverick had left quickly after seeing the two together; it was as if he had never been there. I felt the jealousy radiating off him, confirming suspicions I'd had before. But in all honesty, I was pleased he'd gone. The bitter and twisted part of me was glad he had given up so easily – it was one less competitor.

Lila. My mind hopped back to her but it didn't last long. No matter my feelings for her, she was not here now and a new challenge presented itself. I could feel that place within myself that I damped down as much as I could, flutter its way out of its cage. I could feel a twisted smile break out on my face as I thought about it. I always liked to win, especially when it made others unhappy. Normally I fought it, not wanting to give into my bitter side, but I couldn't help its delicious allure this time.

Turning my attention back to the dance, I realised that the song had finished and Lorian was moving towards me at the edge of the dancing circle. Her plain cotton blouse was tucked into her heavy skirt and it swished as she skipped over to me. She was light on her feet as though she was still hearing music, silent to everyone but herself.

My feet began to move of their own accord to meet her, like a moth drawn to a flame, but before I could reach her someone stepped in front of me. I didn't know who he was, but I didn't particularly care. Reaching out I grabbed at the man in question, but my hand didn't touch his shoulder. I tried again, and again my hand passed straight through him. My hand was cold as I drew it back to my side. Stepping around the spirit, I came to stand beside Lorian. The spirit was whispering something to her urgently. I couldn't hear what he was saying but it was obvious that Lorian could.

Her face was drawn as she listened wide-eyed to the stranger; the lightness that the dancing brought her dimmed as the minutes progressed. As the carefree look she had moments before dwindled and extinguished, so did the man in front of me.

The spirit had materialised, drawing enough energy of the surrounding people to become lucid. He had obviously focused his energy on Lorian, directing all his power to ensure that she was the only one that could hear him. She was now chalky pale; her skin – practically white to start with – was now nearly translucent. Her knees crumbled beneath her she slid to meet the damp grass. Putting my hand out, I managed to slide it beneath her arms just before she could hit the grass. I held her light frame to my chest but I could feel the dead weight of her body. She couldn't hold herself up; she couldn't even seem to make her body cooperate with what she wanted it to do.

"Lorian, are you okay?"

I could feel the worry and fear simmering off her as panic rose in her veins. Scooping her up I pushed through the now-gathered crowd, striding towards the gated side of the town that led to the forest and the only person who might understand what could be happening. And why a spirit might manifest itself just minutes before the veil was to seal itself.

"Don't worry, Grandma Wren will know what to do."

"I didn't know," she muttered as if pleading with me to understand.

I could feel that she wanted me to console her, knowing she wanted absolution for whatever she believed she was blamed for. I was certainly confused, not just by the events but by what Lorian could feel such guilt for; it didn't seem like she would ever go against what was asked of her. I knew that I had to get her to Grandma Wren as soon as possible. The fear escalating within her bubbled into me as her mind raced to piece together the encounter that she had just had. She kept repeating the same words, staring blindly in front of her as we made our way up the grassy bank to the cottage at the edge of the forest.

As I reached the wooden door, I could see that it had been left ajar, a smoky scent wafting out of the small opening. Grandma Wren was obviously home and had a fire lit. She sometimes left the door open so people knew she was there if they needed her, and I most certainly did at this point.

Without knocking, I pushed through the entrance to the little cottage calling her name.

Grandma Wren defied every notion that she was old. She suddenly appeared, all but striding across the small living room.

"What has happened?" she snapped, her eyes drawn to Lorian within a second of us entering the doorway. Lorian was still muttering repeatedly under her breath. "Get her on the sofa by the fire, now," Grandma Wren instructed. She must have been making ointments in the kitchen before I came in as she waved her wooden spoon with remnants of herbs stuck to it as if brandishing a sword.

Moving around her, I placed Lorian on the sofa that I had slept on the night before. As I lowered her, I could feel her shaking, Goddess, she was having a hell of a few days.

"What happened?" Grandma Wren repeated as she replaced the wooden spoon on the table, wiping her hands on the front of the apron she was wearing over her plain dark skirt.

"We were in the last of the festivities when it happened. She had been dancing with Feren…"

"Yes, I know this. Maverick told me," she interrupted, clearly exasperated as she looked at Lorian, who was now curled in a tight ball on her side.

"Maverick told you?" I asked in bemusement.

"Yes, he was here, but never mind that. What happened? Dancing couldn't have done this – she used to dance all the time."

"A spirit materialized in front of everyone. It must have drawn energy from everyone around us, but Lorian seemed like she was the only one that could hear it."

"No…" Grandma Wren stilled and visibly paled. "What did the spirit look like, Emerys? Be specific."

"Well, I don't really remember his face, but he was about five inches shorter than me and was wearing funny clothes; you wouldn't see anything like them around here. They were formal." I tried to recall every detail I could, explaining the buttoned jacket and shining shoes.

Grandma Wren turned her attention back to Lorian and spoke gently as if trying to draw her out. "Lorian, my little bird."

It was funny hearing the pet name that both she and Neave used for someone that had only been here a few days. Grandma Wren only ever called anyone by it if she knew them well or if they were family. Neave, on the other hand, seemed to use it for anyone she seemed to like, who were few and far between.

"What did Hugh say?"

Who on earth was Hugh? None of this was making sense. But Lorian seemed to register who was in front of her as Grandma Wren spoke.

Breaking out of her trance, she threw her arms around Grandma Wren and began to cry. I had never seen anyone act in such a way, especially not to an elder. Everyone in Sòlas treated them with the utmost respect, even if they didn't like them.

"It's my fault, Maria – he says it is and I knew it was deep down. I never did enough, never made them happy. Then they took it out on him as well because of me; it was my fault he did it and I helped. Oh, Maria what am I going to do? He says he will find a way to make me suffer as he did."

"Shhh, it's going to be okay, little bird, we will sort it. He can't harm you, I promise. After tonight, he will be gone. Let me make you some tea while you sit with Emerys. You are safe here."

The women embraced each other, then Grandma Wren went into the kitchen. Wiping the tears from her face, Lorian sat delicately on the edge of the sofa.

I tentatively eased down next to her, ensuring there was enough distance between us, so she didn't feel I was intruding on her space. "Are you okay? Who was that, Lorian?"

I didn't want to push but I was worried, I could feel her fear as I asked the question, but I also felt the threat that Grandma Wren seemed to think this spirit posed. I tried to quieten my need to know and decided not to press. "You don't have to say, I shouldn't pry, but I am worried, Lorian."

"It's okay. Thank you for helping me. You always seem to be there when I'm in trouble."

Taking a deep breath, Lorian voice came out in a small hushed whisper as she explained who the spirit was. "It was my brother… He … is angry as he was punished for something that happened a long time ago and I wasn't, but he feels I should have been too. I can't talk about what, Emerys. I'm sorry, but thank you for helping me, again."

Grandma Wren came back into the room holding a tray with a teapot and three cups and saucers. Lorian smiled as she saw it and I could feel her mood lift slightly. "You kept it, after all this time…"

"Of course, it is my favourite. I normally only get it out for special occasions."

Grandma Wren smiled and set down the tray that held the small, delicate set of china covered in rosebuds on the small coffee table. Lorian was smiling.

"Emerys?" Grandma Wren drew my attention away from Lorian's pretty face towards her. I could see amusement, and something else within her eyes. "Would you please pour the tea?"

"Oh, of course."

Moving to the edge of the sofa I leant over the table and gently began to pour the tea. It was vervain, I realised, to help with Lorian's anxiety.

"So, tell me what happened again," Grandma Wren asked Lorian.

Taking a deep breath, Lorian relayed the story to Grandma Wren, who listened intently, only interrupting when she had a question. There were only a few moments when I grew confused and realised that they were relaying something to one another that had happened in the past.

The early evening drew on as we sat and spoke about everything. Lorian learnt about my power – that I was able to feel what another feels, but also make small suggestions to change another's behaviour. She seemed to calm down after talking about it, having realised that she had felt the slight tingle that my emotional suggestions produced when I had tried to calm her.

Around seven-thirty in the evening, she went into her room and came back out with a big leather journal.

"What's that for?" I asked her, looking inquiringly at the book.

Before answering, she looked at Grandma Wren who gave a small nod and encouraging smile. I don't know why she would feel the need to cover up whatever it was she had.

"It is a journal that Maria gave me."

It always took me a second to realise who she was talking about when she used Grandma Wren's first name.

"Oh I see, so what do you do with it?" I prompted. She seemed to feel it was important, by the way she was gripping it to her chest.

"I write down how I am feeling and what happened in the day," she replied, tilting her head to the side and looking at me as though I was from another planet. "Do you never do that?"

"It is like the book of shadows you keep, Emerys, but this is non-magic based. Lorian has always found it helpful to vent into the safety of pages," Grandma Wren chipped in, explaining in a way she knew I would understand. The small reprimand within her voice told me not to ask about the things she wrote within the pages.

"I used to be teased horribly by my brother for writing things down."

For a moment, Lorian lost herself in thought but then seemed to give herself a mental nudge and came back to the present. Curling her legs under herself she settled back down next to me and opened up to the first page. There was a small note written in Grandma Wren's hand. I couldn't see what it said, but a small smile turned up her lips as she turned to a clean page, and she began to write.

"Now go and practice your scrying spells please, Emerys. There is a bowl to use for water, as I know you find that easiest, over on the side. Do it behind the sofa so I can see you."

"But I haven't needed to practice for years! I know how to perform a scrying ritual, I've finished my lessons," I protested, but Grandma Wren gave me a long look meaning she wasn't in the mood to argue.

Lorian

"What is scrying?" I asked as I watched Emerys.

"It is where you are either looking for something or someone in an element you feel drawn to. Now let him begin," Maria explained.

She took a watch out of her pocket so that I could only just see it – she kept it half-covered in one hand and flicked her other hand over it. I wanted to ask what she was doing, but it felt as though it was something personal.

It was fascinating watching Emerys set up his circle – it was the same as the ritual last night, just on a smaller scale. He gathered the salt he needed to draw the circle and outlined it on the floor, leaving a small gap so he could enter. Stepping inside it, he closed the circle behind him by joining the two open ends; only when this was done did he speak to the four elements.

Sitting cross-legged in the middle of the salt circle, Emerys took the small bowl of water he had placed on the floor in front of him and added a few drops of oil to it. He became very still, the only movement coming from his shallow breathing. Maria explained in hushed whispers that he was interpreting what the oil was 'telling' him.

Suddenly there was a shift in the room, I could feel it – it had to be the magic Emerys was drawing. He was staring into the water, but when I looked at his face his eyes were black. As quickly as I could, I clambered up from my chair and rushed over to him.

"Stop, Lorian!" Maria shouted. "Do not break the circle. It will be detrimental to Emerys if you do. This isn't normal – he is channelling a lot of energy, more than I have seen him handle before."

"But what is happening to him?" I cried, kneeling at the edge of the circle. Emerys was deadly still, not moving a muscle, and I could barely see him breathe.

"He is scrying, Lorian. We must be careful and not disturb him. I haven't seen him draw this much energy before," she repeated. "Obviously what he needs to see is important."

Maria came behind me and put her bony hand on my shoulder, I could smell the ointment she always rubbed into her hands to ease the arthritis that had begun to riddle her joints. Her touch soothed my frayed nerves just enough that I could clear my head and calm down.

Emerys started to grumble, drawing our attention back to him. Maria eased herself into a crouching position and started talking to him. "What is it Emerys, what do you see?" she coaxed,

"Black, everything is black," he muttered. "I'm cold, so cold, help me, please. I can't move." His voice was laced with panic as he repeated the same four sentences over and over again.

"We have to draw him back, this isn't right. I didn't think

he would go this deep into the void. He is normally more controlled. He can't control the vision." I could hear the worry in Maria's usually calm voice.

"What do we have to do?" I would do all I could to help Emerys to repay all the times he had helped me.

"I need to follow him and coax him back." Maria began to prepare a second circle behind Emerys.

"How do you do that?"

Maria placed a bowl in front of herself and filled it with water from the jug Emerys had used. "I am going to have to scry for him and see if I can follow him."

"Can I not go too? He has helped me so much I can't stand here and do nothing."

Maria hesitated a moment. "You have never done this before. I would have to go with you and it would take so much energy for us both to go, I honestly don't know if I will make it myself. I have become weaker with scrying as of late, my age is catching up with me."

"Then let me do it. Talk me through it – there must be a way that you can talk to me but allow me to find him?"

Maria thought for a moment and then came to a decision: "There is one way, but you will be tired, if not hurt, after. Are you sure you want to do this?"

"Yes." I swallowed my fear. I didn't care about consequences – I had been hurt multiple times within the past few days of turning up here and Emerys had always been there to help me. It was time I did the same for him. He was still muttering, although it was now incoherent. All of a sudden, he let out an ear-piercing scream.

"Hurry now – sit in this circle. I am going to connect one behind you with just a small gap so it will filter a small amount of energy into mine. Now look into the water and repeat this chant." Maria started to chant the same chant that Emerys had spoken.

I repeated the chant twice through until darkness engulfed me. I could feel myself begin to panic. Jumping back in my sitting position, I met a firm hand on my back.

"Be still, Lorian, this is normal. Now think of Emerys. You have to think of only him. You are safe, I have you." Her hand reassured me, but I still felt the trepidation of entering uncharted waters. What happened if I got lost like Emerys?

"You won't get lost, I promise. I have you. Now focus…" Maria spoke softly as if from afar, it was odd how she knew what I was thinking, I thought to myself. But remembering her words, I focused solely on Emerys.

Blinking, a light began to come into focus, but only a small light. It cast a grey glow over the walls. I was in a stone room – actually, to be precise, I was inside something in a stone room. I realised I was in a glass dome; glass was even under my feet.

Looking up, I could see what looked like a giant cork right above me, small holes covering the bottom. I peered out, and I noticed there were other domes similar to the one I was in. They looked like glass bottles, and there was something moving in each of them. Glancing around cautiously, I moved to one side of my dome. It was hard to see in the gloom but I could just make out the outline of figures moving as if they were arguing, on the other side.

Tentatively, I called out, "Emerys? Emerys is that you?"

One of the figures turned, responding to my call. "Lorian?"

The figure moved cautiously towards me and came into view. It was Emerys and he wasn't alone. "How are you here?"

he said, rushing towards me.

"Maria told me how to reach you – you have to come back. She said you are channelling too much energy. You were crying out in pain and we need to get you back. Maria said we have to hurry."

"But I can't leave her here…"

Emerys motioned behind him towards another figure. It was a woman, similar to me in age, I thought. She was looking at me, perplexed.

"Emerys, you have to go. I told you, you have to go!" the young woman pleaded.

"Lila, I can't leave you!" Emerys turned back to her. "It's my fault you were out late and I didn't walk you home. I have to get you out of here."

I knew I had heard that name before – Emerys and Maverick had been talking about her. But who was she?

"You can't do anything as you're not actually here. You scried for me and found me. You need to be physically here to be able to help me. And anyway, I'm not myself, I've told you…"

I really was confused, how could this girl not be herself? She was standing in front of me and she looked fine, if not a little worn out. She continued talking and I fell further into confusion.

"I am just essence. Go now, you must go with this woman – she will help you."

"But—" Emerys started.

"No, you must go now, you have been here too long already."

"Emerys, please. You were in so much pain you have to come with me. Maria said it's urgent!" I pleaded along with the girl. I had a sense of distance pulling at me and I was growing tired.

"No!" Emerys shouted, turning and striding away to the other side of the glass dome. His anger was almost malleable and he used it. Drawing it to himself he began blasting the glass with spells and his fists.

The girl ignored his outburst as if it were normal and turned to look at me. "You have to get him to go with you."

"But how? I don't know what I am doing. I've never done this before."

Shock shadowed her face. She was about to confirm my suspicions that it was odd within this world not to know how to use magic.

"You should know how to do this by now, at your age. I've never met anyone who didn't understand the basic principles." She gave me a strange look but then seemed to realise I truly didn't understand. "Okay, here is what you should do. Get him to take your hand and he will be forced to follow you back when you chase the line back to reality. You have to do it now."

Turning, she strode over to Emerys and engulfed him in a hug.

"Take my hand, Emerys, please…" I could hear the fatigue in my voice.

He was standing so close to Lila, his jaw set as he battled his internal torment. I could also see he knew I was growing tired and wouldn't be able to carry on much longer. Lila picked up his hand and reached out for mine. Emerys was about to protest but before he could utter a word, Lila placed Emerys' hand in my outstretched one. Then everything went black.

Opening my eyes, I could see we were back in the cottage, still holding hands, with Maria's hand still on my back, all of us sitting in one big circle of salt on the floor.

Before any of us could ask any questions, the door of the cottage flew open and Maverick, Connie and Neave filled the doorway.

Maverick

T aking the book had been all too easy, Grandma Wren trusted that none of us would go snooping, but this wasn't something I was prepared to leave alone, especially if someone I cared for could get hurt.

I felt guilty as I slipped into Lorian's room and took the book from where she unimaginatively kept it under her pillow. I rolled my eyes at how easy it was. I thought Grandma Wren had caught me as she came out of the kitchen and stared at me as I stood by the fire, but she eased back into conversation.

Slipping into the barn with Xaviran, I looked at the small book that Lorian had held so dearly. Taking a deep breath, I flipped it open and began to read.

21st December 1918
  Dear Diary,
  Tonight was the night of the winter show. I thought it had gone really well when we came offstage; everyone in the audience and the

rest of the dancers seemed happy with the performance. However, that was until Mother and Stepfather came backstage. I knew something was wrong the moment I saw them; their faces were tense and they had that fake smile... No, strained – that was the word I wanted, their smiles were strained.

'A disappointment,' they said. I was a disappointment to them and the family. My form was so bad and I wouldn't dance again. Mother told Miss K. that I would not be attending lessons from now on. Miss K. tried to reason with Mother, but once she's made up her mind she cannot be reasoned with, and after all, she holds the purse strings. If she decides not to pay for me to have lessons, there is nothing more I can do about it. I hate her for it, I hate her for taking away the one thing I love, and I hate Stepfather too. He just stood there smirking.

I am sick of this family and what they stand for. The only comfort I have is that they are going away for Hugh's fencing tournament tomorrow and have said I'm not allowed to attend as I needed to think about the embarrassment I caused them tonight. Honestly, I feel so much happier that I might have a day or two to myself. Of course, I will have to be careful, as the matron will be watching.

I hope tomorrow is a better day, no more crying.

Lorian

I put down the small book, frustrated. Lorian's family made my skin itch and a dark fury stir inside me. But nothing seemed unusual about Lorian from what I had read so far; apart from her belonging to a cruel, ruthless family that seemed to have little care for what made her happy. There was nothing to suggest that she was going to be of any trouble. Maybe she just had poor luck to get into the situations she had.

Sighing, I resolved to read a few more entries.
29ᵗʰ December 1918

Dear Diary,

I hate this man. I know my father wasn't always there for me but my new stepfather has infiltrated my mother's already-cold heart and has just seemed to make her grow even colder, more cruel.

I am still not allowed back to Miss K's school even after Miss K. pleaded for me to be allowed back; and I have now been told I have to stay in my room when I am home.

I know Hugh hates him too. I can see it in his eyes when his back is turned, but he's tried to stay in his good books, to get close to him. I don't know why, but I know Hugh is up to something.

Lorian

I flicked through the tightly handwritten pages until another entry caught my eye. There was nothing remotely different about the page in the sense it was still all handwritten, but it was the smudging in places that made me pause; the way it was scattered across the middle of the page was as if someone had been crying as they were writing and the ink had run. And the fact that it wasn't finished. Lorian hadn't even signed her name… She'd stopped mid-sentence.

I could feel my stomach start to churn as I started to read…

8th April 1919

Dear Diary,

It's been quite a few days since I have written, but I haven't been well enough.

He took it further this time. I thought he had stopped the last time I got sick, but I should have known, since he was still asking questions about herbs and plants. I really didn't think he would do it again.

Hugh cut me with the garden fork just over my chest and I don't know where he got it from, but he rubbed monkshood straight into the cuts.

Oh the pain! My stomach was burning and I was so dizzy.

How could he be so cruel? How could I have given him all the knowledge he needed?

The doctor... the doctor, he said that my heart, it might—

And that was where the entry ended.

Flicking a month or so ahead, I decided to read one more entry:

9th June 1919

Dear Diary,

What has he done? What have I done? This is all my fault. I told him everything I knew about plants, about herbs and he did it. I should have known after everything he did to me that he would take it too far.

He killed Mother and Stepfather.

This is my fault, all my fault. I hated them, yes, but never would I have done something like this.

Hugh is going to a detention centre but because he is underage and with my family's influence, he is going to be held under the care of my uncle, as am I.

I am scared, oh how I am scared. Why is no one in this family kind? Why can't Maria, Ivan, Elijah and Gwen come with me?

I hope things get better...

Lorian.

I read over that entry multiple times before I could even process my thoughts.

I had to get to Grandma Wren's quickly.

Maverick

I didn't know what I had just walked into, but there was Lorian, Grandma Wren and Emerys all sitting in a salt circle on the floor, all in a chain. Grandma Wren had her hand on Lorian's back and Lorian had her arm reaching out in front of her holding Emerys'.

Mum was first to break the awkward silence that was enveloping the room.

"What's happened?"

Grandma Wren tried to rise but she was weak. Rushing to her side, I made an opening in the circle with an athame, a small sacred knife, and helped guide her back to her chair.

"Emerys was scrying and got stuck," she said, turning to Lorian as she sat down. "I am sorry, dear. I don't know what happened, but I couldn't see anything or hear you, let alone get you to hear me."

"What, how?" I asked. "You've done it before, dozens of times. And what do you mean, get Lorian to hear you?"

I looked back towards Emerys and I could see that he

looked drained. He was leaning on Lorian as she guided them both over to the sofa. Emerys slumped down, looking more exhausted than I had ever seen him after he'd performed magic. It was no surprise that Lorian was weary as she had only performed a rite once: last night.

"It's Lila, she's trapped," Emerys said, exhausted.

"What? You found her? But I thought you couldn't see her when you tried before?"

"Enough, for now. They need to rest," Mum said, bringing a pot full of the never-ending supply of tea and sandwiches into the room. "Maverick, take the old tray back into the kitchen please, while I start a fire."

I picked up the tray and noticed it carried the tea set Grandma Wren only used for special occasions. Placing it back on the small oak worktop, I wandered back into the other room, not bothering to clean up its contents. Stopping as I got to the door, I decided it would be better to give them all some space and not all cram on to the limited furniture. The room was aglow with the flickering of flames from the lamps Mum had lit; she was now crouching low over the grate, coaxing the smouldering kindling to catch alight.

Lorian was sitting next to Emerys, and they were both sipping tea. Lorian looked a lot better after she had had some spicy cinnamon tea, but Emerys still looked peaky.

"Why is she here? And performing magic with you?" Connie hissed from the now-closed front door. Her face was twisted into a disgusted scowl, which was fixed on Lorian. "Why Grandma? Why her?"

"Enough, Connie." Mum spoke quickly in the authoritative voice that she only rarely used, rising from where the fire now roared to life.

"No, why her? Why is she so special?"

Connie was walking further into the room now, and even though she was small I could see that she was intimidating Lorian. Then, as though she wanted Lorian to witness her power, she turned herself into a boy that I had never seen before. His hair was dark and he was wearing what looked like a very old, but formal outfit. He was wearing a jacket with just two buttons on the front, a white shirt, waistcoat and trousers, and his shoes shone brighter than I thought was possible.

When Lorian saw the boy, she froze. The small amount of light that had begun to fill her eyes after the tea snuffed out.

I wondered who it was that could cause such a reaction.

Suddenly, the fatigue that seemed to sap all her strength melted from Grandma Wren. She emanated power, more so than the night before, when I had confronted Lorian. She was the witch she once was. The words that came out of her mouth seemed to make even the house quiver in fear.

"Enough," she boomed. "How dare you to come into my house and intimidate my guests. Leave, now!"

Emerys was standing in front of Lorian as though he was going to defend her from my sister. Mum and I seemed to be the only ones that didn't know what was going on.

But Connie wasn't done. She now turned into Lila, causing Emerys to buckle into a heap on the floor. Connie knew how upset he had been over Lila's disappearance and she was using it against him.

Sending my dark fury towards Connie, I engulfed her in seconds, confining her, choking her. She broke concentration and collapsed on the floor coughing, trying to draw breath. She turned back into her true form.

Stalking over to her I picked her up, but still, I didn't release her from my choking constraints. "How dare you ever bring that up, you sick little girl," I hissed. "You'd better get out of here now or I will ensure you will never do your little trick again." Her eyes were wide and, she nodded slowly between coughs.

As soon as I released her, Connie scuttled out of the door as fast as she could. Emerys looked like he had been punched. There was a look of dumbfounded shock on his face.

"Emerys, are you okay? I don't think she meant to hurt you like that."

He was sitting in front of Lorian, a heap on the floor, his eyes fixed on the door where Connie had escaped.

"She did and you know it. She blames me. You know she was close to Lila, like a big sister – she is blaming me for her disappearance." Emerys spoke clearly but quietly, the pain and disappointment evident in his voice.

"I am sure she doesn't, Emerys. As you said, she is just hurting because she was close to Lila." Mum tried to console him, resting a reassuring hand on his shoulder. "Come and sit back down and take a minute to calm yourself. You are drained."

"No, I must go, I have to look for her. I know she isn't safe now – I have to find her."

Pushing past me he stumbled through door. I went to follow after him but was stopped by Grandma Wren.

"Not now, Maverick. We need to explain what we all saw. It might be the only thing that gets Lila back." She moved to sit by Lorian, who had silent tears running down her face. "Shhh now, little bird, it's okay, she doesn't understand."

"Who was it that Connie turned into? Who was that boy?" I

interrupted. There were too many secrets surrounding Lorian and I just had to know what this one was. My anger had started to bubble up; I was infuriated that Grandma Wren was forbidding me to go and help Emerys just when he needed it.

"Not now, Mav—" Mum began, but Lorian cut her off.

"No, it's fine – he was my brother. He showed up when I was dancing earlier. I was walking towards Emerys after dancing with Feren and then – there he was, right in front of me, like the day he—"

She broke off and looked towards the floor, as if ashamed by what she was about to say. Grandma Wren picked up where she left off.

"He was arrested, you see, and it's something he feels Lorian should own up to as well. We will have the time to talk about this later."

"I know who he is!" I whirled round to face Lorian, my dark fury stirring again. "I've read about him. You helped him kill your mother and stepfather, didn't you Lorian?"

"I—I—" Lorian began to stammer.

"Don't you lie, I know you did. I read it in your little book of secrets…"

I tossed the book towards Lorian, but before I could see it hit the floor, Grandma Wren stood directly in front of her.

"I've told you before, boy, no one disrespects my guests. Especially not Lorian."

"But she is a murderer—"

"You don't know what you are talking about, coming in here and throwing your weight around like a child. And control your temper."

She was staring at me with such unwavering intensity. The

whole room was filled with mist, dark and thick fury swirled around our waists. Closing my eyes, I took three deep breaths.

"Now you listen, and listen well. Lorian had no part in that hateful deed. Yes, she may have unknowingly explained about the properties of plants and herbs to Hugh, even though he was so cruel to her. She believed she could have had a friendship with him through it. But what she didn't know was that he was testing the plants out to see how they worked, how they might kill someone."

Grandma Wren turned and looked down at Lorian where she was sitting looking at her hands, as her silent tears fell. "She had nothing to do with it. Now you hand that book over. How would you like someone reading your book of shadows? I thought you were up to no good earlier, but I wanted to trust you wouldn't be doing such an invasive thing as snooping in her room," she said, taking the book from me. "If I ever catch you reading this or looking through her things again, I will ensure all the elders will punish you, you hear me?"

Realisation dawned on me when Grandma Wren explained the significance of the book. A feeling of shame washed over me. The tension in the room was so thick it was practically choking me.

"You saw Hugh because the veil is now thin, Lorian," Grandma Wren explained, "but more so, we are prone to more malicious visitors during Samhain. Do not worry – the veil will solidify more this evening. You have nothing to fear from him." Grandma Wren eased some of the tension that visibly sat on Lorian's shoulders.

Over the next hour, copious amounts of tea and cake were consumed. Grandma Wren and Lorian recited what they had seen when they scried with Emerys, and what had happened to him causing him to be so agitated.

"Well at least we know she isn't in the woods behind your house. That's where we were going to look next," I said around a mouthful of cake.

"No, I didn't think she would be. But how about showing Lorian the statue out in the woods?" Grandma Wren proposed, flicking open the metal trinket she always carried and drawing a strange rune on top of it.

Lorian's face looked puzzled as she watched her – I noticed that Grandma's habit had become more frequent recently.

"I think the walk may calm you both and allow you to process everything that has happened recently." She changed the topic so quickly it took me a moment to understand what she was saying.

"But it is late now. Should we really go?"

I really didn't want to take Lorian for a walk through the woods and spend time with her when I was trying to keep my distance.

"Yes, tonight. There are things there that need to be seen. And it is only seven – you have plenty of time."

It was apparent that Grandma Wren and Mum wanted to talk alone and I could see that Connie had really shaken Lorian.

"Come on then…"

My voice was a little gruff but I didn't really care. Too many things had gone wrong since Lorian had showed up. I led her out of the house and round to the back towards the woods beyond.

Lorian

⟨ ❧ ⟩

Maverick seemed so distant, almost as if I had done
something wrong.

"Where are we going?"

I looked at him out of the corner of my eye – his jaw was
set and obviously he was in some sort of daydream, his eyes
showing that distant, unfocused look. He shook himself.

"You'll see, it isn't much further."

And that was it, he retreated back into his non-verbal state.

We walked for a while longer, through the thick undergrowth that blanketed the forest floor. We had left the path
and the forest had got more shadowed. The only light came
from the small lantern Maverick carried. The dense moss,
thick ferns and wild undergrowth engulfed our footfall, not
betraying a sound. The trees scaled high above us, reaching
towards the overcast clouds, as if racing one another to reach
the grey sky above.

Then all of a sudden, as if out of nowhere, the trees started
to thin. They opened out onto a large clearing filled with

wildflowers cast alight in a silvery glow from the moon. As we moved further into it, I could see that on the far-left side was a pool of water, no bigger than The Huntress fountain in the far corner of our estate, but this pool had a small running stream leading back into the deep forest.

"This is beautiful." I inhaled deeply, filling my lungs with the sweet scent of the forest. "I have never seen anything so beautiful."

"Yes, well, it was apparently an old graveyard from your time, on a grand estate. Yours, I would assume," Maverick said bitterly as if the clearing's beauty did not affect him.

"What do you mean my estate? How could it be and why would you even think that?"

In confusion, I took another look around the clearing to see what could have given him the impression that it belonged to my family. But if this was the graveyard, I wouldn't recognise it – Mother never let me go there, not even to visit Father.

"Drawn to it, like a magnet. I knew you would be, straight away. And you heard – Sólas was built on or around your old town and your estate extended into the forest," Maverick grumbled under his breath.

It wasn't so much that I was drawn to it, in fact, it was the most hideous thing I had ever laid my eyes on. I just couldn't believe something like that existed. Standing roughly eight feet tall was a stone statue, a statue of a dancer. The horrific part was that the statue resembled me.

"How?" I whispered.

"You will have to ask Grandma Wren that. I didn't even know it was you until I saw you dancing the other day."

His voice had lost the hard edge to it now and it had been replaced with more of a whimsical tone.

"You mean you've seen this hideous thing before?"

Turning to look at him, I saw that Maverick had fallen back into the far-off look he'd had earlier. He was staring straight at the statue that stood only two feet taller than him.

"Hideous? I wouldn't say that. I used to come here as a kid, often, and just sit and wonder what her life was like."

I don't know why he was suddenly so talkative after being so grumpy on the walk there, and not just that, but he was letting me in on something that was private. I felt compelled to try and explain to him, even if it was only a small part of how that girl felt.

"Lonely, that's what it was like for her."

"That was not how I pictured it for her."

Moving away from the statue, we crossed the short distance to the water and sat by its edge. It was a shame there was no colour there; I could just imagine the deep blues and the glistening greens that would be created when the sun hit the water and the algae beneath. Then there would be the deep purples, yellows and a variety of colours from the wildflowers that burst from the forest's edge. It would truly be spectacular.

"How did you picture her?" I asked, intrigued by the notion that someone would be imagining what my life was like.

"Well…" He paused, as if debating whether he should continue. There were warring emotions in his eyes.

"Please, I would like to know what you thought…"

"Fine," he sighed. "I imagined that she would have had loads of friends and really encouraging parents, who were always there for her, always on hand if she needed them; that she loved to dance and she entertained everyone with it. There, that was – still is – what I think."

He turned away as if embarrassed by the confession, but

I could see the longing in his eyes as he looked back at the statue.

"Well, one thing was true," I said. "I did entertain people with dance. I did shows with a group of other dancers my age."

"Really?"

"Yes, I just wish the rest was true. I wish my mother was like yours."

"You really wouldn't want her to be your mum, trust me." The disapproval in his voice was alarming.

"Why would you say that? I have never met anyone more dedicated to helping people."

"That's the thing – she helps *other* people, but never me or Connie. She pawned me off on you to deal with my wounds while she treated Emerys."

"But Emerys' were worse, weren't they? And they needed a special treatment I couldn't give," I threw back at him. "Stop being so selfish. Your mother is kind and she wants to help others when they need it."

"She barely even glanced at my wounds, Lorian. She couldn't have known how bad they were. She just saw they were burns, so told us to use the ointment she would put on any other burn, whether from steam or fire."

"But—"

"No, don't defend her, please don't..."

Maverick's anger on the subject confused me but I kept quiet. We sat like that, quiet and tense, for a while, both processing what the other had said until he finally spoke. It was so quiet that I almost missed it.

"I just wish she could be happy..."

That was when I remembered what he had said before about

people there never truly being happy and being fickle, bitter things at heart. Then why was I here? Why would I be brought back? And why was I – oh what was the word – 'preserved' like Grandma Wren had said?

The moonlight was beginning to fade, covered by a sudden curtain of clouds, and a chill breeze rustled through the leaves. It had grown later than I thought. We must have been there for a good hour or two. I had been too caught up in my own thoughts and imaginings. A headache was starting to grow behind my eyes. *Must be from lack of sleep*, I thought.

"Maverick, I would like to go back now. Could you take me?"

I turned towards him but he'd gone. How had he just disappeared? He had been there a second ago. Standing up, I looked around the clearing but the twilight was causing strange glows and shadows. I couldn't see to the other side, even the statue wasn't visible.

"Surely you could get back to the comfort of Grandma Wren's?"

His voice sounded far away, echoing off the trees so I couldn't tell where it was coming from. I could tell he was angry, but I didn't know he had suddenly turned on me. Maybe it was because I had performed magic with Maria and Emerys. I could see he wasn't happy about it, along with Connie.

"I don't know what you mean, Maverick! Please don't leave me – I don't know how to get back!" I cried out.

The twilight had descended quickly and the already grey gloom of the day made it harder for me to see anything.

"Run little bird!"

The wind carried his words to me, willing me forward to

run. I could feel it, a cold heat brushing against my ankles. Wiping tears from my eyes, I tried to clear my vision and what I saw terrified me.

There, wrapping itself around my ankles, was a huge black snake. I tried to kick it away but it broke away into a mist and reformed again, curling around my leg. I knew what it was, and the realisation was sickening. It was Maverick's power. He was using his power on me and that frightened me more than the snake. I was vulnerable, unable to protect myself from it. And I had heard how dangerous it could be.

Finally, my legs seemed to move. I nearly tripped as I pushed them to move faster, as if they weren't ready to take all the effort, but were being led.

Thrusting myself through the surrounding trees I tried to look for things I recognised, but everything looked the same, especially without any colour. I couldn't tell the difference between the flowers and trees and in the fading light, I couldn't see any of the textures and patterns that might have given me some idea of what I was passing. I kept pressing on, kept running, for when I did stop, I could feel the heat of the thing that followed me.

"Keep going now, Lorian…"

His voice sounded so forced – rough and strained – as though Maverick was fighting for his voice to be heard. And then the wind whispered his snarl:

"…or I will catch you."

Oh how I wished it was only the wind I was out-running and not the madman I had felt so drawn to.

My feet began to scream at me to stop, my legs faltering from being pushed to run so hard. I had never run like this. The only thing I had pushed myself to do was dance and I was not cut out for running; my strides were all over the place, causing me to keep stumbling. The undergrowth was fighting against me, rearing its ugly head just where I was about to step.

I tripped and stumbled over dense, moss-covered roots, colliding with the hard base of a tree. Glancing around from where I had propped myself up, catching my breath, I tried to look for any landmarks that looked familiar. Nothing. Nothing but an old building peeking through the gloom. Its white stone walls reflected the dim moonlight but most of the building was covered with thick vines and ivy. It snagged at my memory, something was familiar about it. But I had no time to dwell on it as the black mist twirled itself around my thighs.

Hauling myself up I flew forward in my best attempt at a sprint. Just when I felt like I wasn't going to be able to run any more, I glimpsed the light in the windows of a cottage in the distance. Seeing it gave me renewed hope and energy. I forced myself to run a little faster. I don't know how I had navigated my way home and not run deeper into the forest, but I was so pleased, my heart sang.

Stumbling through the last of the trees, I started to make my way up to the wooden porch when someone grabbed my arm and pulled me back. Turning, I expected to see Maverick's cruel face, but it was Emerys that I came face to face with. He had been crying.

"Are you okay?" I panted, my horror momentarily forgotten as my worry for him rose.

"What is happening? What's wrong?" he countered.

"Maverick, he... um..."

"He what, Lorian?" I could hear the challenge in his voice.

"He chased me out of the forest with his mist," I whispered, shaking off the chill that rose within me.

"He did what? Why would he do that?"

"I don't know, but I don't want to think about it now," I could barely contain my nerves, let alone have Emerys go barrelling off. "What is wrong, Emerys?"

"I—I don't know. You saw where she was – I just don't understand. I know where she is, but at the same time don't. I know she is in a glass dome but at the same time, I don't know where that is."

He broke down again, crumpling to the floor. Catching hold of him I brought his head to my shoulder, rubbing his back in circles and smoothing the back of his hair. I was still panting, trying to catch my breath and calm my own nerves. Looking back at the trees I tried to see if Maverick had followed me out, but all I could see was the darkness beyond.

"Shhh, it will be okay. I promise we will find her. I promise you, Emerys, I will do everything I can to help."

We sat for a moment in silence, my breathing evening out. The only noise was the rustle of leaves, and Emerys as he cried, cried for his loss and for Lila.

Maverick

My anger had flared so brightly whilst I sat at the pond-side with Lorian, I didn't even try to fight it. She had caused so much trouble since she showed up and now I was telling her all my childish thoughts. Why was I so insufferably drawn to her? I didn't fight the call of my dark fury – I just let it consume me; although I knew I shouldn't, I knew what it was asking. I knew chasing her through the trees was cruel but it was as though my dark fury took control, blinding me to what I was doing. It felt good for it to be released, but in those moments I wasn't in control; even my voice wasn't my own. That had never happened before. I had tried to fight it, tried to tell her to keep running, but that was all I could say, before my dark fury blocked me out. I didn't know what was happening.

When I got back to the cottage there they were, Emerys and Lorian, locked in an embrace. Emerys was crying. I watched them for a while, Lorian whispering to Emerys, watching him beginning to calm down. His face was turned towards me, and finally his tears stopped running.

I couldn't stay hidden any longer, I had to know what happened. I stalked out of the bushes to make my presence known. Leftover anger still simmered in my veins; I still felt wired. It was strange as normally, exhaustion would have set in by now.

As I moved into the open, I could see that they were so caught up in their moment that they hadn't noticed me.

"Well, you two look cosy."

It came out more aggressively than I had meant it to; my confused feelings had thrown me. I couldn't take it back now.

Emerys looked up in a daze and wiped his face on his sleeve. "Oh shut up, Mav. Lorian was comforting me – you can obviously see that."

"Sure, whatever you say."

Why was I talking like this? I had seen that she had been clearly comforting him.

"Don't you dare shrug him off like that. He is supposed to be your best friend and honestly, I thought you would worry about him more."

Lorian's tone shocked me, halting me in my tracks. The only other time I had heard her talk with such strength was when she tended to mine and Emerys' wounds. After what had just happened in the forest, I was surprised she was speaking to me at all.

"I don't pry like some people. If I ask if he is okay and if he says yes, we leave it."

"But you didn't even do that!"

"That's because I don't honestly care, Lorian! I told you we are all bitter at heart," I shouted back at her with full force.

I expected her to cower away like she had done all the other times but instead, she stood tall, facing me; nothing like the girl that had just run out of the forest.

"I am fed up with you trying to intimidate me like you did in the forest. That was just cruel. Everyone has always tried to do that to me throughout my life and I am fed up with it. But frankly, the not caring for another person is beyond me, especially someone you consider your friend." I found the way she spoke hilarious but she was serious – I didn't dare to laugh. "Maybe you truly are bitter at heart and maybe, really, you want it to be true so you don't have to let anyone in."

She held her hand out to Emerys and gestured for him to follow her. They both entered Grandma Wren's house without another word.

I stood there, stunned at her words. I must have been out there for a good two minutes staring at the closed door. The humourless laugh that erupted out of me had taken me by surprise.

Mum suddenly appeared looking worried. "Maverick? Why are you crying?"

It took me a moment to realise what she was saying and feel cool, wet tears prickling my cheeks. I hadn't cried in years, not since I was a small child, but now, as the breeze drifted past me, it tracked my tears.

"I—I—I don't know," I stammered, but really I did.

I knew that Lorian was right. I was bitter, and it wasn't due to the incantation that plagued the land. No, it was due to the person that I was. The revelation broke me, not just skin deep, but all the way to my core.

Swiping a hand across my face I turned and walked away from Mum, leaving her there at the door without any explanation.

Emerys

L orian was still holding my hand as she practically dragged me into the living room. It looked as if no one was in the house any more; the small rooms were so close to one another you would know if someone was there. We had passed Neave as she was leaving, but I didn't know where Grandma Wren or Connie were.

Lorian looked furious as she paced in front of the dying fire. She kept shaking her hands out by her sides as if she was trying to release the tension that was radiating off her, muttering under her breath with each pass.

"Are you okay? You know he didn't mean any harm in what he said out there. Maverick has always been like that."

I tried to console her as I sat on the edge of the sofa, watching her pace. She must have forgotten that I was there, for when I spoke she looked at me blankly, having to blink a few times as if clearing a haze from her vision. Her face screwed up and the venom in her voice showed that the anger hadn't dissipated yet.

"No, I am not okay. How dare he be so callous? How can he be your friend when all he does is be spiteful to you?"

"That is how he has always been. He didn't have the best time when he was younger—"

"Not everyone does, but you don't see others treating people as disgustingly as he does."

She began to pace again. I was sure she would wear out the carpet.

The clock on the mantelpiece began to chime midnight. The evening had gone by so fast, I was still surprised that everyone was out. Maybe Neave had gone back home for the evening to ensure Connie was okay. It looked as though we wouldn't be going to bed for a while though. Lorian's anger was still in full flow and showing no sign of stopping soon. I was surprised that she was capable of holding so much anger.

"You need to calm down. Maverick didn't mean anything by it," I said weakly, no fight left in me.

I was still feeling a little raw and embarrassed from crying. I didn't normally cry in front of anyone, let alone someone I had only recently met. Although, there was something about Lorian that made me feel at ease, as if I had known her for a long time.

"How can I calm down? I just don't understand how he could have been like that. Ugh…"

Lorian threw her hands in the air and turned to face me. I could see and feel how angry she really was. Her normally shy smile was nowhere in sight, yet a cruel twist to her mouth was set.

"If he was treated the way he treated you, I think he would realise how lucky he is to have you."

"He understands, Lorian. We have been friends for as long

as I could crawl. We wouldn't abandon one another. It's not as if I don't do the same to him sometimes, but I'll talk to him tomorrow about it, okay? Come, sit down. You must be exhausted – it's late."

Lorian glanced at the clock and sighed. "I guess you're right."

Slumping down next to me on the sofa, she visibly deflated as her anger left her. I have never seen anyone able to release their anger as quickly as she did; it was as if she'd snuffed out the candle that fuelled it.

Changing the subject, I went back to something that I had overlooked earlier: "So why were you coming back in a hurry from in the woods?"

I saw her face crumple in tense lines and thought her anger was about to flare again, but instead she let out a long sigh. I felt just a slight tingle of her unease and a fear that I knew she was trying to keep hidden.

"Maverick took me to look at the old statue he found in the woods, but then on the way back I was chased by this mist snake. It wasn't until I kicked it and it dissolved then came back again that I realised it was his magic."

"The dancer? I will talk to Maverick tomorrow about the mist snake, okay?"

She nodded, but didn't say anything. I took this as my cue to carry on.

"We used to go there as kids; Maverick the most as he got more time off and it was just behind Grandma Wren's."

"Did you notice anything about the dancer?"

She glanced at me, and I could see the apprehension in her eyes, but I couldn't tell why it was there.

"What do you mean? What would I notice? It is just an old statue of someone from the original town."

"It's me," she whispered. "I don't know why it's there, but it's me. The plaque had my name on it, and it says it was dedicated to me from my old dance school. I don't know why they would have dedicated something to me – I wasn't even that good."

As the memories came, she pulled a small vial out of her pocket and quickly took the herbs she used to help her nightmares. I didn't really know what to say. The statue that Maverick and myself had spent so much time contemplating and making stories about was Lorian, the girl that was sitting right next to me. The statue must be a hundred years old and Lorian was younger than me.

I tried to quieten my thoughts and ease hers. "Well, I think you were obviously better than you thought you were, or they wouldn't have done it would they? Plus, I know I don't know anything about dancing, but I know when you danced with Feren last night, you looked like you knew what you were doing."

"Yes, I used to dance, and honestly I loved it, but I know I was never very good."

A small dip in her mood bristled against my powers.

"And how do you know this?"

Putting my arm around her shoulders, I brought her to my side. It was my turn to return the favour and try to ease some of the sadness that was weighing on her.

"I was told. Many times. But that is not important now."

Standing up, she moved back over to the fireplace and added a few logs to the fire in sure motions, as if she had tended it many times before. I could hear quiet sniffles as she began to cry but I daren't go to her. She had moved away for a reason and I wasn't going to push her further.

I could feel the sadness emanate from her in waves; that was the thing about being an empath – you were attuned to others' most intimate feelings. One thing I couldn't put my finger on was why she was feeling guilty; underneath all the sadness there was an undercurrent so dangerous that once you were caught in it you would be swept up by it … or dragged under.

That was what was happening to Lorian, her sadness was slowly turning into guilt for some unknown reason and I could feel that she would be trapped there for a long while if she went in any further. Though I would have left her to her sorrow, I knew I could not leave her to this. As Maverick said, we were all bitter in our hearts, and there was one thing about empaths, we could revel in leaving people to wallow in their feelings. Even though I hated to admit it, there was a part of me that was relishing seeing her so sad, as if I fed off those emotions. I tamping that feeling down and locked it away.

In the end, I decided that even if Lorian wanted to be further away from me, she shouldn't be. I pulled her to my chest as she had done to me not long before, and spoke to her softly. "Why do you feel grief, Lorian?"

I could feel her tense in my arms. "How—how did you know I was feeling that?"

"I am an empath, Lorian, remember? I can feel what you are feeling," I reminded her.

Pulling her head away from my chest, she looked at me wide-eyed.

"I can feel your guilt and I could have left you to it, but you would have been stuck in it for a long time. It is dangerous to feel that kind of regret. What do you have to feel guilty about? Nothing can be that bad, could It?"

Breaking away, she walked towards the little room next to

223

the kitchen and called 'goodnight' over her shoulder before shutting the door, leaving me in the silence of the cottage with only the crackle of the fireplace for company.

I knew I had overstepped my mark when I sensed her feelings. She'd already said Maverick used his power on her, but I just couldn't help it. It was like she was broadcasting directly to me.

Lorian

3600 moons 17 days

Dear Diary,

   Things have been strange recently. Emerys has taken to scouring the city for Lila at a frantic rate. Since the news of her possible location, there has been a huge uptake on the search but that has since dwindled as no further clues or leads have come to light. I can see the disappointment in Emerys' face every time I see him. But I also hear the cruel comments that have started up again about him and how he has something to do with it. I am so scared I will become like them and what then? What will I have if I can't smile, can't laugh, can't dance – because for surely I would not dance as it would bring me no joy with this curse?

   Maria says I have nothing to worry about, but I am not so sure. This place feels as though you wouldn't survive with anything other than a cold twisted heart. I just wonder when it will take mine.

   The other night when Maverick chased me out of the woods, I was sure I had seen buildings that seemed familiar to me but I can't make out why. There was also one when I was first attacked, but I haven't been able to go and explore there since. I will hopefully get the chance.

Anyway, I will see how the next few days go. I have been having terrible headaches and I am sure they are causing my vision to blur. I think I might need to rest more – I hope it helps. Also, the date system is so strange now. When I asked Maria for the date, she said they measure it by moons and not years now. Something about following the moon cycles.

Lorian
 3601 moons 5 days

Dear Diary,

I managed to take a walk back into the woods with Emerys to see what the familiar building was. It was the small orangery and sunroom that had been on our estate. I didn't go to it often, due to how close it was to the graveyard, but it was a strange place to put it. When Ivan took me it had been beautiful; he told me the orangery had been there before the graveyard had been built and that was why it was so close, but also why no one really bothered with it.

My days have been kept busy at the flower stall with Neave. It is truly wonderful to create all the bouquets for people and other small pouches of herbs, which I didn't know we sold until the other day. Neave makes all sorts for her clients – pouches of different teas to help with different ailments and quick supplies to staunch a wound, like the one I used on Emerys.

Maria, whom I've now started to call Grandma Wren, has been teaching me about all the herbs and plants that I hadn't got around to learning about before, when we were both home at the cottage. I *am so pleased to be able to live with her again, but she isn't always home. There have been more disappearances, and the elders and a council that Neave is on are meeting often to discuss what can be done. I know they have said something about creating protection charms for people to wear, but I don't really understand it all and I haven't seen any yet.*

I believe it has been one and a half months or so since I awoke in this strange world. I don't know whether it would be classed as resurrection but that sounds a little creepy anyway, like I should be some sort of monster, but I think I am starting to get used to it.

I'd best be off to bed – lots to do tomorrow on the stall.

Lorian

3062 moons 12 days

Dear Diary,

Something odd has been happening over the last few weeks. I thought it was just something that would pass, but I am feeling more and more uneasy.

Connie seems to be talking to me more, or at least trying to. I never say much normally – I just either nod or keep on with what I am doing. But she seems insistent on asking me questions about my past. They all seem so innocent, like what was my favourite bird or plant, or what did I like to do when I was younger. But I still feel uneasy, like I am giving away something vital if I answer. Sometimes I cannot answer when she just stares at me. It must have started a couple of weeks after Maverick chased me in the woods. I did voice my concerns to Grandma Wren, but she said it wasn't anything to worry about and that she would not use her power to harm me again or try and hex me. There was such an intensity in her gaze and a powerful anger when she'd spoken to Connie, I knew she wouldn't be crossed.

227

I'm off to the stall again. Another festival is coming up soon, Neave said, *so there will be lots to do.*

Lorian

Lorian

Today I was tasked with bunching herbs and tying them together to make smudge sticks – made up of sage, cedarwood, frankincense, sweet grass, lavender, copal and myrrh – when Maverick burst through the door.

"Where's Grandma Wren, Lorian?" He looked frantically around the kitchen.

"She is out…"

I looked at him and then took in his appearance. He never looked particularly tidy, I guess due to his profession as a carpenter (which I only found out about recently). Today he had mud plastered to his shoes and bottoms of his trousers; he also had dead leaves and twigs stuck in his dark hair.

"Where is she, Lorian? I need her now!"

He scanned the kitchen and strode into the living room, not caring about the trail of mud he left behind him.

Bustling after him, I avoided the mud so as not to spread it around.

"I don't know. She went out with Neave about half an hour

ago, I suppose. She said she would be back for dinner," I blurted, trying to keep up with his long strides.

Pursing his lips, I could see Maverick try and restrain his anger. Feeling as if my feet were moving on their own, I walked towards him and placed my hand on his arm. I felt his shock as he shivered under my touch. I could also see something else that I could not place, but as soon as it came it seemed to disappear. He pulled away, retreating back into the kitchen.

I couldn't let him go in the mood he was in without trying to help if I could, no matter what had happened between us – it just wasn't who I was. I called after him: "Can I help you with anything?" I had never been able to leave other people to deal with their problems on their own. Mother used to say I just liked to interfere, but I didn't think it was that.

Maverick's face was cold and emotionless until a cruel snarl twisted his lip. "Unless you know where Connie is, then no, there is nothing someone like you can do to help me find her. And if you wring that lavender any more it won't be fit for anything."

There was a moment of silence before he sighed. "I'm sorry, Lorian, I just can't find Connie. Let me know if you see her, okay?"

I could see the apology and worry in his eyes and knew they were genuine, but his words still stung.

The rest of the day went in a blur. I replayed the conversation with Maverick over and over again in my mind. There was no reason for me to ponder it as much as I did; I already knew deep down I wasn't much help, but I wanted to be.

I fumbled with the ties on the smudge sticks late into the afternoon, until a broad pair of hands reached around me and put them on top.

"Here, let me do that."

It was Emerys. The softness in his voice made my skin come out in goosebumps. He had come in so quietly, I hadn't even heard the door open.

Releasing the string I let him take over. He made quick work of the binding on the last two smudge sticks and set them aside. I saw a dark shadow across his jaw as if he hadn't shaved in a few days.

"So are you going to tell me what is wrong or continue to stare? 'Cause if you are going to stare, I may leave," he joked, shifting uncomfortably.

Having been caught staring, I could feel myself flare with embarrassment.

Turning away, I looked out of the kitchen window, towards the woods. "Oh, it's nothing, I have just been thinking…"

"About?" he prompted, after he realised I wasn't going to explain.

As I thought about how to tell Emerys about Maverick, and how he had made me feel, how small I felt, I started to pull the crockery out of the cupboard to make some tea. Anything to keep myself busy as I wrestled with my thoughts.

I placed the water over the fire and filled a teapot with loose tea leaves, the aroma filling the kitchen. All the time, Emerys watched me as I moved around.

"I will help you find Lila, Emerys," I said, with more conviction than I felt.

"Thank you," Emerys said after a moment. "But you know you've already said you would help?"

There was pain in his eyes as I handed him his cup of steaming herbal tea. I nodded, remembering my promise.

"You love her, don't you?" I asked.

I know it wasn't really the best thing I could have said but my curiosity over who Lila was and what she meant to Emerys fascinated me.

"I believe I did, Lorian, but I don't know any more. All I know is that I want to get her back safely. She doesn't deserve this, she is so bright, so full of life. She should be back here enjoying it."

As he spoke, he stared into his cup as if it was going to give him the answers he needed. I could see the small flecks of tea that escaped through the sieve bob on the top of the cup as if trying to respond to him.

"You would love to have seen her dance, she was quite like you for that. You reminded me of her the other day…" A smile played at his lips and his eyes seemed to shine a little brighter.

"I think I would like to meet her."

I smiled back at Emerys, his words lifting me. Maybe I would have a true friend there, when we got Lila back.

"But why do you want to go and find her, Lorian? You don't even know her…"

"Because I don't want to feel useless any more, Emerys."

I was worried after I said it that he would judge me; I hadn't been so open with anyone since Elijah.

"I know you feel that often, but you shouldn't, Lorian. You have helped Neave so much and I know Grandma Wren feels the same."

"Stop 'sensing' my feelings, Emerys," I said, grinding my teeth as I left the kitchen, seeking out the cool breeze. My temper was rising and I hated the telltale flush that was on my cheeks.

Out in the fresh air, I felt the anger start to seep out of me as the cold breeze encased my flushed skin. It was starting to get late and the white light of the day was turning grey. I could feel that there was going to be a frost tomorrow, the grass underfoot had already started to stiffen. The hoot of the owls and clicks of the beetles echoed around me as they prepared for the night.

It was so different from the hustle and bustle I would hear out of my bedroom window in Temford. Since I had been reunited with Maria, I had learnt about a whole life I was missing out on, and was learning about a whole new world that I hadn't even begun to imagine.

Sighing, I turned to Emerys. He had followed me out but kept his distance. "Did you know that I didn't have many friends when I was younger? No, there was only one person that I felt comfortable with other than Grandma Wren and Ivan, and that was Elijah. He was the only one that did not make fun of me for wanting to learn about herbs. I suppose it makes sense now, knowing that he was a part of this world. But he also made me feel strong, Emerys. And I want to be that strong person and help you find Lila."

"What happened to him, Lorian? Grandma Wren doesn't speak of him much," Emerys asked carefully.

"Well, apparently after I passed, or whatever you call it now, Ivan got ill. And no matter what Grandma Wren or Elijah did, they could not slow his rapidly impending death. Elijah became melancholy and delusional – he was not the same after my death. He got into fights, and one night he was beaten so badly, he knew he would not survive without his injuries being tended to. So he died alone. But he took part of Maria's heart along with him. She was left with only her teenage daughter to raise by herself. And then the curse swept over the town, causing destruction and decay in its wake."

I could feel tears running down my cheeks.

A crunch of grass underfoot told me Emerys was getting closer. I knew he wouldn't venture too close, but all my anger had left me. Just a sense of loneliness remained.

"I'm sorry, Lorian. Look, I didn't mean to sense your feelings, but I can't always help it. You see … it's just…" he began, but he didn't get to finish his sentence as Maverick strode back around the corner.

"And what are you two doing?! Oh wait, let me guess. You're trying to weasel your way into her knickers too, aye, Emerys?" He spat as he continued towards the door.

Whipping around I strode in after him, climbing the wooden steps. "How dare you even think that!" I shouted.

He turned so fast, I was momentarily startled by the pure hatred on his face.

"What do you think his intentions are, Lorian? Don't you remember what we said about people not truly being happy here? Even Mum – look beyond her smile. Everyone is only out for themselves really." His voice morphed as it had done in the woods, his pupils had grown dark.

I couldn't believe what he was saying. Since turning up in this forsaken place, Emerys had been the only one, other than Maria, that I truly felt safe with.

"You are just angry because you can't find Connie," I retorted, the anger that I had thought had passed flaring in full force.

I glared up into his dark smoky eyes that looked like they would be the colour of a stormy sea. But it couldn't be blue that I was seeing, surely? I quickly snapped out of my daze as he grabbed the sides of my shoulders, squeezing hard, putting his face close to mine he snarled at me like I was one of those deformed creatures.

"Don't you ever talk about my sister – you have no right. Ever since you turned up everything has gone to hell."

"Come on now, Mav, you don't mean that…"

I could hear Emerys' voice trying to calm his friend, as though he was an angry or frightened animal. But I couldn't look at him, I was captivated by Maverick's eyes. The blue had gone but I could see a churning in the depths, a smoky black, mixing and swirling.

"No, I do. I should never have brought her into the town and then let her into the house. This is all happening because of her. You should leave now, Lorian. No one wants you here any more."

I could feel the tears begin to prick my eyes; I did not want to let them fall, but I just couldn't help it. Maverick had obviously noticed too but he showed no emotion, no remorse. His now-grey stormy eyes, that had lightened the more he spoke, were blank. The one place I felt safe and thought I had a home in, was ripped away from me with just a few choice words. I felt myself break, and the small bloom that was appearing within myself disappeared.

"Leave," he sighed.

Maverick squeezed my shoulders and shoved me further towards the woods. Even though it wasn't a hard shove, I slipped, landing on my hip on the damp decking, droplets of mud from his boots hitting my face. I heard a roaring in my ears, but still heard the loud slam of the kitchen door.

Pulling myself to my feet I blindly began to walk, but I hadn't made it through the thicket at the edge of the forest before a hand grabbed my shoulders. Turning quickly, I heard a loud *thwack* as my hand connected with my would-be attacker's cheek, and I knew instantly that it was not the person I had thought it was. It was Emerys.

"Ouch. You got one hell of a swing. Why don't you use that more often?" Emerys was rubbing the side of his jaw.

"Emerys, I am so sorry, I thought—"

"You thought I was Maverick. I get it…"

Taking Emerys' face in my hands I looked him over to ensure I hadn't caught him with my nails. He was okay – my slap mark would fade in a matter of minutes, I was sure. I rubbed a small handkerchief that Maria had given me over my face. I could see Emerys' eyes soften as he watched me try to erase the evidence of the encounter.

"Look, Lorian, I am sorry for what happened between us and I am sorry for what Maverick said."

"You shouldn't have to apologise for him – that is not your place."

"Okay, well I am sorry I didn't step in just now and I am sorry for what happened between us. I should not have been listening to your feelings, they are private. It's just that I feel as though I… need…" Sighing, he ran a hand through his short, tousled hair.

He was obviously struggling with what he wanted to say, but I wasn't going to make it easy for him. I just couldn't. He'd hurt me with what he'd said and then what with Maverick's outburst, I didn't think I was up to rolling over and being forgiving just yet.

"I feel as though I need to look after you, Lorian. I don't know why, but I do."

Turning away from me, he rubbed his hand through his hair once again to the back of his neck. He was obviously uncomfortable but I couldn't just let this drop.

"Why Emerys? Why do you feel like that? You practically said you don't care what happens to me, but I think that is more because you feel guilty about Lila."

I knew I had ventured onto dangerous ground as Emerys' back went rigid and he looked over his shoulder at me with a scowl. But it didn't seem as though he was angry – more sad and regretful and trying to cover it.

"I never said that, though, did I, Lorian? I just have to focus on getting Lila back." His shoulders slumped as though the momentous task was pressing on him.

"I understand," I said, placing my hand on his arm and giving it a gentle squeeze. "But you don't need to do this alone – I will help."

There was a long pause as he considered my words, but hope rose in my chest as I heard him sigh. "You need to learn some basic spells and potions before we go."

"Deal…" Thrusting my hand towards him, we shook on it.

"You go back inside and I will go and talk to Maverick. But I would just go straight to your room if I were you. Grandma Wren will be so annoyed when she hears what he did…"

Maverick

I was fuming, I had only just managed to keep my dark fury at bay so it didn't engulf the room or destroy the whole house with my shock-waves. It was bad enough having two different powers, but being twenty-one and not knowing how to control them fully was just plain embarrassing. Everyone normally knew how to control theirs by the age of sixteen, having had lessons or a similar power to their parents they could be taught at home. If they did manifest a power their parents didn't know about, they could go to Grandma Wren and she would give them extra lessons. I suppose living over three hundred years lets you see the majority of powers that occur. However, her kindness or time didn't seem to extend to me – if anything, she seemed to not want anything to do with my powers. I just got the mandatory lessons and was told to help Mum.

You would have thought that with me developing two powers by the age of three, Grandma Wren would have thought it important to try and tutor me more than any of the others, but it didn't seem so. In fact, I felt as though she just hoped it would go away. Thinking about my lack of control and how they could have helped, just made me angrier.

Strolling through Grandma Wren's house, I picked up the coat I had left on the hook along with the hunting bow and quiver that was propped up by the front door. I needed to go and let off some steam and get away from Emerys. I could feel my heart squeeze at the sight of her falling, but I had to try and do something. I know it wasn't her fault, but deep down I couldn't help thinking all that had happened had something to do with her.

I needed to be on my own. Releasing my dark fury would help me – and mean I would have enough rabbit for a stew in no time. Strapping the quiver on my back, I pushed through the forest undergrowth to a quiet secluded spot.

Sighing, I relaxed and loosened the invisible leash that I had to keep on my powers. They rippled out of me in different shades, quivering as small shock-waves ran through them. This was the only time I truly felt at ease – when it didn't matter that I was showing my feelings and could let my powers run out of me more freely. My dark fury felt like a pack of wolves prowling around me, gently nudging to get my attention, asking to be set free. Although I couldn't set it free too much – it would cause too much trouble and generate too many questions.

Nocking the arrow, ensuring my arrow pinched the bow string securely, I began my hunt out into the forest, letting my dark fury move ahead of me. It practically bayed as it ran, in the shape of wolves in the undergrowth. This was one benefit that I had learnt of this strange ability I possessed, it seemed to sense out the location of living things. The only thing it didn't tell me was what the living thing was, but in a way, I didn't mind – that would take away too much of the fun. The stalking was what I enjoyed the most; it allowed me to focus on something other than the mundane work of every day and forget all the irritations.

Hearing movement up ahead, the wolves having gone silent and still, I stooped low and crept closer to the bushes in the direction of the rustling. Peering through the bushes, I could see a rabbit grazing in the small clearing, unaware that I was there. Drawing up the bow slowly, straightening the arrow, I steadied my breathing in preparation. The anticipation had stilled my dark fury more so that it seemed to be a shimmering haze around me. My fingers were strung tightly on the cord as I prepared to let the arrow fly, when a loud snapping of wood disturbed my prey, causing it to skip off into the undergrowth.

"No, you tell him that I will get her away from the others as soon as I can."

A hushed voice came from my left, causing me to stiffen. It was familiar. Peering round the tall oak that rose in front of where I crouched, I tried to get a better view.

"She is causing too much trouble. Grandma Wren spends all her time with her, Mum hasn't got anything really bad to say and Emerys and Maverick have gone all stupid over her. Even if they bicker and argue they seem to still be under her spell. It is infuriating. I wish it could just finish her and be done with it. Why does he want her so badly?"

Connie stood half-shaded by a tall bush, talking to someone deep in the shadows. I couldn't make out what the other person was saying but I could hear Connie's replies and I knew she must be talking about Lorian. But saying that we had gone stupid over her was beyond me. I found her infuriating and was strangely drawn to her, but nothing more. But what did she mean by 'finish' her? It sounded all wrong, and nothing like the Connie I knew.

"I have already hexed her once, only a simple spell to see how she would react to a few nightmares, so it shouldn't be too difficult to slip her another. Maybe I'll try something a little more powerful this time, maybe a waking nightmare. It'll make her see that boy that scared her so much around every corner."

There was a long pause again. I willed my dark fury to conceal me as I unfolded myself and crept closer to try and hear who Connie was talking to., I could hear the hiss of a voice that even sent chills through me.

"Have it done sssooon, but do not harm her physssically. He can't wait much longerrr…"

I froze when I saw a clawed hand extend and brush the side of Connie's cheek. It looked like a loving caress but it couldn't be, not with her – not with one of the deformed creatures I had encountered earlier. Magda, that was her name – she was once a girl of my own age and I had taken lessons at Grandma Wren's with her. How had this happened to her?

Before they could say anything else, I heard a scuffle and crouched lower behind the bush. Another group of the deformed human-like creatures emerged, dragging something between the four of them, it looked like a heavy sack. As they came further into the light, I could see I was terribly, terribly wrong. It wasn't a sack they carried, but a body: Emerys'. His head was hanging low and he didn't try to struggle. He must have been unconscious, for I knew he would not go willingly.

"What have you done to him?" Connie cried. I watched as she shifted uncomfortably.

241

"We found him wandering the woods. He will regain consciousness sssoon, if we don't hurry and get him back. Too much hope. Massster will like this one – he is strong," hissed one of the creatures holding Emerys' arms.

I knew I should try to help, and I felt my dark fury pull against me as it willed me to do something. But I could feel my energy draining already. I didn't think I could take on all five creatures and Connie, if Connie was siding with them.

"Take him back…" hissed Magda. "Bring her to us sssoon, Connie, or Massster won't want you. Bring her soon and he shall go free, I will tell the Massster of our deal and he will honour it – you have my word."

The creatures moved quickly, delving deeper into the shadows of the forest, but still I was frozen to my spot, willing my dark fury to cloak me for just a little longer. I was beginning to feel drained from the power it took to conceal myself, but I also felt helpless. Emerys was now the latest victim in the series of disappearances and Connie was involved. I couldn't understand how she could let the creature touch her. She had grown up with Emerys and didn't even put up a fight to help him.

Connie looked around her, turned on her heel and strode back towards the town, her black winter walking cloak billowing behind her. At the tree line, there was a glimmer of white light and I realised that she had been using her powers frequently, concealing herself when she met with the creatures. All that time I had been looking for her, she could have been out here meeting those deformed creatures, using someone else's face as cover.

As the sky began to grow even darker, I made my way out of my hiding spot and shrugged off my mask. I must have been there longer than I thought; the frost had begun to set in and my joints ached as I tried to straighten them.

Treading carefully in the receding light I made my way back to Grandma Wren's. I raced the last of the day's light, breaking free of the confines of the forest. I moved towards the cottage that had once felt like home, but was now full of strangers. I felt my anger rise and with it, the remains of my dark fury stir.

I could hear the hushed voices of Grandma Wren and Mum talking inside the cottage. Propping my bow up next to the door, I took off my muddy clothes and boots. I padded towards the living room – I was going to have to tell them everything I'd witnessed. I could hear gentle sobs in between soft muttering coming from the living room. They were obviously comforting someone; maybe Connie had come home and told them everything, maybe she'd been forced to meet that creature.

Pushing the door open I walked over to the fire, my bare skin prickling in the heat.

Something about the room was off; my dark fury rose at the implication that it might be needed, surprising me with its presence after feeling so drained. Glancing around the room I tried to detect what was happening, but nothing seemed obviously out of place.

"Mum, Grandma Wren, what's wrong? Something isn't right, I can feel it."

Moving away from the fire I stood in front of them. Mum wiped her face with her soft handkerchief – she had been crying, which only angered me more. Whomever caused Mum to cry would be made to say they are truly sorry.

"It is nothing you should concern yourself with, Maverick…

"

"I am not going to ignore that you've been crying Mum. Who has upset you? Was it Lorian? I told her to leave, I knew she was trouble."

"Yes, we know you did," Grandma Wren said sharply.

Shocked, I turned to look at her. She had a pillow placed across her legs as though someone had been lying there. Then I saw the flicker of light. It looked like the outline of a person, but I couldn't make out who it was.

"You have caused her great pain with what you did, and we will talk about that later. For now, I need you to sit with me and let your mother go. She needs to rest and tend to Connie."

Watching Mum gently get up, I took the seat across from Grandma Wren. She was gazing down at her lap waiting patiently for another flicker of light, but I could see the tension in her mouth. She was obviously worried but trying to hold it together.

"Mum, Connie is involved somehow with the creatures. You have to be careful around her!" I blurted as she rose. I didn't want to make her more upset but she had to know.

"What? You can't be serious, Maverick! You stay with Grandma Wren, okay? I will get some of the other council members to keep their eyes open and I will find Connie."

I could see the shock in her eyes and heard an alarmed edge to her voice, but tiredness overtook her as she made her way slowly towards the door. The weight of the conversation before her was visible.

"What is happening, Grandma? What is that on your lap?" Small beads of sweat began to break out on my bare skin as my body heated quickly by the fire.

"It is Lorian, Maverick. The magic that Ivan and I used to

preserve Lorian and bring her back to us is being interpreted by her memories."

"But how? I don't understand how this is possible? Wouldn't she just be here now and not be able to travel back and forth?"

Moving to kneel in front of Grandma Wren's knees, I could make out the faint outline of Lorian's body.

"It is possible due to her being needed in both places. You see, Lorian's powers are essential in helping us to break the spell that has been bound to this place for many centuries. I told her this when she announced that she was leaving to find somewhere else to live. You see, Maverick, you cast her out of the house that she had finally started to call home."

Grandma Wren paused and considered her next words carefully. "It is not my story to tell, but I think you should know: Lorian grew up an outcast of her own family; even though she lived in the same house as them, she was never considered part of the family. She was only brought out on special occasions to make her family look 'ideal'."

"I know about how her brother would harm her and rub herbs into her wounds to see what would happen, and that you had to save her when he rubbed monkshood in, poisoning her. That's how she got those scars on her collarbone, isn't it? I read her book of shadows, remember?" I spat.

"Diary, and yes I remember. And don't you forget that you have no right to read that. Don't let me catch you doing something like that again. Could you not take my word that she wasn't a threat?"

Her stern look made me pause, but Grandma Wren's next comment made my heart plummet and my fight evaporate.

"She was my family long before you."

Grandma Wren paused and looked back at Lorian's figure

– she was starting to solidify and come back to herself.

I could not process the idea of not being part of a family and not having a true home; even though mine wasn't perfect and I wanted to burn it down now and then, I still had people I could call family. Now I understood why Grandma Wren was so angry with me. I had made Lorian feel as though she was not welcome.

"Grandma Wren, there is something I need to tell you," I said.

Reaching my hand out, I touched Lorian's hair which was now, very nearly, back to normal.

"No, do not touch her!" I heard Grandma Wren shout, but it was as though she was moving quickly to the back of a tunnel. My vision narrowed but the light seemed to chase me quickly, encasing me.

The next thing I knew, I was standing in a room that was bigger than my whole house. There was a fireplace the size of a barn door and a ceiling that had been intricately engraved; a light fixture fitted to it that looked as though it would weigh a tonne. However, this wasn't the strangest thing. The colour, it seemed off, nothing looked normal. When I looked at the fire it looked alive; its colour made me feel alive, warm and invigorated.

Moving towards the flowers on the mantelpiece, I pressed my nose to them and sniffed. They still smelt the same, but as I looked upon them it seemed I grew calm, and optimistic – more so than I had felt since I was little.

Turning to look at the rest of the room, I was assaulted by more intense feelings. There was a small wooden box on an end table next to the edge of the fireplace. It was so similar to Mum's box that she kept the nuts in by our fireplace. I could feel the smile spread across my face – I just had to know if there were nuts in this one too. But as I reached towards it, a small hand grabbed my wrist.

"You mustn't touch, we are only here to watch."

It was Lorian. Her eyes were as round as the doe's eyes I had seen in the forest earlier that week. I didn't understand what she meant. I hadn't even given much thought to where I was. She must have read my thoughts.

"You are in my memories, Maverick."

She glanced down at my still bare chest and legs, her eyes rising without comment.

"Only to watch…"

The door opened and a small girl skipped inside. Her hair was in two pigtails with fat ribbons in them and she had on a little summer dress. I instantly knew it was Lorian, her eyes were big and round as they'd been when they looked at me just moments before, her sharp nose speckled with freckles.

"I loved that dress. Grandma Wren had made it for me," the Lorian next to me said wistfully. "I wanted to show Mother straight away, so she helped me put it on and I came in here."

Taking my attention back to the little girl, I watched as she raced up to a middle-aged lady sitting in one of the chairs that overlooked the garden. I hadn't noticed her before.

"Mama, Mama," called little Lorian. "Look what Maria made me!"

The older lady didn't even look round at little Lorian, but her sharp voice made the little girl freeze.

"What have I told you about running in the house, Lorian? If you can't act civilised, I will not give you the attention you demand. And stop pestering Maria – she is a servant, nothing more. You should not bother her, you will just get in her way."

The ice-cold tone in which the woman spoke to little Lorian could be felt across the room, and I watched as the little girl's face fell with disappointment.

"Yes, Mama," little Lorian replied in a small voice and turned to walk away, large droplets running down her chubby cheeks.

My heart broke, and my dark fury answered with its own menacing response. In the next instant, a cloud of darkness engulfed my feet and began to rise.

"Don't…"

Grown-up Lorian's hand was on my arm again and it was as if my dark fury answered to her; it slowly began to recede and in a matter of seconds it was as if it was never there.

"How could she talk to you like that, even as a child? You were what, four? And she didn't even look at you."

I could still feel anger and protectiveness bubbling under my skin, making my fingers tingle.

"That was just her, and this is just a memory. Do not let it bother you – you can't change it."

But the hurt lingered deep in Lorian's eyes; it had stayed with her all through her life. And I brought that feeling back to her today. I had enticed her back into her memories, only to cause her more pain.

"I am sorry, Lorian," I whispered, looking back on the scene of the older woman gazing out of the window.

I wondered what she could be thinking, what could draw her attention enough that she didn't even want to look at her own daughter. What was it that she could want more, when it looked as though she had everything most people dreamt of owning?

"I didn't mean to make you feel as though you were not wanted."

"It's okay, Maverick, I understand. You were protecting your family, I saw it in your eyes. I am a stranger that has come into your lives unexpectedly and over the past two months, I have basically moved in. But you see…"

Sighing, Lorian shook her head and looked back towards her mother. There were very few similarities that I could see between them; her mother had smaller features all together: smaller eyes, nose and mouth. The only thing they both had was straight hair, but her mother's was white like Emerys' and Lorian's was a strange tone. It was neither closer to grey nor black.

"What is it, Lorian?" I asked, after a few minutes of her gazing at a woman she thought she would never have to see again.

"I have never felt as though I had a place. I loved them in a way, yes, but I was never truly one of them. I do not understand why I am in a time that is not my own, Maverick, but I really do hope you will allow me to try and make a place for myself here."

I did not know what to do with this declaration of hope, but my bitterness towards her seemed to dull. Maybe it was due to seeing her memories, or maybe it was because I just realised she was lonely. Now I understood why she projected herself as weak and timid all the time, it allowed her to make herself less visible. So I said the only thing and made the only promise that I thought I would be able to keep:

"I will try and help you find your place, Lorian."

Lorian placed her hand on my arm and the room narrowed again, and then I was met with the welcoming smells of Grandma Wren's cottage.

Lorian

W ithin the next instant we were in the living room of Grandma Wren's cottage. I didn't know how to get us back from my memories but I guess we'd been lucky. I don't know how Maverick had got there with me, but I was just glad that he hadn't seen some of the other, more troublesome memories that I had re-lived within the time I was asleep.

Looking around the room I took in all the reassuring sights of the small cottage: the clock on the mantelpiece, the plates on the wall and the tablecloths that all reminded me of home. I was lying on Grandma Wren's lap with Maverick crouched in front of her. I was directly level with his face and I could see that he was still dazed from the trip, but his eyes began to refocus on the room around him.

"Are you okay?" I croaked out.

"Yes, are you?"

Nodding I tried to sit up, but my head began to spin.

"Careful, Lorian, you will need time to adjust to being back within this reality. Let me move from under you and I will make you some tea."

I eased myself up, letting Grandma Wren rise. It shocked me again to see her this much older. Why hadn't I noticed she looked older before? Her hair was now grey, but had once been a beautiful chestnut brown, and she stooped where she once stood tall and proud. Mother used to say she stood above her station and that she should not draw so much attention to herself. I had always admired her; she was so gentle at heart but could be firm when needed, and never rude. She also knew when it was better to not say anything at all, or when to speak up.

"I still can't get my head around it. How did we even get there?" Maverick began, looking totally bewildered.

I wanted to put him at ease, but I didn't know what had happened and how we'd managed to go back into my memories.

"I don't know, but you have to promise not to mention it again. It was a long time ago and it should be left there," I said quickly.

I did not want to have to go through, analysing what had happened. Elijah used to want to know exactly what had happened at home when I would go running to him crying. I never knew why he wanted the specifics, but I hated reliving the humiliation my mother put me through.

"Okay, but why did everything look odd?"

I could tell he wanted to know more but decided to focus on a more trivial question.

"Odd? But it wasn't odd, that is what everything is like where I am from; that is colour. You would have seen blues,

251

browns, yellows. That was the colour of my dress – yellow."

"Yellow?"

"Yes, it's one of my favourite colours; that and green, which you would have seen when you looked at the flowers' stalks."

"It made me feel happy seeing you in that dress – the colour of it, I mean."

"Yellow always made me feel happy and calm, that is why it is one of my favourites. Tell me more about the colours you saw, and what you felt."

Tucking my legs under me, I curled up on one end of the sofa and Maverick took the other. As we began to talk. My nerves dissipated and I began to enjoy our conversation.

We sat there talking about all the different colours he had seen and what they meant to me. I was surprised by how much I revealed. When he mentioned the wooden box, I explained they were all different browns. I told him about the times I had climbed into the wardrobe, which was the same colour as the box, to write about the flowers in the garden. I couldn't help but document all that Maria told me before I forgot it.

"So that is what the world would have looked like for you all the time? That is what was in the stories that Grandma Wren told us – the colour of the flowers and what it felt like to see them. They're nothing like I thought," Maverick said, after a lull in our conversation. It must have been getting late and we hadn't seen Grandma Wren since she brought in the tea.

"Yes, you get a feeling about something from its colour, but the feelings are different for everyone and they are different in different situations."

Yawning, I curled up more tightly on the end of the sofa, using my arm as a pillow. I was suddenly very tired. As I began to drift off to sleep, I was sure I heard Maverick say something and place a blanket over me, but I couldn't be sure what he'd said before I drifted off.

I was woken abruptly by the clanking of crockery in the kitchen. Stretching, I rolled my neck, trying to ease the crick that had formed from sleeping with my head propped on my arm. Straightening my blouse, I walked through to the kitchen to see if I could help with the breakfast.

"Afternoon, sleepy bird."

Neave was at the kitchen stove, taking the kettle off to fill the teapot that was set on a tray with the tea set.

"Afternoon? How long have I been asleep?"

Looking out of the window, I could see dark grey clouds covering the sky. "What time is it?"

"It's two o'clock. You've been asleep since midnight, or so Maverick mentioned before he left for work this morning. Now come and have some tea with Grandma Wren and me before I leave to gather some supplies for the upcoming festival. We have a few things to talk about – like what happened before Maverick entered your memories last night." I could see the worry etched between her eyes.

Moving out to the back porch we wrapped ourselves in blankets and joined Grandma Wren. I began pouring the tea into the china teacups decorated with rosebuds whilst everyone settled.

"Did you sleep well, Lorian?" Grandma Wren asked as I handed her a cup.

"Quite, thank you. What is the festival that is coming up?" I asked. It wasn't that long since Halloween, or Samhain, as they called it. The time had gone fast over the last few months – so much had happened while I was working on the flower stall and trying to learn about their magic. Connie was disappearing all the time, and I could tell Neave was worried about it, but honestly, I was more than happy for her to stay away.

"The winter solstice, or Yule as you may recognize it as, is on the twenty-second of December. It's only a few weeks away now and we help supply the decorations for the festivities. I will have to go through the festivals with you – we have a few. The next after Yule is Beltane." Neave took a sip of her peppermint tea and screwed up her nose. "This needs a touch more lemongrass. Excuse me while I get it."

"Do you remember the wreaths we would make to decorate the kitchen at Christmas?" Grandma Wren asked.

"Oh yes, holly, ivy, and … oh, why can't I remember?" I looked into my tea as if I would find the answer floating there, as Emerys had done previously.

"Mistletoe," Grandma Wren chuckled, "you always forgot the mistletoe. Then we would sometimes use evergreens. Do you remember those?"

I couldn't for the life of me remember their names. "I can see them; I can see us adding sprigs to the wreath. They all look similar, but one has a thicker white stalk, was that rosemary?" My eyes were screwed up tightly as I tried to recall the names – I could picture them so clearly.

"Good. Now, what do the others look like?" she prompted, her voice calm as I concentrated. I could remember her doing this when I was first learning the plant types, she never minded if I couldn't remember and gave me as much time as I needed. She always said I already knew the answers – I just had to practice recalling the information.

"One has needles close together and cones, and if I remember correctly, it's called pine?"

I looked up at Grandma Wren and a smile crossed her lips. She nodded, encouraging me to carry on. I could feel my chest swell as it used to whenever I pleased her.

"There is one with thin needles and lots of chalky blueberries all over it. Is it cedar? And then that must mean the thicker flat needles are juniper?"

"Not quite, but I suppose it has been a rather long time since you had to remember those. You had them the wrong way around: the chalky berries and thin needles all close together are juniper and the flat, soft ones are cedar." She smiled brightly at me, she knew I would reprimand myself for getting them wrong.

"It only feels like yesterday," I said looking up at her. "You know, being back in your original cottage. I miss it sometimes – just the simplicity of it, where I understood everything that was happening. Even with the fever, at least I understood. Why am I here, Grandma Wren? Why did you and Ivan put me to sleep? And what happened whilst I was remembering yesterday?"

These questions had plagued me for so long, but I had been too scared to ask – as if uttering the words would cause some spell to break the normality of the last few weeks and I would be taken away from the place I felt comfortable in. Well, as comfortable as I could in the circumstances.

Grandma Wren went very still all of a sudden. She was looking at me, but it was as if she wasn't really seeing me. Moving to her side, I placed my hand on hers. Looking back at her face I could see her slowly disappearing.

"Enough, Lorian. Move away, she needs a moment."

Neave had come back out silently, making me jump out of

my stare. I could smell the lemongrass on her hands as she eased me away.

"Wh—what is happening to her?" I stammered out, perching on the edge of the chair opposite.

I wanted to look away, look at anything other than what was happening in front of my eyes, but I couldn't. There was a loud crash as someone slammed the front door. I could hear their heavy footfall.

Maverick. And he was angry.

"I'm going to kill him – he has gone way too far this time. You will never guess what—What is going on?!"

His anger was almost tangible and a dark mist was slowly thickening at our feet. Maverick was losing his temper, fast.

"She is not of this time. Grandma Wren is revisiting some other place."

Maverick was obviously on the same train of thought as I was. "Spit it out, Mum – now is not the time to talk to us in riddles. Is what is happening to Grandma Wren, what happened to Lorian last night?" he ground out through clenched teeth, moving towards Grandma Wren's side.

"Don't touch her, you will disrupt the journey and confuse her. Not exactly… Lorian's was due to the spell cast on her. Come and sit and I will tell you what is happening."

Neave pulled a chair up next to me but didn't sit in it. Instead, she took the one next to Grandma Wren, as if protecting her from being touched again. Maverick sat next to me, tentatively. The conversation we'd had made me feel relaxed around him – even with his current sour mood.

"What is going on?"

"Well first off, Maverick, this isn't Lorian's fault. I can see you think it is and you must stop it – it makes her upset."

Neave cut off Maverick's protest before it could even form on his lips – obviously a mother's talent. But how did she notice it affected me so much? Obviously, it would take him some time to not blame me for everything, but that didn't stop it stinging a little.

"Then what is happening, Mum, if it isn't the same as what happened to Lorian? Why is Grandma like that?" Maverick was starting to lose his temper, and the thick black fog was still growing – it now pooled around our knees, leaving a slightly singed smell as it moved around us.

"She is in another time, like Lorian last night, but this of her own doing."

As she looked at our confused faces, she could tell we still weren't understanding what was happening, so she tried another approach.

"Maverick, as you know, Grandma Wren is a time-caster, she can manipulate and see backwards or forwards in time. That is what she is doing now – she has gone back to another time that she feels she needs information from."

Glancing back at Grandma Wren, the glimmer of her body was becoming more dense. "How do you know she has gone back somewhere?"

"She only fades when she goes back, as you did last night, otherwise she…" she paused… "she sort of hums."

Both Maverick and I were silent – even though just the night before, we had travelled into my memories, none of us knew what to say. Grandma Wren was in another time, but what could have made her go back there?

"We'll just have to wait for her to finish what she is doing. Whatever it is that she wants to see must be important, as she normally only does this in private. For some reason, it seems as though the thought overtook her and drew her in this time. But don't worry, it just means it needs to be seen. Let me pour you some more tea and we shall wait for her. It can take a while for her to come back around afterwards."

We waited as the night grew darker and the chill started to creep into our bones. Maverick recounted for me what had happened in the woods the night before, regarding Emerys' capture and Connie's involvement. The betrayal was written plainly across Neave and Maverick's faces. Things were starting to happen that I knew would bring danger to this family, I just hoped I hadn't caused them.

Maverick

I t took Grandma Wren hours to retrieve the information she wanted. It was now half-past seven in the evening and she had only come round for half an hour before she went back in, and what she did say hadn't made any sense. She'd just muttered about cleaning rooms and collecting laundry. I hadn't ever seen anything like it before – she didn't even recognise us – but what was even more strange was her calling me Ivan.

I'd never even known Ivan. I only knew the stories I'd been told about him and I had only ever seen one photo. But I didn't miss how Lorian's face had grown sad and distant at the mention of his name. She obviously missed him. She had known him and Grandma Wren long before any of us were around, so it must have been difficult to wake up and only find one person she recognised.

It took me a while to calm down after seeing Grandma Wren like that, and I know I shouldn't have blamed Lorian but I couldn't shake the feeling it was all because of her. Grandma

Wren was now sitting down at the kitchen table looking more like herself; the distant look that had clouded her face was lifting, and she was talking more coherently, but it was as if she was still in the past.

"Miss Lorian, where are you?" Grandma Wren shot up and began searching around the kitchen as if she had lost something. "I can't find my book."

"It's okay, I'm here."

Lorian entered from the glowing living room where she had just taken in more logs. She had quickly learnt how to create a fire and took it upon herself to light one every evening. "What book is it that you can't find?"

"I don't know why you are bothering – it's like she doesn't even recognise us," I said bluntly.

Lorian looked over her shoulder, giving me a look that I didn't even think she could pull: pure disdain. "Shut up, Maverick. She recognises me."

Turning back to Grandma Wren, she asked again, "What book, Maria? Sit down and let me find it for you."

Lorian helped Grandma Wren get comfortable on one of the worn wooden chairs. She was calling her Maria as though not to confuse her. Grandma Wren looked at Lorian, blinking quickly as if trying to clear her vision.

"Is that you, Miss Lorian? It is my herb and spell book, the one you look through."

"It is time to come back to us now, Grandma. We need you back in our time," Mum prompted. "She doesn't normally take this long to come round…"

I could hear the worry laced in her voice and she had begun to wring her hands. She didn't know what to do, didn't know how to help Grandma Wren get back. The look she gave Mum was one of pure confusion, as though she had never seen her before. I could see Mum blanch and her brows pull closer together.

Lorian started to plead with her: "It's me, Maria, but it isn't the time you think it is. That was three hundred years ago. Please come back to me now, I need your help. We need your help!"

"Help with what, my bird?"

"We need to get Emerys and Lila back, and we can't do that without you."

"I need my book, Miss Lorian."

It was starting to annoy me, hearing Lorian being called 'Miss' again. It reminded me of all the infuriating stories Grandma Wren would tell me about her previous employers.

"Okay, I will find it."

Sighing, Lorian got to her feet and turned to Mum. "Where does Grandma Wren keep her book?"

"I don't know what book that is, I don't think I have ever seen one like that. She normally just keeps a book of shadows, but I've never known her to have one about herbs." Mum looked puzzled. "She does keep a trunk under her bed, though. I assume it could be in there as I think that's where she keeps her personal things."

"I'll go look – you stay here and talk to her. She only seems to recognise you," I said quickly, getting up from the chair opposite Grandma Wren.

I couldn't stay there and watch helplessly any longer. I strode the short distance to her bedroom. Her room always surprised me as she didn't have many belongings or knick-knacks on the surfaces; and the only photo was a faded one of her and her husband on their wedding day, which sat by the bed in a worn frame.

Moving to the side of her bed, I slid the old trunk out. On instinct, I let my dark fury loose, feeling for any protection spell. Nothing. Carefully, I prized open the worn buckle that held the trunk closed. All her possessions were neatly arranged inside: photographs, books, old clothes, jewellery. Grandma Wren seemed to have stored everything she'd collected through the centuries in the trunk.

Picking up a faded bundle of photographs held together by string, I looked at the one on top. It was of a group of people in white aprons wearing black. None of them looked happy to be there – in fact, they looked miserable. Curiosity overwhelming me, I pulled at the neatly tied bow and shuffled through the rest. There were more photos of the same group – some included men in suits with white gloves and the shiniest shoes I had seen. But not one of them were smiling; even in the less formal photos, no one wore any other expression other than grim.

"They were the house staff in my family home."

Spinning round, I was suddenly inches away from Lorian's face. She was peering over my shoulder at the photos, a wistful look on her face. "How is it you know about photographs but not electricity?"

"I didn't hear you come in," I blabbed, tucking my hair behind my ears. I had been caught looking through Grandma Wren's things and not just for the book she wanted. It was something Mum hated and I just knew Lorian would tell her I'd been looking. She wouldn't be able to keep her mouth shut.

"Grandma Wren used to show them to us all the time and explain how you used to be able to capture images."

I had longed to be able to do that, capture images of things that may not last so I could look back on them; like Xav as a foal, or our family at Christmas.

"It's okay, I won't say you looked. Here, I will show you one of Maria and Ivan." She picked up another bundle of photos tucked in the box and untied the string.

"We shouldn't be looking at them, I shouldn't have looked in the first place…"

"It's okay, Grandma Wren wouldn't mind. These are my photos anyway."

Flicking through the photos she discarded many before she found the one she was looking for. "Here, this is Ivan and Grandma Wren in my garden. Ivan loved the outdoors and the moments he could have Grandma Wren out there with him. They would always argue about where to place each of the herbs so they wouldn't be noticed." Handing me the photo, she continued with a giggle, "You see, my mother didn't agree with a herb garden – she wanted bright colours and bold statement plants. *"Why would you plant something you could buy?"* she would always say. So Ivan took it upon himself to plant a few herbs here and there where she wouldn't notice. She never cared much about the plant names, just that they looked right."

She returned the remaining photos to the box but didn't ask for the one she had given me. It contained a small woman with her hair tied back in a tight bun. The man next to her was taller but still slender, you could see he was strong. He had his sleeves rolled up and his shirt collar open just like I wear mine – in fact we looked startlingly similar. The only difference was he wore braces on his trousers and didn't have a birthmark on his cheek.

263

"I didn't realise the similarity between you before until now," she said, looking at the photo then at me. "You could be twins. I suppose with everything else happening, I didn't make the connection. Have it, Grandma Wren won't mind."

"No, I couldn't, it's not mine to have."

I went to place the photo back with the others but Lorian's hand covered mine. It was cold and pale against my large, tanned hand.

"She won't mind, I promise. She would like Ivan to be remembered by someone other than her."

I could feel a warmth spread in my chest at her gesture – I had never had anything of the family's to call my own.

Turning back to the box, she rummaged through some of the books, knowing exactly what she was looking for.

"There it is…" She pulled out a small leather-bound book and presented it to me. "Here, go and give this to Grandma Wren. I will put the photos back."

Out of the corner of my eye, I saw her slip a photo into the pocket of her skirt. I was about to ask, but thought better of it. If these really were her photographs, it was none of my business who was in them.

Looking back down at the little book I now cradled in my hands, I could just make out the fading script on the cover: *'Recipe Book'*.

"It was called that in case my mother came down to the kitchens looking for me. She wouldn't give it a second glance if she thought it was a real recipe book."

She returned the trunk back under the bed and looked at me turning the book over in my hands.

I couldn't begin to wonder what it must have been like for Grandma Wren and Grandpa Ivan to keep their magic secret.

I ambled back into the living room where Grandma Wren and Mum now sat quietly talking.

"Oh, you found it. Thank you, Ivan!" Grandma Wren exclaimed, snatching the book from my hands.

"I am not Ivan," I replied, but Grandma Wren ignored my comment and tugged a little harder on the book.

I reluctantly let go of it. Since Lorian had given it to me, my dark fury had stirred and I didn't want to let it go lightly. The book was full of magic – that was for sure.

Lorian came back into the room a few minutes after me and went over to Grandma Wren who was frantically shuffling through the pages of the book. Soft grumblings came from the delirious old lady as Lorian waited by her, patiently.

After ten minutes, Lorian finally spoke. "Let me see if I can help, Maria. What is it you are looking for?" she asked quietly, as if talking to a spooked animal.

I didn't know how much longer I could stay and watch – it seemed as though Grandma Wren really was stuck in the past and we wouldn't get her back this time.

I decided to leave. Pulling the front door open, I was greeted with the chilled cold air of winter – it was going to snow, I could smell it. No one looked up as I left.

Trudging back home, it was as though he knew I was coming. Xaviran, my faithful friend, was waiting for me in the stables attached to the side of my home. He always seemed to know when I was going to be coming to see him. I felt guilty that I hadn't had much time to ride him lately – what with the festivals and helping Grandma Wren, and Emerys being taken, it had all really thrown my routine off.

"What is happening, Xav? I feel so angry all the time, and now Emerys is gone, I don't even have anyone to let it out with. Hunting isn't helping and Feren always seems to be sniffing around. Feren is asking about Lorian, and I know I shouldn't feel like this, but I don't want him near her."

Xaviran let out a huff of warm air – he wasn't going to listen to me unless I gave him an apple first. Fishing around for an apple in the side room where I kept a few treats, I produced a small, unripe offering.

"I'm sorry, but this is all that is left in there." Xaviran huffed but took the apple nevertheless. "What should I do? I feel like I am going to explode if I have to spend more time around her, but then I am drawn – Gods, am I drawn to her…"

Sighing, I pushed a hand through my thick hair, tucking it behind my ears. Sitting with a thud on a large bale across from Xaviran's stable, head in my hands, I grumbled about Xav's inability to comment on the subject. All the while he looked at me unyieldingly, as if I had gone completely mad. With another great huff, he came to the gate of his stable and began kicking. His persistent loud banging on the hardwood jostled me from my meandering thoughts.

"What?" I snapped at my tall black horse.

He had been my most loyal friend for many years, someone whom I could rely on to take my anger and dish it right back at me. He was as committed to me as I was to him.

"If you come out, you will have to go back soon. I should check on Grandma Wren."

Unlatching the stable door, I had only opened it an inch when the great brute kicked it hard, one last time, knocking me to the floor. He ran out of the open barn doors and into the darkness. Brushing the dust off from my trousers, I ran out into the field. Xav would never run off very far, knowing I was the only one to take care of his ill-tempered ways.

"Fine, get your fat ass over here and we can go for a ride."

But Xav just huffed and looked away from me. He liked to play games and test my patience, but I knew what irritated him the most.

Letting my dark fury loose, I morphed it into a small weasel and let it scurry up to him. It took him a few moments to realise it was there but when he did, he jumped back and started pounding the floor with his feet. He gave the best imitation of a scowl I have ever seen a horse give and trotted back over to me.

Laughing, I rubbed the side of his neck. "You love it really, you nearly got in that time." Xav gave a slow blink and pushed his nose under my neck. "Oh come on – you're not afraid of him. You just pretend you are, you great lump."

Xav huffed in my face but turned and presented me with his side to mount. Pushing up, I swung my right leg over his back and settled myself, taking a handful of mane instead of the usual leather rein he so detested. I smirked, thinking of the one and only time I tried to tack him up and the destruction he wrought on the stable.

As soon as Xaviran felt my pull, he cocked his head to the side as if listening to something on the cold winter's breeze and then he was off at a gallop, not waiting for me to kick him on or guide him. He could obviously see better than me as dark outlines flew past us in the gloom.

He took so many different twists and turns that I couldn't tell where we were going; I was even unsure when we had entered the forest. Closing my eyes, I let my dark fury loose once more; these past few months had seen me use it more than ever and it was now hungry to get out as often as it could. Even though I had my eyes closed, I could feel it take on the form of a black wolf running beside Xaviran – its favourite form it seemed. I couldn't see my surroundings but my dark fury gave me a heightened sense of what was around us. I could smell the moss on the floor, feel the density of the trees that we sped past and feel the heavy moisture in the air.

I didn't know how long we had been riding, but I was frozen to the bone and my dark fury had faded long ago. I was unable to keep it released for such long periods of time. I felt drained and I hadn't even been doing most of the work. Xav slowed to a walk and then stopped behind a few bushes.

"I bet you are tired now, boy. How are we going to get home?" But he wasn't paying attention to me – instead, he was looking deep into the shadows up ahead. Sliding from his back, I moved closer to the bushes and listened. Everything was pitch black, the moon couldn't penetrate the dense forest and my eyes were unable to adjust to anything not directly in front of me. I focused on what I could hear.

"It is too soon to get another."

"But more and more hearts are filling; soon we won't be quick enough to extinguish what plagues them."

A conversation drifted to me on the breeze. Even though it now had a reptilian hiss, there was no mistaking whose voice it was. Emerys was out there talking to someone.

Xaviran started to stamp his feet and nudge me on the shoulder. Reaching up, I pulled his nose down to my face, pressing my cheek to it, trying to calm him but he wouldn't settle. I couldn't hear the voices any more, but I wanted to wait a little longer before I moved off.

I waited for another five minutes and, satisfied that we wouldn't be heard, I stood to mount Xav again. Just as I was swinging my leg over, I felt two clawed hands dig into my back. I didn't even have a chance to let out a murmur of a shout before I was thrown backwards, hitting a strong tree.

"Stay away, Maverick. You ssshouldn't be out here."

Looking up I was face to face with Emerys, but it wasn't the Emerys I had grown up with. His face was now twisted into a cruel snarl, his teeth were elongated and broken, and he had a deep open wound across his face. He wasn't as disturbing as some of the other creatures I had seen but he had the distinctive rotting smell that lingered on all of them and the telltale hiss in his voice.

As he spoke I realised his tongue was forked like a snake and it seemed to flick in and out as if he was scenting with it. I couldn't draw my eyes away.

"I can smell your fear, and also your anger and confusion at ssseeing me," he went on. His form took on a smoky outline and he seemed to fade to an unusual grey, but it also seemed as though he let off a slight glow, breaking the darkness of the night. "You shouldn't have come out here, Maverick, this is no place for you. You might get lost … or would being found be worssse?"

It had been only a day since he had been taken but he wasn't the same Emerys as before.

"What do you mean? Why would I worry about getting found when I was never lost?"

"Oh but you are, you are all lossst. How about I find you?" Emerys reached for my chest with his broken jagged nails and began to run a thin line down my exposed skin. "You see, it is sometimes what is held in the heart that we don't realise is there, that is the most poisoning."

He was talking in riddles and my chest burned from where he was clawing at it, but I couldn't bat him away. He was still stronger than me and with my dark fury in short supply, I felt weak. I wouldn't be able to get past him and up on to Xaviran fast enough. And it seemed as though Xav had been as shocked to see Emerys as I was; he just stood there huffing to himself and stamping his feet. Maybe it was because he knew it was Emerys – he was one of the only people he would let touch him.

"Let's see what you truly feel, Maverick." Without a moment's hesitation, he dug his fingers into the centre of the diagram he had drawn on my chest. His fingers slid in between my bones and down into the soft tissue. "You see, this allows me to delve deeper than normal. I can now feel exactly as you do, not just a hint. I feel you're scared and I can see what you hide the most," he whispered in my ear.

Images of Lorian, Mum and Connie all flashed before my eyes and I heard the pounding of Xaviran's feet as he finally bolted. I was alone.

"Ah, your anger at another catching her attention is truly appetising."

His form was now flickering in and out as he spoke, his misty white eyes wide as he savoured everything I felt. My horror mounted as he drank everything in and I was becoming more tired. So tired.

"Oh don't you worry about dear Connie, she is doing just fine for herssself," Emerys sneered. "And you need not worry about Lila either, she is perfectly okay."

Emerys let out a low whistle and another creature stepped up to his side. Blinking, I tried to focus on the new threat. This creature was smaller than Emerys and undoubtedly female, her threadbare clothes barely covering her exposed chest. Glancing up at her horrifically scarred and mottled face I could see that she once would have been beautiful, but it wasn't until I met the cloudy grey eyes that I truly became afraid. It was Lila.

"You see, we are together now. No need to look, the Massster has reunited us and shown us what our powersss can really do," Emerys hissed at me, drawing my attention away from the cold eyes of the girl I once knew.

The images went on through my worst fears to my deepest desires.

"You really can be quite cruel when you want to be. What did Feren ever do to deserve you wishing to curssse and maim him? And then you go all tender to Lorian wishing only to pleassse her. It is rather pathetic that that whore can take your attention when she desires another."

My mouth felt woolly and my tongue fat – I couldn't form words and my eyes were beginning to close. Although I wanted to stay awake and focus on the threat, I was also relieved as the darkness took me, ending the pain.

When I awoke, I was moving quickly through the gloom, trying to focus on the lamps up ahead but I couldn't get my bearings. I could feel someone's thighs pushing against my side as I lay over the horse. My chest was still burning and I could feel a wet sensation flowed underneath me then running down the horses flank.

Tucking my arms underneath me, I tried to push myself up to see where we were heading when a rough hand pushed me back down, making the wounds in my back from Emerys' hands flame.

I could feel my panic begin to mount. What if Emerys had taken me? The voice that came both comforted and angered me.

271

"Don't move, we are almost back at Grandma Wren's."

It was Feren, and from the rhythm of the horse, I was sure he was riding Xav, which was very strange as he never let anyone but me or Emerys ride him. But it was also comforting knowing Xav hadn't abandoned me and had gone to get help.

Before I could make any sort of complaint, we were stopping and Feren was swinging his leg over to dismount.

"Don't try and move yet, Mav. Let me get your mother to help."

I could just see Feren disappearing inside Grandma Wren's cottage. I wasn't going to wait for Mum to help me get off my own horse.

Sliding back, I let out a shout as my chest scraped against Xaviran, making him huff and jostle. "It's okay, boy, I am okay," I murmured to him as I rubbed his side.

With my feet now planted on the ground, I felt as though I could topple over at any minute. Letting go of Xav's mane, I tried to take a step but I quickly realised that without the horse's support I would not be able to hold myself up.

The back door flew open and Mum stood there bathed in the warm white glow of the lights. Before I could even try and take another step towards her, she was flying down the steps.

She pushed her head and shoulders under my arm. "Get his other side, Feren. He is still bleeding and it looks as though he's lost a lot of blood already."

Mum was trying to keep her voice level and matter-of-fact, but I could hear the slight tremor that accompanied her words.

They guided me up the steps and into the kitchen. I could hear Lorian talking softly to Grandma Wren, who seemed to be back to her normal self now, I heard Lorian say that she was going to refill the tea and her soft footfall as she began to enter the kitchen. As her small frame filled the doorway, the teapot that she was holding slipped from her fingers. I watched as if in slow motion as it shattered on the floor.

"Lorian, what is it dear?" Grandma Wren looked over her shoulder to see what expensive piece of china Lorian had broken. "Into Lorian's room with him, Neave, it is quieter in there and you will have enough space to work," she commanded.

Before I could even begin to protest, I was hustled into Lorian's sparse room. Nothing appeared to have changed from when Lorian first arrived. The wardrobe that I had made a few years ago was still there; she also had a shelf on the wall that held a few ornaments, a pair of old dance slippers, a candle and a little glass pot I hadn't seen before. The whole room reminded me of Grandma Wren's.

"Put him on the bed. Feren – fetch me some hot water and some yarrow, cayenne pepper and bentonite clay, so I can make a poultice. Lorian, help me remove his shirt." Mum was firing off instructions as f if she was dealing with a full staff of healers.

"I will help Feren gather what you need, let me know if there is anything else," Grandma Wren said from the doorway, retreating back into the kitchen with Feren when she saw the situation. She still had a slight wistfulness about her voice, but I could tell she was now safely back with us and not stuck in some other time.

"Now, Lorian!"

I was startled at the forcefulness of Mum's voice. Lorian hadn't moved from where she was standing just inside the doorway. Her face was white and her eyes round but she tentatively knelt before me and began helping Mum strip off my shirt. I guess the rush that had taken over her when the creatures attacked hadn't shown its face this time.

The blood I'd lost was starting to dry, causing my shirt fabric to stick to me. They had to soak it to be able to pull it off. As she carefully peeled each piece away, I could feel Lorian's hands shaking.

It seemed as though it would never end, but finally the last piece was removed and the ragged shirt was stripped from my torso. Mum ordered everyone from the room and began to soak my wounds. I caught a glimpse of the tears that traced a silent path on Lorian's cheeks as she gathered up the rags of my shirt and followed the others out.

"Someone will have to re-dress your wounds and put some more salve on them every few hours to prevent infection. Whatever went into you seems to be breeding bacteria quicker than a normal wound. Now sleep and we will wake you when we need to change the dressing. And then, I want to know exactly what happened." Mum's voice trembled with barely contained anger, so my guess was that I was going to be okay.

Surprisingly, I drifted off to sleep easily, my body was so weak from the blood loss and the draining of my dark fury. But the sleep was fitful; it wasn't that I was woken every few hours by Mum, Grandma Wren or occasionally Lorian, it was more that I kept replaying over and over what had happened with Emerys. Something was obviously happening to the missing people to make them become these creatures, but I just couldn't understand what.

Before I came to any conclusions, my mind drifted off into a silent blackness once again but it didn't last long, with a loud screeching sound outside my door jostling me awake. When it sounded again I could just make out the voice. It was Mum talking and I had never heard her so angry.

Trying to haul myself out of bed I nearly landed on the floor; I couldn't get myself up, I couldn't go and see what was happening. Frustrated, I hauled my useless body back on to the bed.

Listening closely, I began to piece together what was happening. Mum was throwing Connie out. Raised voices threw words with abandon. Then a loud slamming of the door indicated Connie had left. I could still just make out Mum's voice.

"I did what needed to be done. For all we know, it could be her doing that, bringing the creatures here, and pinpointing who to take. It could be the reason that Emerys is gone. I don't want her anywhere near this family." Mum spoke in a hushed angry manner.

"I understand," Grandma Wren said.

I heard a second bang and then a low creaking as my door was tentatively opened. I expected to see Mum and took in a deep breath, preparing to tell her what had happened to me. But I was greeted by Lorian's tentative gaze.

"I am sorry, Maverick, but your Mum has asked me to put some more salve on your wounds. She's gone out to collect some more herbs to make some more salve and Grandma Wren is resting. "Don't worry, she has left me instructions on how to put it on and to re-dress your wounds. I also assume you heard the argument?"

I nodded. "I guess Connie won't be coming back…" I winced as I tried to readjust myself on the bed.

"No, your mum said her betrayal is too great to allow her anywhere near the family again."

Without another word she helped me lean forward, apologising when I hissed at the pain.

"It is not your fault, Lorian, stop saying sorry," I snapped. I knew I shouldn't have as she was only trying to help, but it was infuriating that she kept apologising for something she hadn't done.

Slowly and carefully, she unwound my bandages and moved round to dress the puncture marks on my back. After she was done, she placed some clean bandage on my back and then guided me back onto the bed.

"Aren't you going to do my front first before you put the bandage on?"

I was confused by the process she was performing; it was so different from Mum's. Even though Mum was gentle, I could barely feel Lorian's feather-like touch. I only knew she was administering the salve because her hands were colder than my body and I could feel them tremble ever so slightly.

"You do not need to worry, you won't hurt me any more than I already am." I tried to keep my voice low and gentle but I knew I was not the best at it, so in a last attempt to try and ease her worry, I covered her small hand with mine.

"I will lean you forward again to wrap the rest, but if you lie back I believe you will be more comfortable while I treat your front. What happened, Maverick?" Her voice was pitched low to keep from disturbing Grandma Wren in the next room.

As I lay back, I watched her examine the wound on my chest. Even in the low candlelight, I could see the colour draining from her face. Her eyes were shining with unushered tears. I suppose it was the first time she had really seen it; now that it has stopped bleeding excessively she could make out what was drawn there.

A hexagon shape surrounded the centre of my chest and in the middle, intricate swirls shaped like snakes were, etched deeply into my skin. Lorian carefully applied the thick salve, the lumpy texture obscuring the feagal once again. The symbol of fear.

"You do not need to tend to my wounds again – I will tell Mum not to let you. I can see it makes you upset." I was trying to comfort her; I could see it was making her uncomfortable to be dressing the marks that now covered my body.

Wiping a tear from her cheek with the pad of my thumb, I eased up and her small hands adeptly adjusted the gauze on my front. As I leant forward for her to see my back more easily, she wrapped the bandage firmly around me.

"I am not afraid of helping to tend to those who need it, I have done it before. It is more that I do not understand why you were branded. I may not know what the symbol means but I know a brand." Her voice was strong and even.

"It is called the the feagal and it symbolises fear," I said.

"But why would they … want to brand you with that?"

I gathered what energy I had and tried to explain the use of the symbols as simply as I could. "If it is used in accompaniment with other symbols in a ritual, it can help someone overcome a fear. But on its own, it is supposed to instil fear."

This is what was worrying me the most. Why would he brand me with a symbol that would slowly eat away at me, bringing my deepest fears to light?

"But who would do that?" That was the question that had been humming at the edges of everyone's thoughts since last night.

"Help me into the living room and let me explain to

everyone what happened."

Maverick

I talked to everyone about what I'd witnessed, about how it seemed as though the transition into the creatures made an individual's powers grow or persuaded them to use powers to harm others. Mum exploded into a rage I had never seen before, Lorian quietly wept and Grandma Wren just sat, silent and grave. I felt exhausted.

Once back in the bedroom, Lorian checked my wounds and applied some more ointment. "They are looking better, they have stopped weeping and bleeding now, but they still have pus stuck to them. I will ask Neave to bathe them out again for you later."

Binding me back up and covering me with the blankets, Lorian turned to leave.

"Thank you, Lorian. I don't know why you are being so kind to me after everything I've said, but thank you." I closed my eyes and willed sleep to take me.

"You did it for me…"

Her soft response was so quiet I could have misheard her,

but I was sure I'd heard it right. How could she remember the first night, when I pressed herbs to her skin to heal her bruises? She was barely conscious from the tonic Mum had given her to help with the shock. I was sure she'd thought it was Emerys that tended to her. Before I could ask the question, I heard the quiet snick of the latch closing.

Shortly after, Grandma Wren came in carrying a tray with some tea and sandwiches on it. It was obviously lunchtime and I had slept for a few hours, but I still felt as though I could sleep the rest of the winter away, let alone have the strength to make it to the kitchen.

"I thought you might be hungry."

My stomach grumbled in response and she smiled, placing the tray on my lap. Picking up one of the sandwiches. I took a bite: egg and fresh watercress covered my taste-buds. It was one of the things Grandma Wren would always give us when we were feeling low.

"You lost quite a lot of blood but that isn't what's causing you to feel so weak. I'm afraid it's the magic that Emerys used…"

The question had been rattling around my head throughout the night – why couldn't I feel my dark fury, the added strength I was so used to having? But I knew I hadn't spoken it aloud, not even when I recounted the events earlier this morning. Grandma Wren was so intuitive and always seemed to know what I really wanted to know, even before I did.

"Magic? Emerys wouldn't use magic against me unless it was a joke. Surely it's the loss of blood that caused this?"

Propping myself up higher on the pillows, with a wince, I finished my sandwich. Emerys had used magic and branded me in the process, but I didn't want to believe it. I wanted to believe he was still in there somewhere.

"As I said, you did lose a lot of blood, but when Emerys started to absorb your deepest emotions, it drained you. Do you know if he's ever done anything like this before?"

I dropped the second half of the sandwich, scattering egg over the sheets. "You can't be serious. I know you say we are all vicious at heart, but Emerys wouldn't do this to someone. I honestly don't even think he knows how to do it."

My wounds gave a deep throb, as if reminding me that it was Emerys that had caused them. He obviously knew how to hurt someone now.

The silence stretched between us while Grandma Wren contemplated what I had just told her.

"Well, he either knew and never told you, or someone has told him now. This is dark magic, Maverick, and it is all the more deadly with someone who possesses Emerys' powers. You have to be careful."

"Something is seriously wrong with him, we have to do something," I said meekly.

"And we will, I promise you." Her cold, fragile hand clasped mine, sealing her promise.

"What did he mean by being found? I have never heard him talk like that before." It was something that had been bothering me since I had run into him in the woods.

"I am not certain yet." She looked off into the distance as if listening to something. Shaking her head, she turned back to me. "You get some rest. I will get Lorian to bring you some cold water. Drink your tea, it will help you sleep. You'll feel better tomorrow, I think."

Once Grandma Wren had left the room, I pondered on what had happened. Emerys said that his 'Master' – which was disturbing in itself – had a lot of power. The only individual I knew with power like that, was the Stravaig.

A while later, Lorian came in with a wooden tray that had seen better days. Pushing all thoughts of the Dark One aside for a minute, I tried to bring my mind to happier thoughts.

"I have brought you some water and a few biscuits I found left in the jar."

Lorian turned to leave once the tray was safely on my lap and she had removed the one Grandma Wren had brought in.

Reaching out, I caught her hand in mine. "Will you stay with me awhile and talk?"

The hesitation in her eyes was easy to see and I felt my chest squeeze. I'd put that there with how I had acted, but I was determined to make amends. My feelings were closer, and seemed easier to identify.

"Sure," was all she said, as she perched on the edge of the bed, resting the tray on her lap.

Dusk was fast approaching, as it always did at this time of the year. It only felt like a moment ago that I had woken up at lunchtime. As I gazed at the quickly darkening sky – it was only three in the afternoon – I noticed that it had been snowing.

"I'm sorry, Lorian."

"What for?" The puzzlement caused her nose to wrinkle slightly and she pursed her lips into a slight pout that made her look like a small child trying to decide what sweet to have. I had to suppress a smile that tried to creep onto my lips.

"I haven't made you feel the most welcome since you have been here."

"I understand really. I have disrupted you and your family." She was obviously uncomfortable, fiddling with the used dishes on the tray. "You need to rest and I am tired – this headache just won't go away. Try and sleep, Maverick."

She retreated to the door and blew out the candle that was lit on the bedside table.

Taking up the water, I took a sip and nearly spat it out. It had obviously been soaked in herbs and the sourness made me gag. Gulping it down before I changed my mind, I tried to settle back to sleep. I still felt exhausted, but it eluded me. I had obviously rested enough for now, and my mind was too busy.

I was haunted by the memories of my meeting with Emerys and conversations with Lorian that had never taken place. And there was one question that kept playing over and over throughout the dream:

"If I am I lost, what does it mean to be found?"

Lorian

3601 Moons 27 days

Dear Diary,

Over the next few weeks, we will begin to prepare for the festivities coming up, but that isn't what I am writing about. Since Maria had her trip into the past she has been different, more distant, especially to me. And she keeps getting that pocket watch out. I don't understand what it is for. She never had it before I came to Sòlas.

When I asked her what was wrong, she sidestepped the question, similar to when I asked about the pieces of colour I have seen, and my headaches and blurred vision. I know she said I'd have to help bring colour back and surely, if I am beginning to see it, something is happening, but she just won't talk to me. She just says, 'In time,' and then walks away. And how am I supposed to help bring colour back exactly?

I can't concentrate with these headaches, but I will think of

something.
  Lorian

The next few weeks went by quickly; helping Neave with preparations for Yule took up most of my time, allowing me to keep my distance from Maverick. Since his accident, my concern overwhelmed me; I tried to hide it so as not to smother him but it just made me all the more awkward around him.

When he wasn't having hushed conversations with Grandma Wren, it always seemed as though he was watching me. His wounds had healed enough so that he could work on some wooden projects for Yule but they hadn't distracted him enough. Neave had tasked him with carving the Yule logs with protective runes – apparently he did this every year – and he seemed more content when he was whittling away.

I had never heard of that tradition so spoke at length about it with Grandma Wren. Burning the Yule log was supposed to help ward against lightning and house fires, especially if the remains of the burnt log were kept under the bed in the coming year. Maverick engraved additional protective runes on the wood for good fortune and health.

He had refused to say he wasn't feeling strong enough to cast the right spells but he did say he didn't have the time it would take to prepare each log. This year he was filling a trunk with wooden ornaments to sell instead of the logs.

"Lorian, could you pass me the wreath on the back of the

cart?" Neave called from the stall we had finishing setting up moments earlier.

Drawing me out of my daze, where I was standing looking at Maverick's back as he carved, I clambered onto the rickety cart and picked up two wreaths – one was smaller than the other but it still had a significant amount of detail.

"This one?" I held it out to her as I picked my way across the trimmings that we'd allowed to pile up on the floor.

"Yes, thank you. Could you please pack it up and give it to Feren? Apparently he needed another."

She was preparing a thistle bouquet for a sinister-looking customer, but I still caught her amused eye roll. Avoiding eye contact with the cruel-looking witch, I started wrapping the little parcel in the thin paper we used to protect the flowers until they got home.

"Honestly, I don't know why he would need a third wreath. Surely one or two is enough?"

"Oh, I don't think the wreaths are the reason he is coming back." The devious look on Neave's face made me blush. "It's obvious he is taken with you, Lorian. It's okay to have a little fun."

As I looked at Neave I could see a blue hue drift into her eye as it twinkled, and a light blush warmed her normally pale skin. Before I knew it, my hand was brushing her cheek and a questioning look on her face overtook her humorous expression.

"Everything okay?"

"Oh, umm, yes," I stammered, pulling my hand back. The blush was still there. "Just a smudge," I said quickly.

It was a ridiculous excuse as we didn't have any potted plants or herbs on the stall so she couldn't have got a smudge on her. An easy smile remained on her face as she turned back to what she was doing, dismissing my little mishap.

"Do you really need a third wreath?" I asked when I had finished wrapping the parcel and passed it to Feren's waiting hands.

"Oh you know you can't have too many," he remarked, handing me the coin.

It had taken me a while to get used to the currency they used – instead of half a crown, farthing or sixpence, they used twenty, ten or five shard pieces and they even had a coin called a bonn which was the equivalent to a pound note.

"But surely three is a little over the top?"

"Nah, got to have one on each door." Feren's mischievous grin spoke loudly enough, but his next words still took me by surprise. "Would you like to go to the Yule festival with me, Lorian?"

My face must have given away the little understanding I had of the festivities that were due to take place in the next few days, as he quickly tried to explain.

"It's a bit like Samhain – we have dancing, but people also bring plates of food with them. So? Will you go with me? Or has someone already asked you?"

I knew who he was referring to. Everyone seemed to think there was something going on between Maverick and me, especially since his accident. I know I had been helping him too much and that people would assume things, but I couldn't help it. He needed to be looked after in those few weeks and I wanted to be the one to do it. Seeing him with his wounds had shown me a more vulnerable side of Maverick, but now he was regaining his strength, he was beginning to bury it again. His more cruel, shallow side – what I feared was the real him – could re-emerge any moment.

I managed to catch Neave's eye. She had no doubt heard Feren's question, and as if answering my unspoken plea for guidance, she smiled and gave a nod, then turned her back again, giving us the illusion of privacy.

"It's okay, I see you don't—"

"I would love to!" I cut him off before he finished, my confidence had grown since I first arrived in Sólas.

He had turned to leave, but I could see his smile. And when he turned back around, his eyes were purple.

"What is it, Lorian?" Reaching out he placed his hand on my forearm.

"It's nothing, I'm sorry."

I covered his hand with mine, keeping my voice level as though not to show my surprise. I couldn't try and explain it to him. Maybe I was just imagining it, but after seeing colour in Neave's face just moments before, I wasn't so sure any more.

I could feel someone watching us, and before I even saw their face, I could feel the wave of anger. Maverick had obviously finished his carving and returned to the stall. Neave was putting him to work.

"You can go now, Lorian, Maverick can take over from you. Go and enjoy the rest of the market. Here…"

She pressed some small coins into my hand and I finally dragged my eyes from the back of Maverick's head.

"I can't—"

"You aren't, this is your wage. You earned it, so I am not just giving it to you. And take this and get some dried fruit please," she said with a soft understanding on her face.

She pushed a few more coins in my hand and turned back

to the stall. "Have fun. Goodbye, Feren!" she called over her shoulder, as she began trimming more stems.

Feren dragged me into the throng of the Yule market and soon enough, I was engulfed by all the different smells and sounds. Some were familiar and others new and exciting. The spicy smell of potpourri blanketed me in its familiar scent.

Pushing my way through to the stall, I caught sight of little pots of my favourite Christmas decorations. The dried orange slices, cinnamon sticks, star anise and, of course, the pine cones made my hands twitch. I so badly wanted to reach out and touch them, but I knew better than to do that this time.

"How much for the potpourri?" I called over the crowd to the tall skinny man that was tending it. It seemed as though most of the men around my age that I had encountered were tall, none of them shorter than six feet. Strange.

"Ten bonn."

It seemed quite a lot for the small pot, but I knew my Christmas, or Yule, wouldn't be complete without it. I just knew Grandma Wren would be happy to have it too. Fishing out my small cloth coin pouch I began to shuffle through its contents to find the correct change when a man's hands, I assumed Feren's, clamped over them.

"Bit steep for that don't you think, Michael?"

It wasn't Feren's voice, it was Maverick's. I swear he always seemed to appear out of nowhere. It was getting rather annoying, but for now I was relieved someone was able to voice what I thought about the price. He had his face schooled so it wouldn't reveal his emotions and he kept his eyes on the seller. Feren was nowhere to be seen.

"Ah, Maverick, as you have turned up, I assume this is the young lady everyone is talking about. Lorian isn't it?"

Michael sniggered when he glanced at me, causing Maverick to squeeze my hand.

"Yes, I am Lorian," I answered meekly. I could feel tension in the situation and I didn't understand why.

"You see, I was a little confused when I saw her with Feren and not you."

Maverick's body tensed next to me, but he kept his face blank and his voice calm. "How much are you willing to pay, Lorian?"

He was trying to change the subject, to bring it back to the matter at hand. He used the one thing he knew would draw Michael's attention – money.

I looked down at my small coin purse. I still didn't understand the value of anything so it was hard to come to a sum. I heard Maverick sigh, obviously frustrated with my indecisiveness.

"Give him five bonn. That's still more than it's worth; we could have made some at home if you wanted it so badly." He turned and stalked over to where Feren was now standing. I could see Maverick was arguing with him.

"Here you go!" Michael handed me a wrapped paper parcel. "I will see you at the Yule festivities. Save me a dance," he smirked.

I hurriedly handed him the money and pushed my way through the crowd to where Maverick and Feren were facing each other.

"You honestly are the most stupid person I've met, Feren! She's only been here a few months and you let her wander around on her own?"

Maverick's voice was trembling as he tried to control his temper. However, there was no black smoke this time, so that was a good sign.

"She won't learn if you baby her all the time," Feren retorted. "She is fine, aren't you Lorian?" He didn't wait for my response. "I've got to go and help Mum. You know, only a few days to Yule. Got to prepare. I'll collect you from Grandma Wren's at five-thirty Saturday, okay, Lorian?" With that, he kissed me on the cheek and disappeared into the crowd.

I was stunned into silence as I pressed my hand to my cheek. What had just happened? No one had ever kissed me – well not like that. It was too forward on the hand, let alone the cheek.

Maverick's barely contained anger erupted from him in a low growl; it was so animalistic and feral I stumbled away. It was clearly so full of frustration.

"You are going to Yule with him?!"

I was transfixed by the swell of darkness emitting from his ankles in a cloud, now he was losing his temper. "It's just a dance, it doesn't mean anything."

I tried to keep my voice calm but he was frightening to look at. Maverick's top lip was curled and he was slightly crouched, as if he was an animal ready to attack. In a flash, he had his hand around my wrist and was pulling me through the crowd to a secluded spot just off the busy square. I saw him wince slightly as his abrupt movement pulled his wounds.

"Do you realise that Beltane is just a few months later?" His face was only inches from mine.

"I don't even know what Beltane is. Stop, Maverick, you're scaring me." I pushed against him with my free hand, carefully avoiding the centre of his chest, anger growing in me. My breath was coming in short bursts.

Maverick took several deep breaths before he answered

me. The darkness that had surrounded his lower half receded as he grew calmer. "Beltane is the festival when the maiden goddess is at her most fertile. It is also expected that we take a partner, if not wed soon after and begin a family." I could hear the defeat in his voice.

"Who do you mean by 'we'?"

"Between the ages of eighteen and twenty-one they expect us to find someone. Not everyone does, but some people believe it is important to do so in this period. It is supposed to be more likely that you will find your true match. Feren is twenty-two next month and it isn't just the prospect of finding a true match that is enticing him to hurry, his mother thinks he should be settled. If he isn't, and hasn't tried to begin a family by Beltane, she will disown him."

"That is awful."

I was still trying to wrap my head around the concept of there being a true match and that they expected their children to find them in such a short period of time, let alone start a family. But I could also feel hope that maybe what I had started feeling towards Maverick could mean something.

"It is the way it is. Some families are more relaxed about it. Mum would like me to find mine, but she understands it takes time. I'm sorry I scared you, Lorian, the whole situation is just so … messed up."

He was still holding my wrist but only loosely now, tracing the area he had gripped with his thumb, erasing any lingering pressure with its soft tingles.

"Neave seems more reasonable than most parents." I placed my hand on his hand, encouraging him to bring his eyes to mine. He had been staring off into the market while he had been talking. "I understand you're angry, Maverick. You now know that I didn't know the commitment I was showing by going to Yule with Feren. Thank you for telling me."

"You are welcome. Just look after yourself when you do go to Yule. A lot of people will be looking for their match. Come on, let's walk back into the market before it closes. I need to look for a few more things."

We walked, weaving in and out of people to the stalls we wished to look at, Maverick being careful not to let people too close to him in case he jostled his wounds. But the crowds had started to dwindle. It hadn't taken me long to realise the market quietened for a few hours around mid-afternoon and then picked up around five for the last hour until the stalls closed, everyone trying to get the last bargain of the day.

We must have been walking for at least half an hour in near-silence. Maverick gave me some time to process my thoughts. We only spoke to say we wanted to go to a stall or about an item or price. The market had quietened my thoughts, but I still felt strange.

"I honestly thought it was just a dance, Maverick. What if Feren thinks it is more?"

"Oh, he will hope it is more, he is quite taken with you, I believe. But if you are worried, you should tell him. But just be careful – he can have a temper."

It seemed funny to me that Maverick would comment on someone else's temper.

"Okay, but how will I tell him? I don't know where he lives."

Sighing, he looked at me. He looked tired but I knew that he was still healing. "Look, I will tell him to drop by later and you can talk to him then – that okay? That way, I can watch in case he gets mad."

Nodding, I resigned myself to what I had to do. I just had

to figure out what to say but I was glad to have the situation more under control. I was also glad Maverick would be close by. I would seriously have to talk to Grandma Wren about the expectations concerning people my age.

"Here, come and try this." Maverick guided me to a stall that was selling miniature pies with little stars and Christmas trees on top.

"Two please, Paul."

Maverick handed over the shards for the pies then handed me one. I had to juggle the small collection of bags with the few purchases I had bought from the market to be able to eat it.

"Oh a mince pie! Thank you."

"So you have had one before then? I wasn't sure if you would have." A smile spread across his face.

"Mother never let us have them, but I would sneak into the kitchen and share one with Grandma Wren whenever I could." I was delighted to be able to have one to myself and not have to hide it.

"Your mother really wasn't very nice was she?"

"She would say I would get too fat to dance. I really despised her."

"I'm sorry, Lorian. Come on – let's not ruin the first bite."

And so we walked through the market, chomping our mince pies, and only when it was getting too dark and the vendors had started to pack up did we make our way home.

Later that evening, Feren stopped by and I had my very awkward conversation about the dance. As expected, he took it badly, annoyed that Maverick had told me the details, but he was annoyed that I didn't want to go with him if that was what was expected of me.

294

We had our little meeting out in the field next to the cottage, the silver moon shining bright and the stars twinkling on the cold December eve. I was grateful that I had my thick woollen cloak and that Maverick was watching from the tree line.

Feren was angry, very angry.

Closing the small distance between us, he pressed his face so close to mine I couldn't make out his features. The low pitch of his voice as he snarled at me for refusing him, made him seem all the more dangerous. That was when I had felt the comforting presence of Maverick behind me. He did not say anything but was just there, keeping me grounded, and for the first time, I could speak truthfully about what I felt. An unexpected feeling bloomed in my chest and when I realised what it was, it only fuelled me more: strength.

"Stop it, Feren. I have told you I did not understand what it entailed in agreeing to go to Yule with you."

I took a step back.

His hand rose quickly and I could see he intended to strike me, but the blow never came. Instead, his arm froze and he flew backwards, tumbling onto the grass, a dark mist dissipating in front of me. Maverick stalked after him.

Rushing after them, I tried to restrain Maverick's arm from delivering a blow of his own as he leant over Feren who lay slumped on the floor. I knew that he had let me stop him, but it made me feel good to know he had acknowledged my wish.

"Don't. You. Ever. Come. Here. Again. You hear me, Feren? If I see you snooping around Lorian, I won't stop next time. I don't care what you did for me."

His voice was almost a snarl, the animal within him present once again. Maverick stood, easing off and allowing Feren to retreat into the night, but not before we heard his response.

"I will be waiting for this to continue, Maverick!"

It was almost as though he wanted to fight. All the animals, and even the wind seemed to stand still for a moment, before returning to their normal routine. The moment was over.

"Are you okay?" Maverick asked, pulling me into a hug.

"Yes, are you?"

I looped my arms around his waist, careful not to put too much pressure on his still-healing chest. It felt nice to be held, his tenderness having returned for a moment.

"Yes." He winced as I leant lightly against him, but he held me close as I tried to pull back. "Are you sure, though? That went worse than I thought. I should have been out here with you throughout it all. I didn't think he would try and hit you. Get in your face, yes, but not hit you." I could tell he was disappointed with himself.

"Honestly, I actually felt strong when I told him to go away. You can't blame yourself either, Maverick, you weren't to know. And you were here when he did try."

Maverick gave me a little squeeze of reassurance and I relaxed further into his embrace.

"You'll be okay, I promise. It was brave of you to stand up to him when he was like that. Honestly, I didn't think you had it in you." He had a little smile on his face.

"I didn't either. But knowing you were behind me gave me all the strength I needed."

We stood like that, enjoying each other's warmth for a few minutes, before we meandered inside and to bed. It was the most at ease I had ever been with Maverick. I just hoped it would continue because I was beginning to fall for him.

The few days before the festival went in a blur of pine, snow and fruit. The bowls of fruit that were dotted around the rooms were always replenished just before they were completely empty and the snow-trodden floors continually swept to stop them getting too wet.

It was the secrecy of it all that felt so unfamiliar – everyone sneaking in and out of their rooms, now that they'd moved in on a more permanent basis. Neave would say she was checking on her home more than usual and Maverick would go to the stables out back, now he'd moved his horse, Xaviran, there.

When I questioned Grandma Wren why they were all dashing around she reminded me of all the small gifts that would be given at Christmas.

"It's the surprise of getting a present, Lorian. Don't tell me you've forgotten about picking me the small pouch of nuts for Christmas?" She grinned at me, her eyes twinkling with mischief.

They were all preparing for Christmas Day. I had begun to pack up my little parcels but hadn't thought anyone would do the same, at least not without telling everyone else what they had got. Mother always loved to tell us what she had got us for Christmas, well before the day arrived.

The market closed for the next two weeks over the holidays, allowing Yule and the new year to be brought in all together. With only an evening before the day itself, everyone seemed to grow quiet. Oddly enough I could feel anticipation amongst the Wrens; all of them seemed to be waiting for something.

"What is it, Grandma Wren?" I sat next to her on the old tattered couch, the fire roaring next to us, chasing off the late-evening cold.

"This is the night when people select who they would like to be with. I trust Maverick has told you of the custom of joining?"

I nodded "He never used that exact term but I understand the concept. But why are you all waiting for it? Isn't it all done at Beltane?"

"Neave still has hope that Maverick will choose, but also Connie is now of an age when her partner will seek her out. We will obviously not know if that happens now, with her gone. You see, this is the time just before Beltane. Beltane helps with the joining of two people but also the conceiving of a child. It is believed that Yule will give the pair the clarity to find one another and Beltane to seal the partnership."

Just as Grandma Wren finished, the clock began to chime and there was a soft slow rap on the door. Grandma Wren moved slowly but surely and pulled the heavy wooden door back. Maverick and Neave had entered the room silently to see who was there to visit. A man about the same age as Maverick, but about four inches shorter, stood in the doorway. His shoulders filled the frame and the blank look on his face made him an unsettling arrival.

"Maverick, Neave, Grandma Wren." He greeted them all in turn but did not even glance in my direction. "I am here to take Connie out, to see if the joining is between us, as I think it is. Is she here?"

"She is not, and will not be from now on. I am sorry she is unable to join with you tonight."

Neave spoke strongly and we could see confusion cloud the young man's eyes, but giving a slight nod he turned and walked away. Grandma Wren closed the door behind him.

"Where would they go if Connie was still here? What happens?" The questions rolled out of me.

"That would be between them."

It was the defeat in Maverick's voice that made me look at him closely. He seemed to have a weight pressing down on him and I knew it was the responsibility of finding his pair. Everyone seemed to hold that idea sacred, and if I had deduced correctly, Maverick's birthday was just after Beltane and he didn't have long to find his.

He strode back into the kitchen and I heard the snick of the back door. "It is officially Yule – maybe he will start to seek them out now," Neave pondered aloud.

I could feel my stomach drop. Even though I hadn't wanted to admit it to myself, I was really falling for Maverick. Even when he was angry, he was unfailingly honest, something I admired. His outspokenness was freeing, no lies or carefully chosen words that had an underlying meaning.

For once I knew what I wanted and what I had to do, and by god, I was going after it.

I went and retrieved a small parcel from my room and strode into the dark trees that circled the house. Looking into the gloom, I hesitated, knowing what lay within, but as I stood there my head gave a pounding throb and a voice that I'd been hearing urged me forward, hurrying me.

I knew he had gone on Xaviran – the hoof prints in the turned-up mud and snow allowed me to follow them with ease. I knew where he was going, where he said he always went to think.

The statue.

Maverick

My breathing was slowly returning to normal. I couldn't stomach being in that house any longer, knowing Mum and Grandma Wren would just sit there waiting for me to see if I would go and find my pair or for the door to knock again. I couldn't even focus on Emerys and the possibility the Stravaig was more than a legend at that moment. Grandma Wren had silenced my theory, saying I should to leave it to her. But I couldn't help thinking that she was hiding something from all of us.

"What should I do, Xav?" Stroking his mane,

I poured myself out to Xaviran under the watchful gaze of the no-longer-nameless statue. It hadn't felt the same to come here since knowing who she was. In fact, it just felt all the more painful, the longing just intensified.

Xaviran raised his head informing me that we weren't alone any more. I could hear the faint snaps of twigs and the rustle of undergrowth as someone approached. Standing, I moved behind the statue, pulling Xaviran along with me. I had grown all-too cautious since my meeting with the deformed creatures and Emerys and I would not let myself be thrown off-guard again.

I situated Xav behind me, protecting my back, and the statue covering my front. I crouched low and used my dark fury to cloak us even further. I waited to see whoever it was come into view. I knew from the lightness of the step and the slightness of build who it was, before they even raised their head to look in my direction. I knew she was looking at the statue but it felt as though her gaze lingered on me.

Lorian had twigs stuck in her hair and the hem of her skirt was torn where she had battled through the undergrowth. I waited a while longer, just watching, as she moved around the clearing before settling on a fallen log. She sat looking at something in her hands, and I was sure she was muttering to herself.

"I think you may have made a few wrong turns getting here?" I called, revealing myself.

"You could say that. Everything looks so different in the dark. I didn't think it was this far when I made the trip during the day." The relief in her face was easy to see as a smile crossed her lips. "I thought you would be here but when I couldn't see you, I feared I would have to try and get back on my own. I wouldn't have known where to start."

"Why did you come looking for me, Lorian?" I sat down next to her and pulled a few twigs out of her hair.

"Thank you." She smiled at my gesture and my heart swelled inside my chest.

She glanced back down at her hands, drawing my attention back to the item she had been gazing at just moments before. It was a small box, just a simple paper parcel, but the way she held it so delicately in her hands, I knew that whatever was inside was special to her.

"I wanted to give you this." She held out the box towards me. "Happy Chris-Yule!"

I could feel the surprise written all over my face, I hadn't expected her to get me anything, especially after I had acted towards her. It was only since Feren that we had come to an unspoken agreement to be nice to one another. Taking the parcel, I let out a sharp whistle which made her jump. In the next moment, I had Xaviran nuzzling against my arm, letting me know he was there.

"Yule greetings, Lorian." Opening one of the saddlebags the Xaviran rarely wore, I removed a paper parcel and handed it to her.

"Is—is that for me?"

"Well, who else would it be for? It definitely isn't for Xav."

The horse let out an indignant snort as if he understood his owner.

"You really didn't have to, Maverick. You've all been kind enough already."

"Oh shut up and open it, Lorian."

Her kind nature really could be infuriating, but a smile tugged at the corners of my mouth. She remained silent and began to untie the twine carefully, savouring the moment.

"Have you never had a present before? Normally people just rip into them," I jested.

"Not a surprise one. My mother would always tell us what it was before the day."

"Well, what is the point in that?"

I turned and started to fiddle with Xaviran's saddlebag. It was starting to get irritating watching her. If she'd taken any longer, I would have torn the paper off myself. Her short intake of breath let me know that she had finally unwrapped the parcel, as a blazing smile spread across her face. The grey garment was folded in the tissue paper and I watched as her hands lightly drifted across it, picking it up carefully as though it would fall to pieces if she held it too tightly. I was lucky Xaviran's saddlebags were a good hiding spot for the presents. What she didn't expect was a small wooden box to fall out.

Picking it up she examined the carving I had engraved onto its lid, like a three-pronged fork.

"It is the rune, algiz. It is a symbol for you to have courage in the face of fear, but also understanding that fear means for you to protect yourself and be on your guard. I thought it was small enough for you to keep on you, maybe with some herbs you need in it."

Gathering both objects up she turned towards me, a broad smile on her lips. "It's beautiful, Maverick, thank you."

I felt my soul stir and soar as I had never felt it before. The feeling was so unusual to me I nearly fell off the log, bumping into Xav. I could suddenly see a future, a plan, one I had never thought I would have, or even dream of having; a family, and one not edged with bitterness or duty.

Leaning closer to Lorian, I met her eyes. They were beautiful and I could still see the colour they were when she'd gazed into the mirror. Her eyes dropped to my lips and I leant a little closer as her eyes fluttered closed. My lips seemed to follow of their own accord.

A sharp intake of breath and Xaviran kicking his feet against the soft dirt ground pulled me out of my daze just before our lips touched. A light breeze had started to pick up, moving the damp fallen leaves around our feet, catching Lorian's hair as her scarf billowed in front of her. Then I caught sight of her eyes.

They shone, so brightly and boldly in the moonlit grove. As I watched, the strange magic spread through Lorian, changing her skin, lips, hair and clothes before me.

"What is happening Lorian?" I tried to shout over the wind that whipped around us.

Her skirt was billowing around her legs, and her now-luminous hair rose like snakes weaving through the undergrowth. Her smile shone brightly as she looked at the silk scarf I had given her, my token for Yule. But concern suddenly clouded her face.

"It is red. How can it be red?"

Her voice was no more than a whisper but the wind seemed to die down, once the transformation had occurred. The strange colours had leaked and bled through the entirety of Lorian and she now seemed to glow like a beacon in the dark grove.

"Red? That is what it is then, the same sort of colour as the fire we saw in your memory. It isn't the only thing that has changed. Your hair, it's the same colour as the scarf."

"What do you—"

She grabbed a handful of her long, knotted hair and drew it in front of her. "But how can that be? I have only seen glimpses of colour since I have been here."

I could hear her panic start to rise and as it did, the colours that had illuminated Lorian began to fade. As quickly as they came, they disappeared, leaching into the colourless ground and disappearing.

"Wait – what is happening? Where is it going? Maverick!"

"It's okay, Lorian, I don't know what happened, but we will

find out. Grandma Wren will know, I am sure." I sat down beside her and drew her to my side.

"How could we explain what just happened?"

"Well, I guess the best way would be to say you changed colour. You know, like the colours we saw in that memory of yours? The yellow and the—well, the other colours. Where is the scarf?"

I saw the bundle of cloth spread over her small feet from where Lorian had dropped it, the box still clutched in her hands. As I pulled it out of the shadows, I looked at it by the light of the moon. The one thing that hadn't changed back was the scarf, it was still the colour that Lorian had described it: red.

"But why didn't this change back?"

Lorian took the fine fabric from my hands and placed it on her lap, twining her fingers in its folds.

"That is also a question for Grandma Wren. Come, we should get back."

Pulling Xav around, I offered my clasped hands to Lorian.

"I don't know if I could get on him – my legs are shaking. Can't we walk? I've never ridden without a saddle."

"Well, this is as good a time as any, it will take too long to go back on foot now. It's already late and we all know what is about. Xav will be quicker and swifter if we come across anything, but he will also be gentle. He will not throw you, I promise."

The reassurance I gave her was small, but it seemed as though it was enough. Tucking the box back into Xav's saddlebag, she nestled her foot into my cupped hands. She hooked up her skirt and I hoisted her up, swinging her leg over Xav's thick body to sit astride him. Even though she said she was nervous, she sat confidently.

"Move forward and I will sit behind you."

The moment we had shared, no matter if it had been interrupted, had shifted something in me and I just knew I needed to be close to her. Her hesitation was slight, but she did as I asked. I sat closely behind her, taking a grip of Xav's mane in one hand and holding her around the waist with the other. Her petite frame stiffened for a moment and then began to relax.

"I won't let you fall, I promise."

As rode steadily into the dense trees, a dark fog began to rise.

"The fog is coming in quicker than I have seen it before, and we used to get pretty bad ones in Temford." Lorian's hand closed around my arm around her waist, as if for reassurance.

"I won't let you fall," I repeated.

Kicking Xaviran to go faster I steered him onto a narrower, winding path that I knew would be quicker. This wasn't any normal fog, it was denser and it smelt of coal and rot. But I knew not to mention it – it would cause Lorian to panic more. The fog continued to rise, distorting the path and muffling the sounds of the forest. The only sound was Xav's thundering feet and Lorian's rapid breathing.

"It smells like smoke, Maverick. This isn't normal, is it?"

"No, but we are nearly there. Don't worry. I won't let you fall," I repeated for the third time.

I didn't know if I could keep us going at this pace, so releasing my dark fury. I wove it round us to try and block the fog from coming too near. But the tendrils fought against each other, performing a dark dance for dominance.

Xav snorted, shaking his head, trying to rid the strange

smell from his nostrils. Lorian began to cough, covering her mouth with the scarf, which still blazed a bright red in the gloom.

A loud creaking noise broke through the heavy silence, then a loud scream. It took me a moment to realise what was happening, the cold damp earth under my cheek and the smell of mud confirming that we had been thrown.

Pulling myself up, I quickly checked for any serious injuries; other than a few scrapes and bumps and my back and chest throbbing, I was okay. I started to search for where Lorian had landed but could see she was just gathering herself up. Rushing to her side, I tried to help her get back to her feet; we had to get moving and quickly. Whatever had sent the fog, would be on us soon.

"Are you okay?"

"Yes, what happened? Are you okay?"

Looking around I tried to locate Xav, He was laying not too far away from us, his body partially hidden by a large tree root. The fog was beginning to clear but the smoky rotten smell lingered. Xav didn't stir.

"Xaviran, come on boy, you stuck?"

Xaviran's laboured, raspy breathing rang in my ears. My knees became soaked as I knelt beside him to feel if his foot was stuck. There was not enough light to see what was wrong, but I knew that whatever I was kneeling in wasn't water. It was thick and when I felt with my hands it was warm. A metallic smell overpowered the lingering smell of the fog.

A low hiss and a muffled squeak drew my attention away from Xav. I could just make out a dark figure holding a smaller one in front of them: Lorian.

"You sssee, I brought friends thisss time, Maverick. I did

warn you, but you jussst couldn't leave it alone. You just had to go chasssing it, didn't you? You want to find what ssshouldn't be there." I could hear muffled sobs coming from Lorian where she was pressed against his chest. "I would have thought you would have had more senssse than coming into the forest at night. I would have thought our lassst encounter would have made that clear. I think my messsage is even clearer this time, don't you? The next time you venture where you shouldn't, it will be you instead of your horssse on the ground. Remember that."

Emerys went to turn and leave, Lorian still pinned to his chest.

"Where are you taking her? She isn't going with you," I snarled at the form of my closest friend.

"Oh but ssshe is, Maverick. You sssee, she isss the problem, she is the one that isss causing all the isssues. This cloth that she wearsss around her neck just provesss that it is infecting our world and we need to preserve how it isss."

Even though I could not see the forest around me, I could hear the restless rustling just out of sight. The creatures weren't happy with what was happening, and it seemed as though whatever instructions Emerys had given them weren't going to keep them still for long. The only thing I could think of doing was shocking them, but that would hurt Lorian. But if I didn't act quickly, they would disappear into the forest and I wouldn't find them.

Then instinct seemed to kick in. I let my dark fury loose, cloaking me and blinding the surrounding creatures. I knew that it wouldn't last long with the powers that they still possessed, but it allowed just enough of a distraction for me to close some of the distance between myself and Lorian.

Grabbing hold of Emerys' arm, I sent a shock wave travelling down my arm and into his. It wouldn't enough to harm him, but it allowed his grip to loosen and for me to pull Lorian free.

Emerys rallied quickly, turning and throwing a hex at us. It travelled so quickly I didn't have time to counter or throw a blocking spell up. I only had enough time to position myself in front of Lorian. The spell hit with the force of a sledgehammer squarely in my back, making my knees buckle under me.

I didn't know how we were going to get out of this. The spell was starting to take hold. I was drifting as if falling into a hole, and that was when the searing pain started; the deeper I drifted the more intense it grew. I could hear Lorian crying through the haze and I desperately tried to claw my way to the top but it only seemed to add to the pain. I let the darkness close around me, succumbing to the burning inside.

A tiny pinprick of light seemed to open up, taunting me, and then with a sudden rush it grew, engulfing me in its white light. I was sure it was all an illusion, a continuation of the torment of Emerys' hex, but as my eyes pried themselves open, I could see that it was now daylight, the white sunlight trickling through the overhead canopy. My head throbbed.

Pushing up on my elbows I heaved, bringing up the contents of my stomach. Regaining my composure and feeling slightly more steady, I looked around, blinking in the light, disorientated. Rubbing my eyes, I managed to clear them enough to focus on my surroundings.

Everything looked calm, as though nothing had happened. Maybe I had dreamt the attack, but that was when I saw Lorian. She was lying just a few feet away, with her arms propped under her head like a pillow. She looked peaceful, but the tension around her eyes lingered. I couldn't stand, so I positioned myself on all fours and began a slow shuffle over to her. Any sort of movement churned my stomach, and my vision was still slightly blurred, I swayed as if seasick.

My slow approach was interrupted when I felt a cold powdery substance on my hands. Looking down, I could make out the thin, now disturbed, circle of a fine powder. Lifting my hand to my nose I sniffed, and as the powder entered my nostrils I instantly began to sneeze and cough: chilli powder.

"You're awake. I didn't know if it would work, but I know I can't leave the circle now I have cast it."

Lorian's raspy voice broke through my coughs and I tried to regain my composure enough to talk. "You cast a chilli circle? But where did Emerys and the other creatures go?"

Looking around, my vision finally back to normal, I noticed that the surrounding trees bore the wounds of claw marks and misused magic, A tree had been ripped from the ground where Xaviran had lain. His body had gone. My heart squeezed at the loss of my dear friend. Finally, my gaze landed on the thin lighter circle that ran around myself and Lorian, perfectly formed, if not a little light on powder.

"You cast a protection circle? I didn't even know you knew how to do that," I said, amazed.

"Crushed dried blueberry leaves. Grandma Wren has been showing me how to look after myself. She said it would protect me if I needed it. She also told me it would help if anyone tried to spell me. I didn't know if it would work but you were asleep for so long, I didn't know how to uncast the circle to get help. We hadn't got to that bit. I didn't think I would have to use it, or at least not until I had practised more."

Cutting the chilli circle with my athame, I moved closer to

Lorian, lifting her chin to look her in the eye. "You saved us, Lorian, it doesn't matter if you didn't know how to close the circle after it was cast, knowing how to cast it in the first place was essential. Emerys and the creatures must have got tired, not being able to pass the protection circle to get to us."

A blush changed the colour of her skin. Instead of a dull shadow, her cheeks reddened. As the blush moved down her throat, I was transfixed by the wonder happening before me. I hadn't noticed until then that there were four deep gouges traced along the side of her neck. Looking down, I saw where she was clutching her side, a slow trickle of blood oozing out between her fingers.

"We need to get you home, you are bleeding!"

Every muscle in my body ached, but mustering all the magical energy I had left, I closed the circle thanking the Goddess and God for their help in protecting us.

"Let me help you. You won't get far, you are too drained from what Emerys did to you," she said.

Forcing myself into a standing position, I leant heavily on Lorian for support. I could see she wanted to ask something. "What is it, Lorian?"

"What happened to you, Maverick? I was so scared, you seemed to just black out and I couldn't wake you. When I sprinkled the chilli powder round you, I couldn't even remember what it did. I just hoped it helped."

"Later…" I sighed. She had obviously been thinking about it for a while, but I didn't think I could answer questions and walk too. "I promise I'll answer, Lorian, but we need to focus on getting back."

I steered us to see if what I feared was true, but as I passed the tree root, Xaviran wasn't there, just the pool of blood that

I had knelt in last night. My stomach dropped and I felt a new wave of nausea wash over me. Had they taken him or had he pulled himself out of the way? I couldn't think about that now – I had to try and get both of us home and get Mum to help. Something still didn't feel right, and even though Lorian had removed the hex, I still felt weak and powerless and Lorian was still bleeding.

Stumbling through the undergrowth, back towards Grandma Wren's cottage, we passed countless trees that had succumbed to the creatures' wrath, though the closer we got to the border of the forest the less we saw. We really had been only a few hundred metres from the cottage.

Emerging from the trees, both of us had to stop. The light was bright as the midday sun edged its way around the sky and we had to let our vision adjust. Though the trees had thinned out, we still needed to become accustomed to the low December light.

A dark figure began to streak towards us, I couldn't make out who it was as my eyes were still adjusting from the sudden light change. I pushed Lorian behind me while I summoned what little strength I had. No matter how weak I was, I would try and ensure that none of those creatures would harm her again.

Raising my arms defensively to fight off the attacker, my eyes adjusted just before I swung to strike the oncoming threat.

"Maverick. Enough. You need to come quickly." It was Mum, the urgency in her voice adding more adrenaline to my veins. "We have been looking for you everywhere. When Xaviran came home without you, we knew something was wrong. We all thought you two would just be having some time together, but as the morning wore on, we knew something must have happened. You would surely make it in time for Yule."

I growled in my throat at her comment about me and Lorian, I was too tired to hear that crap, but Lorian cut me off before I had the chance to respond.

"Where is Xaviran, is he here? Is he okay?"

As Lorian pushed past me, I could feel myself sway and she tucked herself back under my arm to steady me.

"He's in Grandma Wren's barn. We couldn't make it back to our house with him… He isn't good, Maverick."

She turned and began striding back to the barn, urging us to follow. It took us double the time it normally would, I knew most of it was because of me, I just couldn't find the energy to move any quicker.

As we entered the barn, I froze. Xav was laid out on the hay, covered in blood. Grandma Wren was trying to change the soaked hay as Mum tried to staunch the wounds in his sides.

Lorian pressed closer to my side, I could feel her shaking.

Dragging my eyes away from the scene in front of me, I saw the sorrow in Mum's face. ""He needs you now, Maverick. You will calm him…"

Xav was kicking his legs while Mum tried to press herbs into the wounds and he was huffing, exasperated and in pain.

Crouching down, I lay his head in my lap, gently stroking him. "Shhh, it's okay, boy, Mum is only trying to help. You have to let her help, okay?"

I could hear the tremor in my own voice. I caught Mum's eye and I tried to get a reading on what she thought of his wounds. There was anger there, but also deep regret as she gave her head a little shake. A tear escaped me and as it traced its path down my cheek, I looked at my best friend. He looked at me as if pleading for me to take the pain away, and so I let the last of my dark fury loose around him.

I watched as my best friend slipped away, losing myself in his gaze as that defiant light went out. A new feeling bloomed in my chest. One I didn't think I would ever know: shame.

Lorian

3,602 Moons 4 days

Dear Diary,

The headaches are more frequent now. They come on so suddenly and I am sure I am seeing an outline of a person. It looks exactly like the girl I saw when Emerys was scrying. However, as soon as the headaches come and I try to focus on the girl, they are gone within a few moments. No lingering side effects, nothing.

I have asked Grandma Wren, but all she says is to rest and have some chamomile tea. It is just stress.

I'd best go, it is Christmas.

Lorian

Everyone seemed to freeze once Xaviran had fallen still. I could feel the horror bloom in my chest at what I had just witnessed, but one emotion overrode it all: Maverick's loss. I had seen people die around me when I was back in Temford, in the last few months after I had run away. We tried to tend to people with the sickness. Most of the people I tended to were in their last few days of life and I would just make them comfortable, but I couldn't help but feel the loss with each one.

Moving over to him, I carefully crouched down, aware of my wounds but ignoring the pain. He was still stroking Xaviran's neck in gentle soothing strokes, I leant my head on his shoulder, trying to provide him with some sort of comfort. I don't know how long we sat there, but everyone left and twilight seemed to creep in. The cold was starting to bite at my ankles when I finally tried to talk to him. "You should come inside now, I will get you something to eat."

"You know I had him since he was a foal? He was the naughtiest one in the paddock."

"That I don't doubt," I said with a small smile. "Come…" I pulled his free hand as I rose, stretching out my stiff joints carefully from sitting on the cold hay. My side had eased but I could once again feel the small trickle of fresh blood as I moved and reopened the wound. Neave had quickly tended to it as I sat with Maverick, but said she would clean it out again later.

Without another word, he lifted Xaviran's head and placed it gently on the hay, allowing me to guide him back to the house. The heat blazing out of the hearth stung as we entered the cottage. We hadn't felt warmth since we'd ventured into the forest the previous night and our bodies ached as it expelled the cold.

Maverick sat next to the fire, on the big couch that I had slept on when we'd had our first long talk. That felt longer than a month ago, so much had happened since. I found one of the old checked blankets and hung it over his shoulders. He hadn't said anything since being in the barn, his eyes had taken on the glaze of memory.

"Would you like some tea?" I stood in front of him, picking at the torn fabric of my dress with one hand as I clutched my side with the other.

Looking at me, he blinked slowly, chasing away the memories that hung over him. "No," he whispered clearing his throat. "No, thank you."

His eyes drifted to my hands and then to the cuts that marred my skin, visible through the gaps in the torn fabric. Within an instant he was kneeling before me, moving my hands to look at my side. I knew the wound would scar. He was gentle as he pulled the fabric away from it; a few of the edges were stuck and pulled as he moved them. He pressed his finger around the wound.

"What are you doing?" I hissed, as I felt the sharp pain of his touch. I tried to move away from him but he held fast.

His eyes blazed. "I am seeing what damage it caused … hold still." He pressed his fingers into my side once again. I tried not to flinch as he moved his hands. "It is deep, but I don't think it is deep enough to cause any lasting damage. You will have scars though, I'm afraid, and you will need to clean it out. In a way it's good it's still bleeding, pushing out all the dirt. Lucky it didn't get infected like Emerys'."

Standing up, he raised my chin and looked at my neck. "Luckily these aren't as deep. They will fade, but there will always be a small trace."

His eyes caught mine and for a moment we just stood there looking at one another, until he broke away and stared back into the fire.

"Thank you for looking at them. Your mum said they would need looking at again."

He sat again and I knelt in front of him, looking up into his once-again clouded eyes. "I am sorry about Xaviran, Maverick."

The set of his mouth let me know he heard me, as a single tear skirted down his angular face. I chased it away with my thumb and pressed the palm of my hand to his face, drawing his eyes to mine. "I really am sorry, please tell me if there is anything I can do."

"Why would you think you can do anything, and why do you always try and help everyone?" His words would've normally stung, but instead they sounded sad.

"Because sometimes people can feel so alone and think it is better to keep everything to themselves. They just need a reminder that they are not on their own."

His eyes widened as he looked at me. Cupping my face, his voice was almost a whisper. "Your eyes, Lorian. What magic do you possess?"

"Nothing, I possess no magic, Maverick. All I want to do is help you."

"But you do, Lorian, you are different. We may not know what it is yet, but you do possess a special kind of magic." He held my face as he leant his forehead against mine. "Will you stay with me?"

We stayed like that for a long while, the thought of food forgotten. Grandma Wren came in and cleaned our wounds and then left without so much as a murmur. Maverick leant back shortly after, taking my hand and pulling me up to sit next to him. He stared into the fire once again, but pulled me under his arm, holding me close, brushing his lips lightly over my forehead. And that is where I stayed, under the protection of his arm.

Throughout the night, I relived the evening before, waking up feeling Emerys' hands were around my throat, his nails biting into my skin. A searching feeling wove its way through my body.

"Shh, calm down, Lorian, it is only me, Maverick." Maverick held my thrashing wrists as I awoke for the third time that evening, tears pouring down my face. I didn't know if I had woken him or if he had even fallen asleep, but he always seemed awake when I woke up.

"I'm sorry, Maverick, I should be looking after you. You are the one that has been in trouble, then you lost Xaviran, I have nothing to have nightmares over," I hiccuped, patting at my face with the palm of my hand to dry away the tears. I was lying against him, my face turned away so he couldn't see me; my side ached from where it had been pressed into Maverick's hip.

"Look at me, Lorian." His voice was stern as he put his forefinger under my chin, pulling me back to his gaze. "You have every right to have nightmares. What happened last night should never have happened, do you hear me? You should never have been out there."

"I was looking for you…"

"I shouldn't have put you in the position where you had to look for me. You must not go into the forest again, do you hear me, Lorian?"

I gave a small nod, and he nodded in return, satisfied that his message had got through. "You know, I honestly thought Feren had come for you last night when there was a knock at the door. Even when I saw it wasn't him, I still thought he would come, but that was no excuse to leave."

"When are you supposed to find your partner by, Maverick? Why is it so important?"

"Have you never wanted to find your true match, the one that will understand you? That is what the pairing is, and Beltane is supposed to be the easiest to find them. It should guide you to them. But after this Beltane, it will disappear for me, and then I will have the uncertainty of who I will be with."

"But how do you know when you've met your pairing?"

"I suppose it just feels right, like when you cast a spell correctly for the first time. When you cast that circle last night and it held all of them back, how did it make you feel?"

"Safe, but also scared that something like that had worked."

"I guess that is what it feels like then. It's scary, but also thrilling and feels safe."

Our eyes drifted to one another and the blood rushed in my ears as my heart began to beat faster. *Why does he do this to me?* I wondered. My eyes drifted once again to his mouth as they had earlier tonight, but this time I tentatively leant in. It was just a few inches, but I could feel the rush of adrenaline flood my veins in anticipation. His hands tucked a few strands of hair behind his ears, as they always did when he was nervous.

As if his body was reacting to a command that his mind hadn't even thought of yet, he tipped his face down, his eyes widening as he realised what he was doing. There was a slight hesitation before, but to my relief he relaxed, his soft lips tentatively brushing mine.

I carefully placed my hand over the mark Emerys had given him, willing the pain to subside. My lips followed his slight command as they continued to brush together with his in a silent dance. Heat radiated through me gently, as insistently, he pulled me by my waist, gently tucking me into his side. Pain laced through me as my injured side connected with his, a pitiful squeak escaping my lips shattering the moment in an instant.

"I'm sorry, Lorian... I... uh... got carried away. Are you okay?"

Pulling himself away from me, he searched my eyes as though checking for any signs I was upset, but all I knew he would see was the faint trace of need and longing that I could see in his.

"I'm okay, Maverick, I promise."

I cupped his face once again, but this time a slight blush crept up my neck. He watched it as it rose higher, a look of bewilderment flickering into his gaze before he shook it away. Gently, he brushed my neck with his fingertips, causing me to giggle.

"I'm sorry, you know, if that wasn't okay, I have never... well..." I whispered, cautiously.

"That was your first kiss?"

I could feel the blush deepen as I ducked my head so he could not meet my eyes.

"That is nothing to be ashamed of Lorian." Raising my chin to look at him in the eyes as he had done so before, he smiled at me. "Now, take some of your limeflower and ashwagandha – we forgot earlier – and try to get a few more hours of sleep. I will keep the nightmares away, okay?"

Settling back down, I thought through everything Maverick had said about Beltane and pairing. Over the past few months I had begun to feel what he'd described ... with him. I was completely terrified, but when I was with him, I ultimately felt safe. Slipping my hand into the pocket of my skirt I pulled out the bundle of fabric I had left from the beautiful scarf he had given me. It had ripped in the struggle with Emerys, but it still blazed a bright red. The fabric was soft in my hands and floated through them like a breeze on a summer's day. I could feel that Maverick had noticed what I was playing with and shifted, pulling something out of his pocket. The paper was torn but the ribbon held it together.

"Shall I open it now?" he asked. Sadness still marred his face, but there was a trace of gratitude in amongst it. He seemed more peaceful now a few hours had passed.

"Of course, I hope you like it."

I shifted so I wasn't as close to him and waited for him to untie the ribbon. The paper fell open as the ribbon fell away and tissue paper covered the small object within. The timepiece that had belonged to my dear friend looked like a child's toy in Maverick's large, scarred hands.

"It's beautiful, Lorian. Where did you get something like this? I don't believe anyone crafts such things in the town? It looks like what Grandma Wren keeps on her."

"It was my dear friend, Elijah's. It was in my things and I thought you would like it. I was surprised it still works, I know you don't use watches and such for timekeeping, but I hope you like it."

"It's beautiful, thank you."

I watched him as he inspected the object that I had just given him. His skin began to flare a deep tan, a light pink leached into his lips and his hair took on a dark shine. The birthmark on his cheek deepened into a dark brown. A small noise escaped me, and he looked at me with a glint quizzical look in his eyes.

"What is it?

Before I could answer, Grandma Wren entered the room. "You're up la—" She stopped abruptly as she looked at us. "I thought we would have more time, but obviously I misread the signs." She flicked out the pocket watch she always seemed to carry, snipping it shut as though it had bitten her.

"What is it, Grandma Wren? Are you okay?" Maverick's concern was apparent in his voice.

"I do not have long, so listen carefully. I am unable to stay much longer and now you both have a task. The happenings around here have been coming for a long time and they stem from the time colour was taken from this world. That is all about to change."

As she spoke, her outline began to fade.

Panic rose in me.

"What is happening, Grandma? What is happening to you?" I cried.

"She is fading like you did when you were stuck in the memories. What is happening?"

Maverick's hold on me tightened, but I wriggled out from under him and moved to kneel in front of Grandma Wren.

"My time is up, Lorian, I have been here long enough; it is now time for things to change. This watch and the rune you see me draw have kept me here for as long as they can. You remember the questions about the colour you have seen? I can now answer them. You remember what I told you, that you are the one to help bring colour back and set the lost souls free, that your powers are essential?"

"But I don't have any powers. Who are the lost souls? Please don't go. Not now, not when I have just found you again, not when this place is feeling like home!" Tears streamed down my face and I could hear the crack in my voice.

"The creatures, Lorian, they are the people disappearing. Their souls, their essence is trapped somewhere. Now listen carefully, Lorian."

We sat silently as Grandma Wren recited a poem that I remembered from long ago. She used to recite it to me when I couldn't sleep:

It can be found in the smallest of things,
*   You just have to be willing to open your eyes and see.*
*   It can be suffocated easily,*
*   It can paralyse and destroy,*
*   If challenged it can strengthen thee.*
*   Find the former to overcome the latter,*
*   It will allow the curse to shatter.*

"This is your task now, Lorian – only you can do it together. The poem will guide you. I'm sorry I couldn't stay longer, to help you understand more magic before I give this task to you. I'm sorry, but heed this warning, if you should fail, you too will be consumed by the curse. Trust the colours in the mist. Please forgive me."

"Colours in the mist? What colours? What mist? There is nothing to forgive you for. Please stay – I don't understand… "

The tears were coming so quickly I could barely see but I clutched onto her hand, willing her to stay longer.

"There is one last thing. Those that used to be friends may not be the same. Keep your wits about you, Lorian. I wasn't the only one to stay in this time. Your theory was right, Maverick, I'm sorry I have left it so long and I can't tell you more. You look after her, she will need you."

Grandma Wren was flickering in and out so quickly, her form was hazy. If I wasn't looking directly at her, I would have thought she was a trick of the light.

"Lorian, your headaches aren't just normal headaches. Someone is trying to communicate with you. From what you have told me, I believe it to be Lila. You have to relax and let your vision show you,"

Why was Lila trying to talk to me? Maverick had said she was one of those creatures, he had seen her when he was attacked by Emerys. But I didn't have time to ask, Grandma Wren was nearly gone.

"I will, Grandma Wren, I promise…"

I could hear the sorrow and heartache in Maverick's voice but I could not take my eyes off the face of the one person I loved more than anything in this world. I was so confused. Who else would be here? She said Ivan died but there was only one other she would call my friend – Elijah. My heart fluttered at the prospect of seeing him again.

"It is time, Lorian. Will you do one thing for me before I go?"

"Yes, what is it?"

Her voice was a whisper. A lump formed in the back of my throat as I tried to suppress the sobs I knew would come.

"Sit with me awhile. Tell me one of the stories you used to know when you were little."

And so I did, and by the time the story of Elijah the knight and Lorian the fairy was over, she was gone. Only the pocket watch remained where she'd been sitting.

My new life was about to begin without her.

About the Author

E. P. MacLachlan is a British author living in a cottage just outside Bristol with her boyfriend, grey Savannah cat, Tomas and Cocker Spaniel puppy, Ryker. She started writing Colours in the Mist in her second year of University.

You can connect with me on:

🔗 https://www.instagram.com/norys_stories

Printed in Great Britain
by Amazon

74341731R00190